Elisabeth von Arnim

The Adventures of Elizabeth in Rügen

Outlook

Elisabeth von Arnim

The Adventures of Elizabeth in Rügen

1. Auflage | ISBN: 978-3-73262-502-4

Erscheinungsort: Frankfurt am Main, Deutschland

Erscheinungsjahr: 2018

Outlook Verlag GmbH, Frankfurt.

Elisabeth von Arnim

The Adventures of Elizabeth in Rügen

Outlook

THE

ADVENTURES OF ELIZABETH

IN RÜGEN

BY THE AUTHOR OF

"ELIZABETH AND HER GERMAN GARDEN"

New York

THE MACMILLAN COMPANY

LONDON: MACMILLAN & CO., LTD.

1904

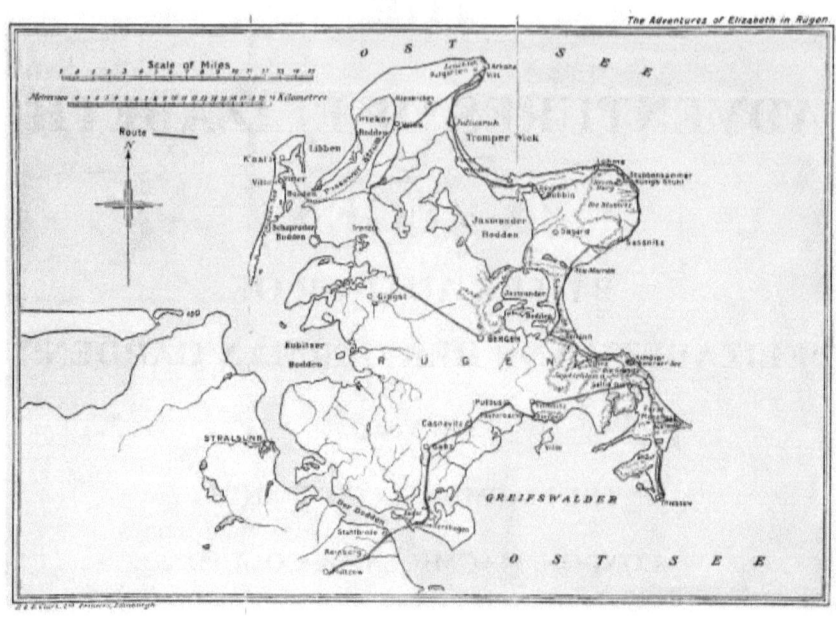

CONTENTS

THE ADVENTURES OF ELIZABETH IN RÜGEN

THE FIRST DAY

FROM MILTZOW TO LAUTERBACH

Every one who has been to school and still remembers what he was taught there, knows that Rügen is the biggest island Germany possesses, and that it lies in the Baltic Sea off the coast of Pomerania.

Round this island I wished to walk this summer, but no one would walk with me. It is the perfect way of moving if you want to see into the life of things. It is the one way of freedom. If you go to a place on anything but your own feet you are taken there too fast, and miss a thousand delicate joys that were waiting for you by the wayside. If you drive you are bound by a variety of considerations, eight of the most important being the horses' legs. If you bicycle—but who that loves to get close to nature would bicycle? And as for motors, the object of a journey like mine was not the getting to a place but the going there.

Successively did I invite the most likely of my women friends, numbering at least a dozen, to walk with me. They one and all replied that it would make them tired and that it would be dull; and when I tried to remove the first objection by telling them how excellent it would be for the German nation, especially those portions of it that are still to come, if its women walked round Rügen more often, they stared and smiled; and when I tried to remove the second by explaining that by our own spirits are we deified, they stared and smiled more than ever.

Walking, then, was out of the question, for I could not walk alone. The grim monster Conventionality whose iron claws are for ever on my shoulder, for ever pulling me back from the harmless and the wholesome, put a stop to that even if I had not been afraid of tramps, which I was. So I drove, and it was round Rügen that I drove because one hot afternoon when I was idling in the library, not reading but fingering the books, taking out first one and then another, dipping into them, deciding which I would read next, I came across Marianne North's *Recollections of a Happy Life*, and hit upon the page where she begins to talk of Rügen. Immediately interested—for is not Rügen nearer to me than any other island?—I became absorbed in her description of the bathing near a place called Putbus, of the deliciousness of it in a sandy cove where the water was always calm, and of how you floated about on its crystal surface, and beautiful jelly-fish, stars of purest colours, floated with you. I threw down the book to ransack the shelves for a guide to Rügen. On the first page of the first one I found was this remarkable paragraph:—

5

'Hearest thou the name Rügen, so doth a wondrous spell come over thee. Before thine eyes it rises as a dream of far-away, beauteous fairylands. Images and figures of long ago beckon thee across to the marvellous places where in grey prehistoric times they dwelt, and on which they have left the shadow of their presence. And in thee stirs a mighty desire to wander over the glorious, legend-surrounded island. Cord up, then, thy light bundle, take to heart Shylock's advice to put money in thy purse, and follow me without fear of the threatening sea-sickness which may overtake thee on the short crossing, for it has never yet done any one more harm than imposing on him a rapidly- passing discomfort.'

This seemed to me very irresistible. Surely a place that inspired such a mingling of the lofty and the homely in its guide-books must be well worth seeing? There was a drought just then going on at home. My eyes were hot with watching a garden parch browner day by day beneath a sky of brass. I felt that it only needed a little energy, and in a few hours I too might be floating among those jelly-fish, in the shadow of the cliffs of the legend- surrounded island. And even better than being surrounded by legends those breathless days would it be to have the sea all round me. Such a sea too! Did I not know it? Did I not know its singular limpidity? The divineness of its blue where it was deep, the clearness of its green where it was shallow, lying tideless along its amber shores? The very words made me thirsty—amber shores; lazy waves lapping them slowly; vast spaces for the eye to wander over; rocks, and seaweed, and cool, gorgeous jelly-fish. The very map at the beginning of the guide-book made me thirsty, the land was so succulently green, the sea all round so bland a blue. And what a fascinating island it is on the map—an island of twists and curves and inland seas called Bodden; of lakes, and woods, and frequent ferries; with lesser islands dotted about its coasts; with bays innumerable stretching their arms out into the water; and with one huge forest, evidently magnificent, running nearly the whole length of the east coast, following its curves, dipping down to the sea in places, and in others climbing up chalk cliffs to crown them with the peculiar splendour of beeches.

It does not take me long to make up my mind, still less to cord up my light bundle, for somebody else does that; and I think it was only two days after I first found Marianne North and the guide-book that my maid Gertrud and I got out of a suffocating train into the freshness that blows round ryefields near the sea, and began our journey into the unknown.

It was a little wayside station on the line between Berlin and Stralsund, called Miltzow, a solitary red building on the edge of a pine-wood, that witnessed the beginning of our tour. The carriage had been sent on the day before, and round it, on our arrival, stood the station authorities in an interested group. The stationmaster, everywhere in Germany an elaborate, Olympic person in white gloves, actually helped the porter to cord on my hold-all with his own hands, and they both lingered over it as if loth to let us go. Evidently the coachman had told them what I was going to do, and I suppose such an enterprising woman does not get out at Miltzow every day. They packed us in with the greatest care, with so much care that I thought they would never have done. My hold-all was the biggest piece of luggage, and they corded it on in an upright position at our feet. I had left the choosing of its contents to Gertrud, only exhorting her, besides my pillow, to take a sufficiency of soap and dressing-gowns. Gertrud's luggage was placed by the porter on her lap. It was almost too modest. It was one small black bag, and a great part of its inside must, I knew, be taken up by the stockings she had brought to knit and the needles she did it with; yet she looked quite as respectable the day we came home as she did the day we started, and every bit as clean. My dressing- case was put on the box, and on top of it was a brown cardboard hat-box containing the coachman's wet-weather hat. A thick coat for possible cold days made a cushion for my back, and Gertrud's waterproof did the same thing for hers. Wedged in between us was the tea-basket, rattling inharmoniously, but preventing our slipping together in sloping places. Behind us in the hood were the umbrellas, rugs, guide-books, and maps, besides one of those round shiny yellow wooden band-boxes into which every decent German woman puts her best hat. This luggage, and some mysterious bundles on the box that the coachman thought were hidden by his legs but which bulged out unhideable on either side, prevented our looking elegant; but I did not want to look elegant, and I had gathered from the remarks of those who had refused to walk that Rügen was not a place where I should meet any one who did.

Now I suppose I could talk for a week and yet give no idea whatever of the exultation that filled my soul as I gazed on these arrangements. The picnic-like simplicity of them was so full of promise. It was as though I were going back to the very morning of life, to those fresh years when shepherd boys and others shout round one for no reason except that they are out of doors and alive. Also, during the years that have come after, years that may properly be called riper, it has been a conviction of mine that there is nothing so absolutely bracing for the soul as the frequent turning of one's back on duties. This was exactly what I was doing; and oh ye rigid female martyrs on the rack of daily exemplariness, ye unquestioning patient followers of paths that have been pointed out, if only you knew the wholesome joys of sometimes being less good!

The point at which we were is the nearest from which Rügen can be reached by persons coming up from the south and going to drive. No one ever gets out there who is bound for Rügen, because no one ever drives to Rügen. The ordinary tourist, almost exclusively German, goes first to Stralsund, is taken across the narrow strip of water, train and all, on the steam ferry, and continues without changing till he reaches the open sea on the other side of the island at Sassnitz. Or he goes by train from Berlin to Stettin and then by steamer down the Oder, crosses the open sea for four hours, and arrives, probably pensive for the boats are small and the waves are often big, at Göhren, the first stopping-place on the island's east coast.

We were not ordinary tourists, and having got to Miltzow were to be independent of all such wearinesses as trains and steamers till the day we wanted to come back again. From Miltzow we were going to drive to a ferry three miles off at a place called Stahlbrode, cross the mile of water, land on the island's south shore, and go on at once that afternoon to the jelly-fish of Miss North's Putbus, which were beckoning me across to the legend- surrounded island far more irresistibly than any of those grey figures the guide-book talked about.

The carriage was a light one of the victoria genus with a hood; the horses were a pair esteemed at home for their meekness; the coachman, August, was a youth who had never yet driven straight on for an indefinite period without turning round once, and he looked as though he thought he were going to enjoy himself. I was sure I was going to enjoy myself. Gertrud, I fancy, was without these illusions; but she is old, and has got out of the habit of being anything but resigned. She was the sop on this occasion thrown to the Grim One of the iron claws, for I would far rather have gone alone. But Gertrud is very silent; to go with her would be as nearly like being alone as it is possible to be when you are not. She could, I knew, be trusted to sit by my side knitting, however bumpy the road, and not opening her lips unless asked a question. Admirable virtue of silence, most precious, because most rare, jewel in the crown of female excellences, not possessed by a single one of those who had refused to walk! If either of them had occupied Gertrud's place and driven with me would she not, after the way of women, have spent the first half of the time telling me her secrets and the other half being angry with me because I knew them? And then Gertrud, after having kept quiet all day, would burst into activities at night, unpack the hold-all, produce pleasant things like slippers, see that my bed was as I like it, and end by tucking me up in it and going away on tiptoe with her customary quaint benediction, bestowed on me every night at bedtime: 'The dear God protect and bless the gracious one,' says Gertrud as she blows out the candle.

'And may He also protect and bless thee,' I reply; and could as ill spare my pillow as her blessing.

It was half-past two in the afternoon of the middle Friday in July when we left the station officials to go back to their dull work and trotted round the corner into the wide world. The sky was a hot blue. The road wound with gentle ups and downs between fields whitening to harvest. High over our heads the larks quivered in the light, shaking out that rapturous song that I can never hear without a throb of gratitude for being alive. There were no woods or hills, and we could see a long way on either side, see the red roofs of farms clustered wherever there was a hollow to protect them from the wild winds of winter, see the straight double line of trees where the high road to Stralsund cut across ours, see a little village a mile ahead of us with a venerable church on a mound in the middle of it gravely presiding over the surrounding wide parish of corn. I think I must have got out at least six times during the short drive between Miltzow and the ferry pretending I wanted flowers, but really to enjoy the delight of loitering. The rye was full of chickory and poppies, the ditches along the road where the spring dampness still lingered were white with the delicate loveliness of cow-parsley, that most spiritual of weeds. I picked an armful of it to hold up against the blue of the sky while we were driving; I gave Gertrud a bunch of poppies for which she thanked me without enthusiasm; I put little posies of chickory at the horses' ears; in fact I felt and behaved as if I were fifteen and out for my first summer holiday. But what did it matter? There was nobody there to see.

Stahlbrode is the most innocent-looking place—a small cluster of cottages on grass that goes down to the water. It was quite empty and silent. It has a long narrow wooden jetty running across the marshy shore to the ferry, and moored to the end of this jetty lay a big fishing-smack with furled brown sails. I got out and walked down to it to see if it were the ferry-boat, and whether the ferryman was in it. Both August and the horses had an alarmed, pricked-up expression as they saw me going out into the jaws of the sea. Even the emotionless Gertrud put away her stocking and stood by the side of the carriage watching me. The jetty was roughly put together, and so narrow that the carriage would only just fit in. A slight wooden rail was all the protection provided; but the water was not deep, and heaved limpidly over the yellow sand at the bottom. The shore we were on was flat and vividly green, the shore of Rügen opposite was flat and vividly green; the sea between was a lovely, sparkling blue; the sky was strewn across with loose clusters of pearly clouds; the breeze that had played so gently among the ears of corn round Miltzow danced along the little waves and splashed them gaily against the wooden posts of the jetty as though the freshness down there on the water had filled it with new life. I found the boat empty, a thing of steep sides and curved bottom, a thing that was surely never intended for the ferrying across of horses and carriages. No other boat was to be seen. Up the channel and down the channel there was nothing visible but the flat green shores, the dancing water, the wide sky, the bland afternoon light.

I turned back thoughtfully to the cottages. Suppose the ferry were only used for ferrying people? If so, we were in an extremely tiresome fix. A long way back against the sky I could see the line of trees bordering the road to Stralsund, and the whole dull, dusty distance would have to be driven over if the Stahlbrode ferry failed us. August took off his hat when I came up to him, and said ominously, 'Does the gracious one permit that I speak a few words?'

'Speak them, August.'

'It is very windy.'

'Not very.'

'It is far to go on water.'

'Not very.'

'Never yet have I been on the sea.'

'Well, you are going on it now.'

With an expression made up of two parts fright and one resignation he put on his hat again and relapsed into a silence that was grim. I took Gertrud with me to give me a countenance and walked across to the inn, a new red-brick house standing out boldly on a bit of rising ground, end ways on to the sea. The door was open and we went in, knocking with my sunshade on the floor. We stirred up no life of any sort. Not even a dog barked at us. The passage was wide and clean with doors on each side of it and an open door at either end—the one we had come in by followed by the afternoon sun, and the other framing a picture of sky with the sea at the bottom, the jetty, the smack with folded sails, and the coast of Rügen. Seeing a door with *Gaststube* painted on it I opened it and peeped in. To my astonishment it was full of men smoking in silence, and all with their eyes fixed on the opening door. They must have heard us. They must have seen us passing the window as we came up to the house. I concluded that the custom of the district requires that strangers shall in no way be interfered with until they actually ask definite questions; that it was so became clear by the alacrity with which a yellow-bearded man jumped up on our asking how we could get across to Rügen, and told us he was the ferryman and would take us there.

'But there is a carriage—can that go too?' I inquired anxiously, thinking of the deep bottom and steep sides of the fishing-smack.

'*Alles, Alles*,' he said cheerily; and calling to a boy to come and help he led the way through the door framing the sea, down a tiny, sandy garden prickly with gooseberry bushes, to the place where August sat marvelling on his box.

'Come along!' he shouted as he ran past him.

'What, along that thing of wood?' cried August. 'With my horses? And my newly-varnished carriage?'

'Come along!' shouted the ferryman, half-way down the jetty.

'Go on, August,' I commanded.

'It can never be accomplished,' said August, visibly breaking out into a perspiration.

'Go on,' I repeated sternly; but thought it on the whole more discreet to go on myself on my own feet, and so did Gertrud.

'If the gracious one insists——' faltered August, and began to drive gingerly down to the jetty with the face of one who thinks his last hour well on the way.

As I had feared, the carriage was very nearly smashed getting it over the sides of the smack. I sat up in the bows looking on in terror, expecting every instant to see the wheels wrenched off, and with their wrenching the end of our holiday. The optimistic ferryman assured us that it was going in quite easily— like a lamb, he declared, with great boldness of imagery. He sloped two ineffectual planks, one for each set of wheels, up the side of the boat, and he and August, hatless, coatless, and breathless, lifted the carriage over on to them. It was a horrid moment. The front wheels twisted right round and were as near coming off as any wheels I saw in my life. I was afraid to look at August, so right did he seem to have been when he protested that the thing could not be accomplished. Yet there was Rügen and here were we, and we had to get across to it somehow or turn round and do the dreary journey to Stralsund.

The horses, both exceedingly restive, had been unharnessed and got in first. They were held in the stern of the boat by two boys, who needed all their determination to do it. Then it was that I was thankful for the boat's steep sides, for if they had been lower those horses would certainly have kicked themselves over into the sea; and what should I have done then? And how should I have faced him who is in authority over me if I returned to him without his horses?

'We take them across daily,' the ferryman remarked, airily jerking his thumb in the direction of the carriage.

'Do so many people drive to Rügen?' I asked astonished, for the plank arrangements were staringly makeshift.

'Many people?' cried the ferryman. 'Rightly speaking, crowds.'

He was trying to make me happy. At least it reassured August to hear it; but I could not suppress a smile of deprecation at the size of the fib.

By this time we were under weigh, a fair wind sending us merrily over the water. The ferryman steered; August stood at his horses' heads talking to them soothingly; the two boys came and sat on some coiled ropes close to me, leaned their elbows on their knees and their chins on their hands, and fixing their blue fisher-boy eyes on my face kept them there with an unwinking interest during the entire crossing. Oh, it was lovely sitting up there in the sun, safe so far, in the delicious quiet of sailing. The tawny sail, darned and patched in divers shades of brown and red and orange, towered above us against the sky. The huge mast seemed to brush along across the very surface of the little white clouds. Above the rippling of the water we could hear the distant larks on either shore. August had put on his scarlet stable-jacket for the work of lifting the carriage in, and made a beautiful bit of colour among the browns of the old boat at the stern. The eyes of the ferryman lost all the alertness they had had on shore, and he stood at the rudder gazing dreamily out at the afternoon light on the Rügen meadows. How perfect it was after the train, after the clattering along the dusty road, and the heat and terror of getting on board. For one exquisite quarter of an hour we were softly lapped across in the sun, and for all that beauty we were only asked to pay three marks, which included the horses and carriage and the labour of getting us in and out. For a further small sum the ferryman became enthusiastic and begged me to be sure to come back that way. There was a single house on the Rügen shore where he lived, he said, and from which he would watch for us. A little dog came down to welcome us, but we saw no other living creature. The carriage conducted itself far more like a lamb on this side, and I drove away well pleased to have got over the chief difficulty of the tour, the soft-voiced ferryman wishing us Godspeed, and the two boys unwinking to the last.

So here we were on the legend-surrounded island. 'Hail, thou isle of fairyland, filled with beckoning figures!' I murmured under my breath, careful not to appear too unaccountable in Gertrud's eyes. With eager interest I looked about me, and anything less like fairyland and more like the coast of Pomerania lately left I have seldom seen. The road, a continuation of the road on the mainland, was exactly like other roads that are dull as far as a rambling village three miles farther on called Garz—persons referring to the map at the beginning of this book will see with what a melancholy straightness it proceeds to that village— and after Garz I ceased to care what it was like, for reasons which I will now set forth.

There was that afternoon in the market-place of Garz, and I know not why, since it was neither a Sunday nor a holiday, a brass band playing with a singular sonorousness. The horses having never before been required to listen to music, their functions at home being solely to draw me through the solitudes of forests, did not like it. I was astonished at the vigour of the dislike they showed who were wont to be so meek. They danced through Garz, pursued by the braying of the trumpets and the delighted shouts of the crowd, who seemed to bray and shout the louder the more the horses danced, and I was considering whether the time had not come for clinging to Gertrud and shutting my eyes when we turned a corner and got away from the noise on to the familiar rattle of the hard country road. I gave a sigh of relief and stretched out my head to see whether it were as straight a bit as the last. It was quite as straight, and in the distance bearing down on us was a black speck that swelled at an awful speed into a motor car. Now the horses had not yet seen a motor car. Their nerves, already shaken by the brass band, would never stand such a horrid sight I thought, and prudence urged an immediate getting out and a rushing to their heads. 'Stop, August!' I cried. 'Jump out, Gertrud— there's a dreadful thing coming—they're sure to bolt——'

August slowed down in apparent obedience to my order, and without waiting for him to stop entirely, the motor being almost upon us, I jumped out on one side and Gertrud jumped out on the other. Before I had time to run to the horses' heads the motor whizzed past. The horses strange to say hardly cared at all, only mildly shying as August drove them slowly along without stopping.

'That's all right,' I remarked, greatly relieved, to Gertrud, who still held her stocking. 'Now we'll get in again.'

But we could not get in again because August did not stop.

'Call to him to stop,' I said to Gertrud, turning aside to pick some unusually big poppies.

She called, but he did not stop.

'Call louder, Gertrud,' I said impatiently, for we were now a good way behind.

She called louder, but he did not stop.

Then I called; then she called; then we called together, but he did not stop. On the contrary, he was driving on now at the usual pace, rattling noisily over the hard road, getting more and more out of reach.

'Shout, shout, Gertrud!' I cried in a frenzy; but how could any one so respectable as Gertrud shout? She sent a faint shriek after the ever-receding

August, and when I tried to shout myself I was seized with such uncontrollable laughter that nothing whatever of the nature of a noise could be produced.

Meanwhile August was growing very small in the distance. He evidently did not know we had got out when the motor car appeared, and was under the pleasing impression that we were sitting behind him being jogged comfortably towards Putbus. He dwindled and dwindled with a rapidity distressing to witness. 'Shout, shout,' I gasped, myself contorted with dreadful laughter, half-wildest mirth and half despair.

She began to trot down the road after him waving her stocking at his distant back and emitting a series of shrill shrieks, goaded by the exigencies of the situation.

The last we saw of the carriage was a yellow glint as the sun caught the shiny surface of my bandbox; immediately afterwards it vanished over the edge of a far-away dip in the road, and we were alone with Nature.

Gertrud and I stared at each other in speechless dismay. Then she looked on in silence while I sank on to a milestone and laughed. There was nothing, her look said, to laugh at, and much to be earnest over in our tragic predicament, and I knew it but I could not stop. August had had no instructions as to where he was driving to or where we were going to put up that night; of Putbus and Marianna North he had never heard. With the open ordnance map on my lap I had merely called out directions, since leaving Miltzow, at cross-roads. Therefore in all human probability he would drive straight on till dark, no doubt in growing private astonishment at the absence of orders and the length of the way; then when night came he would, I supposed, want to light his lamps, and getting down to do so would immediately be frozen with horror at what he saw, or rather did not see, in the carriage. What he would do after that I could not conceive. In sheerest despair I laughed till I cried, and the sight of Gertrud watching me silently from the middle of the deserted road only made me less able to leave off. Behind us in the distance, at the end of a vista of *chaussée* trees, were the houses of Garz; in front of us, a long way in front of us, rose the red spire of the church of Casnewitz, a village through which, as I still remembered from the map now driving along by itself, our road to Putbus lay. Up and down the whiteness of this road not a living creature, either in a cart or on its legs, was to be seen. The bald country, here very bald and desolate, stretched away on either side into nothingness. The wind sighed about, whisking little puffs of derisive dust into our eyes as it passed. There was a dreadful absence of anything like sounds.

'No doubt,' said Gertrud, 'August will soon return?'

'He won't,' I said, wiping my eyes; 'he'll go on for ever. He's wound up. Nothing will stop him.'

'What, then, will the gracious one do?'

'Walk after him, I suppose,' I said, getting up, 'and trust to something unexpected making him find out he hasn't got us. But I'm afraid nothing will. Come on, Gertrud,' I continued, feigning briskness while my heart was as lead, 'it's nearly six already, and the road is long and lonely.'

'*Ach*,' groaned Gertrud, who never walks.

'Perhaps a cart will pass us and give us a lift. If not we'll walk to that village with the church over there and see if we can get something on wheels to pursue August with. Come on—I hope your boots are all right.'

'*Ach*,' groaned Gertrud again, lifting up one foot, as a dog pitifully lifts up its wounded paw, and showing me a black cashmere boot of the sort that is soft and pleasant to the feet of servants who are not required to use them much.

'I'm afraid they're not much good on this hard road,' I said. 'Let us hope something will catch us up soon.'

'*Ach*,' groaned poor Gertrud, whose feet are very tender.

But nothing did catch us up, and we trudged along in grim silence, the desire to laugh all gone.

'You must, my dear Gertrud,' I said after a while, seeking to be cheerful, 'regard this in the light of healthful exercise. You and I are taking a pleasant afternoon walk together in Rügen.'

Gertrud said nothing; at all times loathing movement out of doors she felt that this walking was peculiarly hateful because it had no visible end. And what would become of us if we were forced to spend the night in some inn without our luggage? The only thing I had with me was my purse, the presence of which, containing as it did all the money I had brought, caused me to cast a careful eye at short intervals behind me, less in the hope of seeing a cart than in the fear of seeing a tramp; and the only thing Gertrud had was her half-knitted stocking. Also we had had nothing to eat but a scrappy tea-basket lunch hours before in the train, and my intention had been to have food at Putbus and then drive down to a place called Lauterbach, which being on the seashore was more convenient for the jelly-fish than Putbus, and spend the night there in an hotel much recommended by the guide-book. By this time according to my plans we ought to have been sitting in Putbus eating *Kalbsschnitzel*. 'Gertrud,' I asked rather faintly, my soul drooping within me at the thought of the *Kalbsschnitzel*, 'are you hungry?'

Gertrud sighed. 'It is long since we ate,' she said.

We trudged on in silence for another five minutes.

'Gertrud,' I asked again, for during those five minutes my thoughts had dwelt with a shameful persistency on the succulent and the gross, 'are you *very* hungry?'

'The gracious one too must be in need of food,' evaded Gertrud, who for some reason never would admit she wanted feeding.

'Oh she is,' I sighed; and again we trudged on in silence.

It seemed a long while before we reached that edge over which my bandbox had disappeared flashing farewell as it went, and when we did get to it and eagerly looked along the fresh stretch of road in hopes of seeing August miraculously turned back, we gave a simultaneous groan, for it was as deserted as the one we had just come along. Something lay in the middle of it a few yards on, a dark object like a little heap of brown leaves. Thinking it was leaves I saw no reason for comment; but Gertrud, whose eyes are very sharp, exclaimed.

'What, do you see August?' I cried.

'No, no—but there in the road—the tea-basket!'

It was indeed the tea-basket, shaken out as it naturally would be on the removal of the bodies that had kept it in its place, come to us like the ravens of old to give us strength and sustenance.

'It still contains food,' said Gertrud, hurrying towards it.

'Thank heaven,' said I.

We dragged it out of the road to the grass at the side, and Gertrud lit the spirit-lamp and warmed what was left in the teapot of the tea. It was of an awful blackness. No water was to be got near, and we dared not leave the road to look for any in case August should come back. There were some sorry pieces of cake, one or two chicken sandwiches grown unaccountably horrible, and all those strawberries we had avoided at lunch because they were too small or two much squashed. Over these mournful revels the church spire of Casnewitz, now come much closer, presided; it was the silent witness of how honourably we shared, and how Gertrud got the odd sandwich because of her cashmere boots.

Then we buried the tea-basket in a ditch, in a bed of long grass and cow-parsley, for it was plain that I could not ask Gertrud, who could hardly walk as it was, to carry it, and it was equally plain that I could not carry it myself, for it was as mysteriously heavy as other tea-baskets and in size very nearly as big as I am. So we buried it, not without some natural regrets and a dim feeling that we were flying in the face of Providence, and there it is, I suppose, grown very rusty, to this day.

After that Gertrud got along a little better, and my thoughts being no longer concentrated on food I could think out what was best to be done. The result was that on reaching Casnewitz we inquired at once which of the cottages was an inn, and having found one asked a man who seemed to belong there to let us have a conveyance with as much speed as possible.

'Where have you come from?' he inquired, staring first at one and then at the other.

'Oh—from Garz.'

'From Garz? Where do you want to go to?'

'To Putbus.'

'To Putbus? Are you staying there?'

'No—yes—anyhow we wish to drive there. Kindly let us start as soon as possible.'

'Start! I have no cart.'

'Sir,' said Gertrud with much dignity, 'why did you not say so at once?'

'*Ja, ja, Fräulein*, why did I not?'

We walked out.

'This is very unpleasant, Gertrud,' I remarked, and I wondered what those at home would say if they knew that on the very first day of my driving-tour I had managed to lose the carriage and had had to bear the banter of publicans.

'There is a little shop,' said Gertrud. 'Does the gracious one permit that I make inquiries there?'

We went in and Gertrud did the talking.

'Putbus is not very far from here,' said the old man presiding, who was at least polite. 'Why do not the ladies walk? My horse has been out all day, and my son who drives him has other things now to do.'

'Oh we can't walk,' I broke in. 'We must drive because we might want to go beyond Putbus—we are not sure—it depends——'

The old man looked puzzled. 'Where is it that the ladies wish to go?' he inquired, trying to be patient.

'To Putbus, anyhow. Perhaps only to Putbus. We can't tell till we get there.

But indeed, indeed you must let us have your horse.'

Still puzzled, the old man went out to consult with his son, and we waited in profound dejection among candles and coffee. Putbus was not, as he had said, far, but I remembered how on the map it seemed to be a very nest of cross-roads, all radiating from a round circus sort of place in the middle. Which of them would August consider to be the straight continuation of the road from Garz? Once beyond Putbus he would be lost to us indeed.

It took about half an hour to persuade the son and to harness the horse; and while this was going on we stood at the door watching the road and listening eagerly for sounds of wheels. One cart did pass, going in the direction of Garz, and when I heard it coming I was so sure that it was August that I triumphantly called to Gertrud to run and tell the old man we did not need his son. Gertrud, wiser, waited till she saw what it was, and after the quenching of that sudden hope we both drooped more than ever.

'Where am I to drive to?' asked the son, whipping up his horse and bumping us away over the stones of Casnewitz. He sat huddled up looking exceedingly sulky, manifestly disgusted at having to go out again at the end of a day's work. As for the cart, it was a sad contrast to the cushioned comfort of the vanished victoria. It was very high, very wooden, very shaky, and we sat on a plank in the middle of so terrible a noise that when we wanted to say anything we had to shout. 'Where am I to drive to?' repeated the youth, scowling over his shoulder.

'Please drive straight on until you meet a carriage.'

'A what?'

'A carriage.'

'Whose carriage?'

'My carriage.'

He scowled round again with deepened disgust. 'If you have a carriage,' he said, looking at us as though he were afraid we were lunatics, 'why are you in my cart?'

'Oh why, why are we!' I cried wringing my hands, overcome by the wretchedness of our plight; for we were now beyond Casnewitz, and gazing anxiously ahead with the strained eyes of Sister Annes we saw the road as straight and as empty as ever.

The youth drove on in sullen silence, his very ears seeming to flap with scorn; no more good words would he waste on two mad women. The road now lay through woods, beautiful beechwoods that belong to Prince Putbus, not fenced off but invitingly open to every one, with green shimmering depths and occasional flashes of deer. The tops of the great beeches shone like gold against the sky. The sea must have been quite close, for though it was not visible the smell of it was everywhere. The nearer we got to Putbus the more civilised did the road become. Seats appeared on either side at intervals that grew more frequent. Instead of the usual wooden sign-posts, iron ones with tarnished gilt lettering pointed down the forest lanes; and soon we met the first of the Putbus lamp-posts, also iron and elaborate, wandered out, as it seemed, beyond the natural sphere of lamp-posts, to light the innocent country road. All these signs portended what Germans call *Badegäste*—in English obviously bath-guests, or, more elegantly, visitors to a bathing resort; and presently when we were nearer Putbus we began to pass them strolling in groups and couples and sitting on the seats which were of stone and could not have been good things for warm bath-guests to sit on.

Wretched as I was I still saw the quaintness and prettiness of Putbus. There was a notice up that all vehicles must drive through it at a walking pace, so we crawled along its principal street which, whatever else it contained, contained no sign of August. This street has Prince Putbus's grounds on one side and a line of irregular houses, all white, all old-fashioned, and all charming, on the other. A double row of great trees forms a shady walk on the edge of the grounds, and it is bountifully supplied with those stone seats so fatal, I am sure, to many an honest bath-guest. The grounds, trim and shady, have neat paths winding into their recesses from the road, with no fence or wall or obstacle of any sort to be surmounted by the timid tourist; every tourist may walk in them as long and as often as he likes without the least preliminary bother of gates and lodges.

As we jolted slowly over the rough stones we were objects of the liveliest interest to the bath-guests sitting out on the pavement in front of the inns having supper. No sign whatever of August was to be seen, not even an ordnance map, as I had half expected, lying in the road. Our cart made more noise here than ever, it being characteristic of Putbus that things on wheels are heard for an amazing time before and after their passing. It is the drowsiest little town. Grass grows undisturbed between the cobbles of the street, along the gutters, and in the cracks of the pavement on the sidewalk. One or two shops seem sufficient for the needs of all the inhabitants, including the boys at the school here which is a sort of German Eton, and from what I saw in the windows their needs are chiefly picture-postcards and cakes. There is a white theatre with a colonnade as quaint as all the rest. The houses have many windows and balconies hung about with flowers. The place did not somehow seem real in the bright flood of evening sunlight, it looked like a place in a picture or a dream; but the bath-guests, pausing in their eating to stare at us, were enjoying themselves in a very solid and undreamlike fashion, not in the least in harmony with the quaint background. In spite of my forlorn condition I could not help reflecting on its probable charms in winter under the clear green of the cold sky, with all these people away, when the frosted branches of the trees stretch across to deserted windows, when the theatre is silent for months, when the inns only keep as much of themselves open as meets the requirements of the infrequent commercial traveller, and the cutting wind blows down the street, empty all day long. Certainly a perfect place to spend a quiet winter in, to go to when one is tired of noise and bustle and of a world choked to the point of suffocation with strenuous persons trying to do each other good. Rooms in one of those spacious old houses with the large windows facing the sun, and plenty of books—if I were that abstracted but happy form of reptile called a bookworm, which I believed I am prevented from being only by my sex, the genus, I am told, being persistently male, I would take care to spend at least one of my life's winters in Putbus. How divinely quiet it would be. What a place for him who intends to pass an examination, to write a book, or who wants the crumples got by crushing together too long with his fellows to be smoothed out of his soul. And what walks there would be, to stretch legs and spirits grown stiff, in the crisp wintry woods where the pale sunshine falls across unspoilt snow. Sitting in my cart of sorrow in summer sultriness I could feel the ineffable pure cold of winter strike my face at the mere thought, the ineffable pure cold that spurs the most languid mind into activity.

Thus far had I got in my reflections, and we had jolted slowly down about half the length of the street, when a tremendous clatter of hoofs and wheels coming towards us apparently at a gallop in starkest defiance of regulations, brought me back with a jerk to the miserable present.

'Bolted,' remarked the surly youth, hastily drawing on one side.

The bath-guests at supper flung down their knives and forks and started up to look.

'*Halt! Hah!*' cried some of them, '*Es ist verboten! Schritt! Schritt!*'

'How can he halt?' cried others; 'his horses have bolted.'

'Then why does he beat them?' cried the first.

'It is August!' shrieked Gertrud. 'August! August! We are here! Stop! Stop!'

For with staring eyes and set mouth August was actually galloping past us. This time he did hear Gertrud's shriek, acute with anguish, and pulled the horses on to their haunches. Never have I seen unhappy coachman with so white a face. He had had, it appeared, the most stringent private instructions before leaving home to take care of me, and on the very first day to let me somehow tumble out and lose me! He was tearing back in the awful conviction that he would find Gertrud and myself in the form of corpses. 'Thank God!' he cried devoutly on seeing us, 'Thank God! Is the gracious one unhurt?'

Certainly poor August had had the worst of it.

Now it is most unlikely that the bath-guests of Putbus will ever enjoy themselves quite so much again. Their suppers all grew cold while they crowded round to see and listen. August, in his relief, was a changed creature. He was voluble and loud as I never could have believed. Jumping off his box to turn the horses round and help me out of the cart, he explained to me and to all and any who chose to listen how he had driven on and on through Putbus, straight round the circus to the continuation of the road on the north side, where sign-posts revealed to him that he was heading for Bergen, more and more surprised at receiving no orders, more and more struck by the extreme silence behind him. 'The gracious one,' he amplified for the benefit of the deeply-interested tourists, 'exchanges occasional observations with Fräulein'—the tourists gazed at Gertrud—'and the cessation of these became by degrees noticeable. Yet it is not permissible that a well-trained coachman should turn to look, or interfere with a *Herrschaft* that chooses to be silent ——'

'Let us get on, August,' I interrupted, much embarrassed by all this.

'The luggage must be seen to—the strain of the rapid driving——'

A dozen helpful hands stretched out with offers of string.

'Finally,' continued August, not to be stopped in his excited account, manipulating the string and my hold-all with shaking fingers—' finally by the mercy of Providence the map used by the gracious one fell out'—I knew it would—'as a peasant was passing. He called to me, he pointed to the road, I pulled up, I turned round, and what did I see? What I then saw I shall never—no, never forget—no, not if my life should continue to a hundred.' He put his hand on his heart and gasped. The crowd waited breathless. 'I turned round,' continued August, 'and I saw nothing.'

'But you said you would never forget what you saw,' objected a dissatisfied-looking man.

'Never, never shall I forget it.'

'Yet you saw nothing at all.'

'Nothing, nothing. Never will I forget it.'

'If you saw nothing you cannot forget it,' persisted the dissatisfied man.

'I say I cannot—it is what I say.'

'That will do, August,' I said; 'I wish to drive on.'

The surly youth had been listening with his chin on his hand. He now removed his chin, stretched his hand across to me sitting safely among my cushions, and said, 'Pay me.'

'Pay him, Gertrud,' I said; and having been paid he turned his horse and drove back to Casnewitz scornful to the last.

'Go on, August,' I ordered. 'Go on. We can hold this thing on with our feet. Get on to your box and go on.'

The energy in my voice penetrated at last through his agitation. He got up on to his box, settled himself in a flustered sort of fashion, the tourists fell apart staring their last and hardest at a vision about to vanish, and we drove away.

'It is impossible to forget that which has not been,' called out the dissatisfied man as August passed him.

'It is what I say—it is what I say!' cried August, irritated.

Nothing could have kept me in Putbus after this.

Skirting the circus on the south side we turned down a hill to the right, and immediately were in the country again with cornfields on either side and the sea like a liquid sapphire beyond them. Gertrud and I put a coat between us in place of the abandoned tea-basket, and settled in with an appreciation of our comforts that we had not had before. Gertrud, indeed, looked positively happy, so thankful was she to be safely in the carriage again, and joy was written in every line of August's back. About a mile and a half off lay Lauterbach, a little straggling group of houses down by the water; and quite by itself, a mile to the left of Lauterbach, I could see the hotel we were going to, a long white building something like a Greek temple, with a portico and a flight of steps the entire length of its façade, conspicuous in its whiteness against a background of beechwoods. Woods and fields and sea and a lovely little island a short way from the shore called Vilm, were bathed in sunset splendour. Lauterbach and not Putbus, then, was the place of radiant jelly-fish and crystal water and wooded coves. Probably in those distant years when Marianne North enjoyed them Lauterbach as an independent village with a name to itself did not exist. A branch railway goes down now to the very edge of the sea. We crossed the line and drove between chestnut trees and high grassy banks starry with flowers to the Greek hotel.

How delightful it looked as we got out of the deep chestnut lane into the open space in front of it before we were close enough to see that time had been unkind. The sea was within a stone's throw on the right beyond a green, marshy, rushy meadow. On the left people were mowing in a field. Across the field the spire of a little Lutheran church looked out oddly round the end of the pagan portico. Behind and on either side were beeches. Not a soul came out as we drew up at the bottom of the steps. Not a soul was to be seen except the souls with scythes in the meadow. We waited a moment, thinking to hear a bell rung and to see flying waiters, but no one came. The scythes in the meadow swished, the larks called down that it was a fine evening, some fowls came and pecked about on the sunny steps of the temple, some red sails passed between the trunks of the willows down near the water.

'Shall I go in?' inquired Gertrud.

She went up the steps and disappeared through glass doors. Grass grew between the stones of the steps, and the walls of the house were damp and green. The ceiling of the portico was divided into squares and painted sky-blue. In one corner paint and plaster had come off together, probably in wild winter nights, and this and the grass-grown steps and the silence gave the place a strangely deserted look. I would have thought it was shut up if there had not been a table in the portico with a reassuring red-check cloth on it and a coffee-pot.

Gertrud came out again followed by a waiter and a small boy. I was in no hurry, and could have sat there contentedly for any time in the pleasant evening sunshine. The waiter assured me there was just one room vacant for me, and by the luckiest of chances just one other leading out of it for the Fräulein. I followed him up the steps. The portico, open at either end, framed in delicious pictures. The waiter led me through a spacious boarded hall where a narrow table along one side told of recent supper, through intricate passages, across little inner courts with shrubs and greenery, and blue sky above, and lilac bushes in tubs looking as though they had to pretend they were orange trees and that this was Italy and that the white plaster walls, so mouldy in places, were the marble walls of some classic baths, up strange stairs that sloped alarmingly to one side, along more passages, and throwing open one of the many small white doors, said with pride, 'Here is the apartment; it is a fine, a big, a splendid apartment.'

The apartment was of the sort that produces an immediate determination in the breast of him to whom it is offered to die sooner than occupy it. Sleep in its gloomy recesses and parti-coloured bed I would not. Sooner would I brave the authorities, and taking my hold-all for a pillow go out to the grasshoppers for the night. In spite of the waiter's assertion, made for the glory of the house, that this was the one room unoccupied, I saw other rooms, perhaps smaller but certainly vacant, lurking in his eye; therefore I said firmly, 'Show me something else.'

The house was nearly all at my disposal I found. It is roomy, and there were hardly a dozen people staying in it, I chose a room with windows opening into the portico, through whose white columns I would be able to see a series of peaceful country pictures as I lay in bed. The boards were bare and the bed was covered with another of those parti-coloured quilts that suggest a desire to dissemble spots rather than wash them out. The Greek temple was certainly primitive, and would hardly appeal to any but the simplest, meekest of tourists. I hope I am simple and meek. I felt as though I must be as I looked round this room and knew that of my own free will I was going to sleep in it; and not only sleep in it but be very happy in it. It was the series of pictures between the columns that had fascinated me.

While Gertrud was downstairs superintending the bringing up of the luggage, I leaned out of one of my windows and examined the delights. I was quite close to the blue and white squares of the portico's ceiling; and looking down I saw its grass-grown pavement, and the head of a pensive tourist drinking beer just beneath me. Here again big lilac bushes planted at intervals between the columns did duty for orange trees. The north end framed the sky and fields and distant church; the south end had a picture of luminous water shining through beech leaves; the pair of columns in front enclosed the chestnut-lined road we had come along and the outermost white houses of Putbus among dark trees against the sunset on high ground behind; through those on the left was the sea, hardly sea here at all the bay is so sheltered, and hardly salt at all, for grass and rushes, touched just then by the splendour of light into a transient divine brightness, lay all along the shore. 'Truly the light is sweet, and a pleasant thing it is for the eyes to behold the sun,' I thought; aloud, I suppose, for Gertrud coming in with the hold-all said 'Did the gracious one speak?'

Quite unable to repeat this rapturous conviction to Gertrud, I changed it into a modest request that she should order supper.

How often in these grey autumn days have I turned my face away from the rain on the window and the mournful mistiness of the November fields, or my mind from the talk of the person next to me, to think with a smile of the beauty of that supper. Not that I had beautiful things to eat, for lengthy consultations with the waiter led only to eggs; but they were brought down steep steps to a little nook among the beeches at the water's edge, and this little nook on that particular evening was the loveliest in the world. Enthusiastically did I eat those eggs and murmur 'Earth has not anything to show more fair'—as much, that is, of it as could be made to apply. Nobody could see me or hear me down there, screened at the sides and back and overhead by the beeches, and it is an immense comfort secretly to quote. What did it matter if the tablecloth were damp, besides having other imperfections? What if the eggs cooled down at once, and cool eggs have always been an abomination to me? What if the waiter forgot the sugar, and I dislike coffee without sugar? Sooner than go up and search for him and lose one moment of that rosy splendour on the water I felt that I would go for ever sugarless. My table was nearly on a level with the sea. A family of ducks were slowly paddling about in front of me, making little furrows in the quiet water and giving an occasional placid quack. The ducks, the water, the island of Vilm opposite, the Lauterbach jetty half a mile off across the little bay with a crowd of fisher-boats moored near it, all were on fire with the same red radiance. The sun was just down, and the sky behind the dark Putbus woods was a marvel of solemn glory. The reflections of the beech trees I was sitting under lay black along the water. I could hear the fishermen talking over at the jetty, and a child calling on the island, so absolute was the stillness. And almost before I knew how beautiful it was the rosiness faded off the island, lingered a moment longer on the masts of the fisher-boats, gathered at last only in the pools among the rushes, died away altogether; the sky paled to green, a few stars looked out faintly, a light twinkled in the solitary house on Vilm, and the waiter came down and asked if he should bring a lamp. A lamp! As though all one ever wanted was to see the tiny circle round oneself, to be able to read the evening paper, or write postcards to one's friends, or sew. I have a peculiar capacity for doing nothing and yet enjoying myself. To sit there and look out into what Whitman calls the huge and thoughtful night was a comely and sufficient occupation for the best part of me; and as for the rest, the inferior or domestic part, the fingers that might have been busy, the tongue that might have wagged, the superficial bit of brain in daily use for the planning of trivialities, how good it is that all that should often be idle.

With an impatience that surprised him I refused the waiter's lamp.

THE SECOND DAY

LAUTERBACH AND VILM

A ripe experience of German pillows in country places leads me to urge the intending traveller to be sure to take his own. The native pillows are mere bags, in which feathers may have been once. There is no substance in them at all. They are of a horrid flabbiness. And they have, of course, the common drawback of all public pillows, they are haunted by the nightmares of other people. A pillow, it is true, takes up a great deal of room in one's luggage, but in Rügen however simply you dress you are better dressed than the others, so that you need take hardly any clothes. My hold-all, not a specially big one, really did hold all I wanted. The pillow filled one side of it, and my bathing things a great part of the other, and I was away eleven days; yet I am sure I was admirably clean the whole time, and I defy any one to say my garments were not both appropriate and irreproachable. Towards the end, it is true, Gertrud had to mend and brush a good deal, but those are two of the things she is there for; and it is infinitely better to be comfortable at night than, by leaving the pillow at home and bringing dresses in its place, be more impressive by day. And let no one visit Rügen who is not of that meek and lowly character that would always prefer a good pillow to a diversity of raiment, and has no prejudices about its food.

Having eased my conscience by these hints, which he will find invaluable, to the traveller, I can now go on to say that except for the pillow I would have had if I had not brought my own, for the coloured quilt, for the water to wash with brought in a very small coffee-pot, and for the breakfast which was as cold and repellent as in some moods some persons find the world, my experiences of the hotel were pleasing. It is true that I spent most of the day, as I shall presently relate, away from it, and it is also true that in the searching light of morning I saw much that had been hidden: scraps of paper lying about the grass near the house, an automatic bon-bon machine in the form of a brooding hen, and an automatic weighing machine, both at the top of the very steps leading down to the nook that had been the night before enchanted, and, worst shock of all, an electric bell piercing the heart of the very beech tree under which I had sat. But the beauties are so many and so great that if a few of them are spoilt there are still enough left to make Lauterbach one of the most delightful places conceivable. The hotel was admirably quiet; no tourists arrived late, and those already in it seemed to go to bed extraordinarily early; for when I came up from the water soon after ten the house was so silent that instinctively I stole along the passages on the tips of my toes, and for no reason that I could discover felt conscience-stricken. Gertrud, too, appeared to think it was unusually late; she was waiting for me at the door with a lamp, and seemed to expect me to look conscience-stricken. Also, she had rather the expression of the resigned and forgiving wife of an incorrigible evil-doer. I went into my room much pleased that I am not a man and need not have a wife who forgives me.

The windows were left wide open, and all night through my dreams I could hear the sea gently rippling among the rushes. At six in the morning a train down at the station hidden behind the chestnuts began to shunt and to whistle, and as it did not leave off and I could not sleep till it did, I got up and sat at the window and amused myself watching the pictures between the columns in the morning sunlight. A solitary mower in the meadow was very busy with his scythe, but its swishing could not be heard through the shunting. At last the train steamed away and peace settled down again over Lauterbach, the scythe swished audibly, the larks sang rapturously, and I fell to saying my prayers, for indeed it was a day to be grateful for, and the sea was the deepest, divinest blue.

The bathing at Lauterbach is certainly perfect. You walk along a footpath on the edge of low cliffs, shaded all the way from the door of the hotel to the bathing-huts by the beechwood, the water heaving and shining just below you, the island of Vilm opposite, the distant headland of Thiessow a hazy violet line between the misty blues of sea and sky in front, and at your feet moss and grass and dear common flowers flecked with the dancing lights and shadows of a beechwood when the sun is shining.

'Oh this is perfect!' I exclaimed to Gertrud; for on a fine fresh morning one must exclaim to somebody. She was behind me on the narrow path, her arms full of towels and bathing things. 'Won't you bathe too, afterwards, Gertrud? Can you resist it?'

But Gertrud evidently could resist it very well. She glanced at the living loveliness of the sea with an eye that clearly saw in it only a thing that made dry people wet. If she had been Dr. Johnson she would boldly have answered, 'Madam, I hate immersion.' Being Gertrud, she pretended that she had a cold.

'Well, to-morrow then,' I said hopefully; but she said colds hung about her for days.

'Well, as soon as you have got over it,' I said, persistently and odiously hopeful; but she became prophetic and said she would never get over it.

The bathing-huts are in a row far enough away from the shore to be in deep water. You walk out to them along a little footbridge of planks and find a sunburnt woman, amiable as all the people seem to be who have their business in deep waters, and she takes care of your things and dries them for you and provides you with anything you have forgotten and charges you twenty *pfennings* at the end for all her attentions as well as the bathe. The farthest hut is the one to get if you can—another invaluable hint. It is very roomy, and has a sofa, a table, and a big looking-glass, and one window opening to the south and one to the east. Through the east window you see the line of low cliffs with the woods above till they melt into a green plain that stretches off into vagueness towards the haze of Thiessow. Through the south window you see the little island of Vilm, with its one house set about with cornfields, and its woods on the high ground at the back.

Gertrud sat on the steps knitting while I swam round among the jelly-fish and thought of Marianne North. How right she was about the bathing, and the colours, and the crystal clearness of the water in that sandy cove! The bathing woman leaned over the hand-rail watching me with a sympathetic smile. She wore a white sun-bonnet, and it looked so well against the sky that I wished Gertrud could be persuaded to put one on too in place of her uninteresting and eminently respectable black bonnet. I could have stayed there for hours, perfectly happy, floating on the sparkling stuff, and I did stay there for nearly one, with the result that I climbed up the cliff a chilled and saddened woman, and sat contemplating the blue tips of my fingers while the waiter brought breakfast, and thought what a pitiful thing it was to have blue finger tips, instead of rejoicing as I would have done after a ten minutes' swim in the glorious fact that I was alive at all on such a morning.

The cold tea, cold eggs, and hard rolls did not make me more cheerful. I sat under the beeches where I had had supper the night before and shivered in my thickest coat, with the July sun blazing on the water and striking brilliant colours out of the sails of the passing fisher-boats. The hotel dog came along the shingle with his tongue out, and lay down near me in the shade. Visitors from Putbus, arriving in an omnibus for their morning bathe, passed by fanning themselves with their hats.

The Putbus visitors come down every morning in a sort of waggonette to bathe and walk back slowly up the hill to dinner. After this exertion they think they have done enough for their health, and spend the rest of the day sleeping, or sitting out of doors drinking beer and coffee. I think this is quite a good way of spending a holiday if you have worked hard all the rest of the year; and the tourists I saw looked as if they had. More of them stay at Putbus than at Lauterbach, although it is so much farther from the sea, because the hotel I was at was slightly dearer than—I ought rather to say, judging from the guide- book, not quite so cheap as—the Putbus hotels. I suppose it was less full than it might be because of this slight difference, or perhaps there was the slight difference because it was less full—who shall solve such mysteries? Anyhow the traveller need not be afraid of the bill, for when I engaged our rooms the waiter was surprised that I refused to put myself *en pension*, and explained in quite an aggrieved voice that all the *Herrschaften* put themselves *en pension*, and he hoped I did not think five marks a day for everything a too expensive arrangement. I praised the arrangement as just and excellent, but said that, being a bird of passage, I would prefer not to make it.

After breakfast I set out to explore the Goor, the lovely beechwood stretching along the coast from the very doors of the hotel. I started so briskly down the footpath on the edge of the cliffs in the hope of getting warm, that tourists who were warm already and were sitting under the trees gasping, stared at me reproachfully as I hurried past.

The Goor is beautiful. The path I took runs through thick shade with many windings, and presently comes out at the edge of the wood down by the sea in a very hot, sheltered corner, where the sun beats all day long on the shingle and coarse grass. A solitary oak tree, old and storm-beaten, stands by itself near the water; across the water is the wooded side of Vilm; and if you continue along the shingle a few yards you are away from the trees and out on a grassy plain, where lilac scabious bend their delicate stalks in the wind. An old black fishing-smack lay on its side on the shingle, its boards blistered by the sun. Its blackness and the dark lines of the solitary oak sharply cleft the flood of brilliant light. What a hot, happy corner to lie in all day with a book! No tourists go to it, for the path leads to nowhere, ending abruptly just there in coarse grass and shingle—a mixture grievous to the feet of the easily tired. The usual walk for those who have enough energy—it is not a very long one, and does not need much—is through the Goor to the north side, where the path takes you to the edge of a clover field across which you see the little village of Vilmnitz nestling among its trees and rye, and then brings you back gently and comfortably and shadily to the hotel; but this turning to the right only goes down to the shingle, the old boat, and the lonely oak. The first thing to do in that hot corner is to pull off your coat, which I did; and if you like heat and dislike blue finger tips and chilled marrows, lie down on the shingle, draw your hat over your eyes, and bake luxuriously, which I did also. In the pocket of my coat was *The Prelude*, the only book I had brought. I brought it because I know of no other book that is at the same time so slender and so satisfying. It slips even into a woman's pocket, and has an extraordinarily filling effect on the mind. Its green limp covers are quite worn with the journeys it has been with me. I take it wherever I go; and I have read it and read it for many summers without yet having entirely assimilated its adorable stodginess. Oh shade of Wordsworth, to think that so unutterable a grub and groveller as I am should dare call anything of thine Stodgy! But it is this very stodginess that makes it, if you love Wordsworth, the perfect book where there can be only one. You must, to enjoy it, be first a lover of Wordsworth. You must love the uninspired poems for the sake of the divineness of the inspired poems. You must be able to be interested in the description of Simon Lee's personal appearance, and not mind his wife, an aged woman, being made to rhyme with the Village Common. Even the Idiot Boy should not be a stumbling-block to you; and your having learned The Pet Lamb in the nursery is no reason why you should dislike it now. They all have their beauties; there is always some gem, more or less bright, to be found in them; and the pages of *The Prelude* are strewn with precious jewels. I have had it with me so often in happy country places that merely to open it and read that first cry of relief and delight—'Oh there is blessing in this gentle breeze!'—brings back the dearest remembrances of fresh and joyous hours. And how wholesome to be reminded when the days are rainy and things look blank of the many joyous hours one has had. Every instant of happiness is a priceless possession for ever.

That morning my *Prelude* fell open at the Residence in London, a part where the gems are not very thick, and the satisfying properties extremely developed. My eye lighted on the bit where he goes for a walk in the London streets, and besides a Nurse, a Bachelor, a Military Idler, and a Dame with Decent Steps— figures with which I too am familiar—he sees—

> ... with basket at his breast
> The Jew; the stately and slow-moving Turk
> With freight of slipper piled beneath his arm....
> The Swede, the Russian; from the genial south
> The Frenchman and the Spaniard; from remote
> America, the Hunter-Indian; Moors,
> Malays, Lascars, the Tartar, the Chinese,
> And Negro Ladies in white muslingowns

—figures which are not, at any rate, to be met in the streets of Berlin. I am afraid to say that this is not poetry, for perhaps it is only I do not know it; but after all one can only judge according to one's lights, and no degree of faintness and imperfection in the lights will ever stop any one from judging; therefore I will have the courage of my opinions, and express my firm conviction that it is not poetry at all. But the passage set me off musing. That is the pleasant property of *The Prelude*, it makes one at the end of every few lines pause and muse. And presently the image of the Negro Ladies in their white muslin gowns faded, and those other lines, children of the self-same spirit but conceived in the mood when it was divine, stood out in shining letters—

> Not in entire forgetfulness.
> And not in utter nakedness....

I need not go on; it is sacrilege to write them down in such a setting of commonplaceness; I could not say them aloud to my closest friend with a steady voice; they are lines that seem to come fresh from God.

And now I know that the Negro Ladies, whatever their exact poetic value may be, have become a very real blessing to an obscure inhabitant of Prussia, for in the future I shall only need to see the passage to be back instantaneously on the hot shingle, with the tarred edge of the old boat above me against the sky, the blue water curling along the shore at my feet, and the pale lilac flowers on the delicate stalks bending their heads in the wind.

About twelve the sun drove me away. The backs of my hands began to feel as though they proposed to go into blisters. I could not lie there and deliberately be blistered, so I got up and wandered back to the hotel to prepare Gertrud for a probably prolonged absence, as I intended to get across somehow to the island of Vilm. Having begged her to keep calm if I did not appear again till bedtime I took the guide-book and set out. The way to the jetty is down a path through the meadow close to the water, with willows on one side of it and rushes on the other. In ten minutes you have reached Lauterbach, seen some ugly little new houses where tourists lodge, seen some delightful little old houses where fishermen live, paid ten *pfennings* toll to a smiling woman at the entrance to the jetty, on whom it is useless to waste amiabilities, she being absolutely deaf, and having walked out to the end begin to wonder how you are to get across. There were fishing-smacks at anchor on one side, and a brig from Sweden was being unloaded. A small steamer lay at the end, looking as though it meant to start soon for somewhere; but on my asking an official who was sitting on a coil of ropes staring at nothing if it would take me to Vilm, he replied that he did not go to Vilm but would be pleased to take me to Baabe. Never having heard of Baabe I had no desire to go to it. He then suggested Greifswald, and said he went there the next day; and when I declined to be taken to Greifswald the next day instead of to Vilm that day he looked as though he thought me unreasonable, and relapsed into his first abstraction.

A fisherman was lounging near, leaning against one of the posts and also staring straight into space, and when I turned away he roused himself enough to ask if I would use his smack. He pointed to it where it lay a little way out— a big boat with the bright brown sails that make such brilliant splashes of colour in the surrounding blues and whites. There was only a faint breeze, but he said he could get me across in twenty minutes and would wait for me all day if I liked, and would only charge three marks. Three marks for a whole fishing-smack with golden sails, and a fisherman with a golden beard, blue eyes, stalwart body, and whose remote grandparents had certainly been Vikings! I got into his dinghy without further argument, and was rowed across to the smack. A small Viking, appropriately beardless, he being only ten, but with freckles, put his head out of the cabin as we drew alongside, and was presented to me as the eldest of five sons. Father and son made a comfortable place for me in a not too fishy part of the boat, hauled up the huge poetic sail, and we glided out beyond the jetty. This is the proper way, the only right way, to visit Vilm, the most romantic of tiny islands. Who would go to it any other way but with a Viking and a golden sail? Yet there is another way, I found out, and it is the one most used. It is a small launch plying between Lauterbach and Vilm, worked by a machine that smells very nasty and makes a great noise; and as it is a long narrow boat. If there are even small waves it rolls so much that the female passengers, and sometimes even the male, scream. Also the spray flies over it and drenches you. In calm weather it crosses swiftly, doing the distance in ten minutes. My smack took twenty to get there and much longer to get back, but what a difference in the joy! The puffing little launch rushed past us when we were midway, when I should not have known that we were moving but for the slight shining ripple across the bows, and the thud of its machine and the smell of its benzine were noticeable for a long time after it had dwindled to a dot. The people in it certainly got to their destination quickly, but Vilm is not a place to hurry to. There is nothing whatever on it to attract the hurried. To rush across the sea to it and back again to one's train at Lauterbach is not to have felt its singular charm. It is a place to dream away a summer in; but the wide-awake tourist visiting it between two trains would hardly know how to fill up the three hours allotted him. You can walk right round it in three-quarters of an hour. In three-quarters of an hour you can have seen each of the views considered fine and accordingly provided with a seat, have said 'Oh there is Thiessow again,' on looking over the sea to the east; and 'Oh there is Putbus again,' on looking over the sea to the west; and 'Oh that must be Greifswald,' on remarking far away in the south the spires of churches rising up out of the water; you will have had ample time to smile at the primitiveness of the bathing-hut on the east shore, to study the names of past bathers scribbled over it, besides poems, valedictory addresses, and quotations from the German classics; to sit for a little on the rocks thinking how hard rocks are; and at length to wander round, in sheer inability to fill up the last hour, to the inn, the only house on the island, where at one of the tables under the chestnuts before the door you would probably drink beer till the launch starts.

But that is not the way to enjoy Vilm. If you love out-of-door beauty, wide stretches of sea and sky, mighty beeches, dense bracken, meadows radiant with flowers, chalky levels purple with gentians, solitude, and economy, go and spend a summer at Vilm. The inn is kept by one of Prince Putbus's foresters, or rather by his amiable and obliging wife, the forester's functions being apparently restricted to standing picturesquely propped against a tree in front of the house in a nice green shooting suit, with a telescope at his eye through which he studies the approaching or departing launch. His wife does the rest. I sat at one of the tables beneath the chestnuts waiting for my food—I had to wait a very long while—and she came out and talked. The season, she explained, was short, lasting two months, July and August, at the longest, so that her prices were necessarily high. I inquired what they were, and she said five marks a day for a front room looking over the sea, and four marks and a half for a back room looking over the forest, the price including four meals. Out of the season her charges were lower. She said most of her visitors were painters, and she could put up four-and-twenty with their wives. My luncheon came while she was still trying to find out if I were a female painter, and if not why I was there alone instead of being one of a batch, after the manner of the circumspect-petticoated, and I will only say of the luncheon that it was abundant. Its quality, after all, did not matter much. The rye grew up to within a yard of my table and made a quivering golden line of light against the blue sparkle of the sea. White butterflies danced above it. The breeze coming over it blew sweet country smells in my face. The chestnut leaves shading me rustled and whispered. All the world was gay and fresh and scented, and if the traveller does not think these delights make up for doubtful cookery, why does he travel?

The *Frau Förster* insisted on showing me the bedrooms. They are simple and very clean, each one with a beautiful view. The rest of the house, including the dining-room, does not lend itself to enthusiastic description. I saw the long table at which the four-and-twenty painters eat. They were doing it when I looked in, and had been doing it the whole time I was under the chestnuts. It was not because of the many dishes that they sat there so long, but because of the few waiters. There were at least forty people learning to be patient, and one waiter and a boy to drive the lesson home. The bathing, too, at Vilm cannot be mentioned in the same breath with the glorious bathing at Lauterbach. There is no smiling attendant in a white sunbonnet waiting to take your things and dry them, to rub you down when you come out shivering, and if needful jump in and pull you out when you begin to drown. At Vilm the bathing-hut lies on the east shore, and you go to it across a meadow—the divinest strip of meadow, it is true, with sea behind you and sea before you, and cattle pasturing, and a general radiant air about it as though at any moment the daughters of the gods might come over the buttercups to bleach their garments whiter in the sun. But beautiful as it is, it is a very hot walk, and there is no path. Except the path through the rye from the landing- stage up to the inn there is not a regular path on the island—only a few tracks here and there where the cows are driven home in the evening; and to reach the bathing-hut you must plunge straight through meadow-grass, and not mind grasshoppers hopping into your clothes. Then the water is so shallow just there that you must wade quite a dangerous-looking distance before, lying down, it will cover you; and while you are wading, altogether unable, as he who has waded knows, to hurry your steps, however urgent the need, you blush to think that some or all of the four-and-twenty painters are probably sitting on rocks observing you. Wading back, of course, you blush still more. I never saw so frank a bathing-place. It is beautiful—in a lovely curve, cliffs clothed with beeches on one side, and the radiant meadow along the back of the rocks on the other; but the whole island can see you if you go out far enough to be able to swim, and if you do not you are still a conspicuous object and a very miserable one, bound to catch any wandering eye as you stand there alone, towering out of water that washes just over your ankles.

I sat in the shadow of the cliffs and watched two girls who came down to bathe. They did not seem to feel their position at all, and splashed into the water with shrieks and laughter that rang through the mellow afternoon air. So it was that I saw how shallow it is, and how embarrassing it would be to the dignified to bathe there. The girls had no dignity, and were not embarrassed. Probably one, or two, of the four-and-twenty were their fathers, and that made them feel at home. Or perhaps—and watching them I began to think that this was so—they would rather have liked to be looked at by those of the painters who were not their fathers. Anyhow, they danced and laughed and called to each other, often glancing back inquiringly at the cliffs; and indeed they were very pretty in their little scarlet suits in the sapphire frame of the sea.

I sat there long after the girls were clothed and transformed into quite uninteresting young women, and had gone their way noisily up the grass slope into the shadows of the beeches. The afternoon stillness was left to itself again, undisturbed by anything louder than the slow ripple of the water round the base of the rocks. Sometimes a rabbit scuttled up the side of the cliff, and once a hawk cried somewhere up among the little clouds. The shadows grew very long; the shadows of the rocks on the water looked as though they would stretch across to Thiessow before the sun had done with them. Out at sea, far away beyond the hazy headland, a long streak of smoke hung above the track where a steamer had passed on the way to Russia. I wish I could fill my soul with enough of the serenity of such afternoons to keep it sweet for ever.

Vilm consists of two wooded hills joined together by a long, narrow, flat strip of land. This strip, beyond the meadow and its fringing trees, is covered with coarse grass and stones and little shells. Clumps of wild fruit trees scattered about it here and there look as if they knew what roughing it is like. The sea washes over it in winter when the wind is strong from the east, and among the trees are frequent skeletons, dead fruit trees these many seasons past, with the tortured look peculiar to blasted trees, menacing the sky with gaunt, impotent arms. After struggling along this bit, stopping every few minutes to shake the shells out of my shoes, I came to uneven ground, soft green grass, and beautiful trees—a truly lovely part at the foot of the southern hill. Here I sat down for a moment to take the last shells out of my shoes and to drink things in. I had not seen a soul since the bathing girls, and supposed that most of the people staying at the inn would not care on hot afternoons to walk over the prickly grass and shells that must be walked over before reaching the green coolness of the end. And while I was comfortably supposing this and shaking my shoe slowly up and down and thinking how delightful it was to have the charming place to myself, I saw a young man standing on a rock under the east cliff of the hill in the very act of photographing the curving strip of land, with the sea each side of it, and myself in the middle.

Now I am not of those who like being photographed much and often. At intervals that grow longer I go through the process at the instant prayers of my nearest and dearest; but never other than deliberately, after due choice of fitting attitude and garments. The kodak and the instantaneous photograph taken before one has had time to arrange one's smile are things to be regarded with abhorrence by every woman whose faith in her attractions is not unshakeable. Movements so graceful that the Early Victorians would have described them as swan-like—those Early Victorians who wore ringlets, curled their upper lips, had marble brows, and were called Georgiana— movements, I say, originally swan-like in grace, are translated by the irreverent snap-shot into a caricature that to the photographed appears not even remotely like, and fills the photographed's friends with an awful secret joy. 'What manner of young man is this?' I asked myself, examining him with indignation. He stood on the rock a moment, looking about as if for another good subject, and finally his eye alighted on me. Then he got off his rock and came towards me. 'What manner of young man is this?' I again asked myself, putting on my shoe in haste and wrath. He was coming to apologise, I supposed, having secured his photograph.

He was. I sat gazing severely at Thiessow, There is no running away from vain words or from anything else on an island. He was a tall young man, and there was something indefinable and reassuring about his collar.

'I am so sorry,' he said with great politeness. 'I did not notice you. Of course I did not intend to photograph you. I shall destroy the film.'

At this I felt hurt. Being photographed without permission is bad, but being told your photograph is not wanted and will be destroyed is worse. He was a very personable young man, and I like personable young men; from the way he spoke German and from his collar I judged him English, and I like Englishmen; and he had addressed me as *gnädiges Fräulein*, and what mother of a growing family does not like that?

'I did not see you,' I said, not without blandness, touched by his youth and innocence, 'or I should have got out of your way.'

'I shall destroy the film,' he again assured me; and lifted his cap and went back to the rocks.

Now if I stayed where I was he could not photograph the strip again, for it was so narrow that I would have been again included, and he was evidently bent on getting a picture of it, and fidgeted about among the rocks waiting for me to go. So I went; and as I climbed up the south hill under the trees I mused on the pleasant slow manners of Englishmen, who talk and move as though life were very spacious and time may as well wait. Also I wondered how he had found this remote island. I was inclined to wonder that I had found it myself; but how much more did I wonder that he had found it.

There are many rabbit-holes under the trees at the south end of Vilm, and I disturbed no fewer than three snakes one after the other in the long grass. They were of the harmless kind, but each in turn made me jump and shiver, and after the third I had had enough, and clambered down the cliff on the west side and went along at the foot of it towards the farthest point of the island, with the innocent intention of seeing what was round the corner. The young man was round the corner, and I walked straight into another photograph; I heard the camera snap at the very instant that I turned the bend.

This time he looked at me with something of a grave inquiry in his eye.

'I assure you I do not *want* to be photographed,' I said hastily.

'I hope you believe that I did not intend to do it again,' he replied.

'I am very sorry,' said I.

'I shall destroy the film,' said he.

'It seems a great waste of films,' said I.

The young man lifted his cap; I continued my way among the rocks eastward; he went steadily in the opposite direction; round the other side of the hill we met again.

'Oh,' I cried, genuinely disturbed, 'have I spoilt another?'

The young man smiled—certainly a very personable young man—and explained that the light was no longer strong enough to do any more. Again in this explanation did he call me gnädiges Fräulein, and again was I touched by so much innocence. And his German, too, was touching; it was so conscientiously grammatical, so laboriously put together, so like pieces of Goethe learned by heart.

By this time the sun hung low over the houses of Putbus, and the strip of sand with its coarse grass and weatherbeaten trees was turned by the golden flush into a fairy bridge, spanning a mystic sea, joining two wonderful, shining islands. We walked along with all the radiance in our faces. It is, as I have observed, impossible to get away from any one on an island that is small enough. We were both going back to the inn, and the strip of land is narrow. Therefore we went together, and what that young man talked about the whole way in the most ponderous German was the Absolute.

I can't think what I have done that I should be talked to for twenty minutes by a nice young man who mistook me for a Fräulein about the Absolute. He evidently thought—the innocence of him!—that being German I must, whatever my sex and the shape of my head, be interested. I don't know how it began. It was certainly not my fault, for till that day I had had no definite attitude in regard to it. Of course I did not tell him that. Age has at least made me artful. A real Fräulein would have looked as vacant as she felt, and have said, 'What is the Absolute?' Being a matron and artful, I simply looked thoughtful—quite an easy thing to do—and said, 'How do you define it?'

He said he defined it as a negation of the conceivable. Continuing in my artfulness I said that there was much to be said for that view of it, and asked how he had reached his conclusions. He explained elaborately. Clearly he took me to be an intelligent Fräulein, and indeed I gave myself great pains to look like one.

It appeared that he had a vast admiration for everything German, and especially for German erudition. Well, we are very erudite in places. Unfortunately no erudition comes up my way.

My acquaintances do not ask the erudite to dinner, one of the reasons, as insufficient as the rest, being that they either wear day clothes in the evening, or, if worldly enough to dress, mar the effect by white satin ties with horse-shoe pins in them; and another is that they are Liberals, and therefore uninvitable. When the unknown youth, passing naturally from Kant and the older philosophers to the great Germans now living, enthusiastically mentioned the leading lights in science and art and asked if I knew them or had ever seen them—the mere seeing of them he seemed to think would be a privilege—I could only murmur no. How impossible to explain to this scion of an unprejudiced race the limitless objection of the class called *Junker*—I am a female *Junker*—to mix on equal terms with the class that wears white satin ties in the evening. But it is obvious that a man who can speak with the tongue of angels, who has put his seal on his century, and who will be remembered when we have returned, forgotten, to the Prussian dust from which we came—or rather not forgotten because we were at no time remembered, but simply ignored—it is obvious that such a man may wear what tie he pleases when he comes to dine, and still ought to be received on metaphorical knees of reverence and gratitude. Probably, however, if we who live in the country and think no end of ourselves did invite such a one, and whether there were hostesses on knees waiting for him or not, he would not come. How bored he would be if he did. He would find us full of those excellences Pater calls the more obvious parochial virtues, jealous to madness of the sensitive and bloodthirsty appendage known as our honour, exact in the observance of minor conventionalities, correct in our apparel, rigid in our views, and in our effect uninterruptedly soporific. The man who had succeeded in pushing his thoughts farther into the region of the hitherto unthought than any of his contemporaries would not, I think, if he came once, come again. But it is supposing the impossible, after all, to suppose him invited, for all the great ones of whom the unknown youth talked are Liberals, and all the *Junkers* are Conservatives; and how shall a German Conservative be the friend of a German Liberal? The thing is unthinkable. Like the young man's own definition of the Absolute, it is a negation of the conceivable.

By the time we had reached the chestnut grove in front of the inn I had said so little that my companion was sure I was one of the most intelligent women he had ever met. I know he thought so, for he turned suddenly to me as we were walking past the Frau Förster's wash-house and rose-garden up to the chestnuts, and said, 'How is it that German women are so infinitely more intellectual than English women?'

Intellectual! How nice. And all the result of keeping quiet in the right places.

'I did not know they were,' I said modestly; which was true.

'Oh but they are,' he assured me with great positiveness; and added, 'Perhaps you have noticed that I am English?'

Noticed that he was English? From the moment I first saw his collar I suspected it; from the moment he opened his mouth and spoke I knew it; and so did everybody else under the chestnuts who heard him speaking as he passed. But why not please this artless young man? So I looked at him with the raised eyebrows of intense surprise and said, 'Oh, are you English?'

'I have been a good deal in Germany,' he said, looking happy.

'But it is extraordinary,' I said.

'It is not so very difficult,' he said, looking more and more happy.

'But really not German? *Fabelhaft.*'

The young man's belief in my intelligence was now unshakeable. The Frau Förster, who had seen me disembark and set out for my walk alone, and who saw me now returning with a companion of the other sex, greeted me coldly. Her coldness, I felt, was not unjustifiable. It is not my practice to set out by myself and come back telling youths I have never seen before that their accomplishments are *fabelhaft*. I began to feel coldly towards myself, and turning to the young man said good-bye with some abruptness.

'Are you going in?' he asked.

'I am not staying here.'

'But the launch does not start for an hour. I go across too, then.'

'I am not crossing in the launch. I came over in a fishing-smack.'

'Oh really?' He seemed to meditate. 'How delightfully independent,' he added.

'Have you not observed that the German Fräulein is as independent as she is intellectual?'

'No, I have not. That is just where I think the Germans are so far behind us. Their women have nothing like the freedom ours have.'

'What, not when they sail about all alone in fishing-smacks?'

'That certainly is unusually enterprising. May I see you safely into it?'

The Frau Förster came towards us and told him that the food he had ordered for eight o'clock was ready.

'No, thank you,' I said, 'don't bother. There is a fisherman and a boy to help me in. It is quite easy.'

'Oh but it is no bother——'

'I will not take you away from your supper.'

'Are you not going to have supper here?'

'I lunched here to-day. So I will not sup.'

'Is the reason a good one?'

'You will see. Good-bye.'

I went away down the path to the beach. The path is steep, and the corn on either side stands thick and high, and a few steps took me out of sight of the house, the chestnuts, and the young man. The smack was lying some distance out, and the dinghy was tied to her stern. The fisherman's son's head was visible in a peaceful position on a heap of ropes. It is difficult as well as embarrassing to shout, as I well knew, but somebody would have to, and as nobody was there but myself I was plainly the one to do it, I put my hands to my mouth, and not knowing the fisherman's name called out *Sie*. It sounded not only feeble but rude. When I remembered the appearance of the golden-bearded Viking, his majestic presence and dreamy dignity, I was ashamed to find myself standing on a rock and calling him as loud as I could *Sie*.

The head on the ropes did not stir. I waved my handkerchief. The boy's eyes were shut. Again I called out *Sie*, and thought it the most offensive of pronouns. The boy was asleep, and my plaintive cry went past him over the golden ripples towards Lauterbach.

Then the Englishman appeared against the sky, up on the ridge of the cornfield. He saw my dilemma, and taking his hands out of his pockets ran down. '*Gnädiges Fräulein* is in a fix,' he observed in his admirably correct and yet so painful German.

'She is,' I said.

'Shall I shout?'

'Please.'

He shouted. The boy started up in alarm. The fisherman's huge body reared up from the depths of the boat. In two minutes the dinghy was at the little plank jetty, and I was in it.

'It was a very good idea to charter one of those romantic smacks to come over in,' said the young man on the jetty wistfully.

'They're rather fishy,' I replied, smiling, as we pushed off.

'But so very romantic.'

'Have you not observed that the German Fräulein is a romantic creature,'— the dinghy began to move—'a beautiful mixture of intelligence, independence, and romance?'

'Are you staying at Putbus?'

'No. Good-bye. Thanks for coming down and shouting. You know your food will be quite cold and uneatable.'

'I gathered from what you said before that it will be uneatable anyhow.'

The dinghy was moving fast. There was a rapidly-widening strip of golden water between myself and the young man on the jetty.

'Not all of it,' I said, raising my voice. 'Try the compote. It is lovely compote. It is what you would call in England glorified gooseberry jam.'

'Glorified gooseberry jam?' echoed the young man, apparently much struck by these three English words. 'Why,' he added, speaking louder, for the golden strip had grown very wide, 'you said that without the ghost of a foreign accent!'

'Did I?'

The dinghy shot into the shadow of the fishing-smack. The Viking and the boy shipped their oars, helped me in, tied the dinghy to the stern, hoisted the sail, and we dropped away into the sunset.

The young man on the distant jetty raised his cap. He might have been a young archangel, standing there the centre of so much glory. Certainly a very personable young man.

THE THIRD DAY

FROM LAUTERBACH TO GÖHREN

The official on the steamer at the Lauterbach jetty had offered to take me to Baabe when I said I wanted to go to Vilm, and I had naturally refused the offer. Afterwards, on looking at the map, I found that Baabe is a place I would have to pass anyhow, if I carried out my plan of driving right round Rügen. The guide-book is enthusiastic about Baabe, and says—after explaining its rather odd name as meaning *Die Einsame*, the Lonely One—that it has a pine forest, a pure sea air with ozone in it, a climate both mild and salubrious, and that it works wonders on people who have anything the matter with their chests. Then it says that to lie at Baabe embedded in soft dry sand, allowing one's glance to rove about the broad sea with its foam-crested waves, and the rest of one to rejoice in the strong air, is an enviable thing to do. Then it bursts into poetry that goes on for a page about the feelings of him who is embedded, written by one who has been it. And then comes the practical information that you can live at Baabe *en pension* for four marks a day, and that dinner costs one mark twenty *pfennings*. Never was there a more irrepressibly poetic guide-book. What tourist wants to be told first how he will feel when he has embedded himself in sand? Pleasures of a subtle nature have no attraction for him who has not dined. Before everything, the arriving tourist wants to know where he will get the best dinner and what it will cost; and not until that has been settled will there be, if ever, raptures. The guide- book's raptures about Baabe rang hollow. The relief chest-sufferers would find there if they could be induced to go, and the poem of the embedded one, would not, I felt, have been put in if there had been anything really solid to praise. Still, a place in a forest near the sea called *Die Einsame* was to me, at least, attractive; and I said good-bye to the Lauterbach I knew and loved, and started, full of hope, for the Baabe I was all ready to love.

It was a merry day of bright sun and busy breeze. Everything was moving and glancing and fluttering. I felt cheerful to hilarity when we were fairly out in the fields that lie between the Greek temple and the village of Vilmnitz— privately hilarious, of course, for I could not be openly so in the sober presence of Gertrud. I have observed that sweet smells, and clear light, and the piping of birds, all the things that make life lovely have no effect whatever on Gertruds. They apparently neither smell, nor see, nor hear them. They are not merely unable to appreciate them, they actually do not know that they are there. This complete unconsciousness of the presence of beauty is always a wonder to me. No change of weather changes my Gertrud's settled solemnity. She wears the same face among the roses of June that she does in the nipping winds of March. The heart of May, with which every beast keeps holiday, never occupies her respectable interior. She is not more solemn on a blank February afternoon, when the world outside in its cold wrapping of mist shudders through the sodden hours, than she is on such a day of living radiance as this third one of our journey. The industrious breeze lifted up the stray hairs from her forehead and gave it little pats and kisses that seemed audaciously familiar applied to a brow of such decorum; the restless poplar leaves whispered all the secrets of life in her unhearing ears; the cottage gardens of Vilmnitz, ablaze that day with the white flame of lilies, poured their stream of scent into the road, and the wind caught it up and flung it across her sober nostrils, and she could not breathe without drawing in the divineness of it, yet her face wore exactly the same expression that it does when we are passing pigs. Are the Gertruds of this world, then, unable to distinguish between pigs and lilies? Do they, as they toss on its troublesome waves, smell perpetual pigs? The question interested me for at least three miles; and so much did I want to talk it over that I nearly began talking it over with Gertrud herself, but was restrained by the dread of offending her; for to drive round Rügen side by side with an offended Gertrud would be more than my fortitude could endure.

Vilmnitz is a pretty little village, and the guide-book praises both its inns; but then the guide-book praises every place it mentions. I would not, myself, make use of Vilmnitz except as a village to be driven through on the way to somewhere else. For this purpose it is quite satisfactory though its roads might be less sandy, for it is a flowery place with picturesque, prosperous- looking cottages, and high up on a mound the oldest church in the island. This church dates from the twelfth century, and I would have liked to go into it; but it was locked and the parson had the key, and it was the hour in the afternoon when parsons sleep, and wisdom dictates that while they are doing it they shall be left alone. So we drove through Vilmnitz in all the dignity that asks no favours and wants nothing from anybody.

The road is ugly from there to a place called Stresow, but I do not mind an ugly road if the sun will only shine, and the ugly ones are useful for making one see the beauty of the pretty ones. There are many Hun graves, big mounds with trees growing on them, and I suppose Huns inside them, round Stresow, and a monument reminding the passer-by of a battle fought there between the Prussians under the old Dessauer and the Swedes. We won. It was my duty as a good German to swell with patriotic pride on beholding this memorial, and I did so. As a nation, the least thing sets us swelling with this particular sort of pride. We acquire the habit in our childhood when we imitate our parents, and on any fine Sunday afternoon you may see whole families standing round the victory column and the statues in the *Sieges Allee* in Berlin engaged in doing it. The old Dessauer is not very sharply outlined in a mind that easily forgets, and I am afraid to say how little I know of him except that he was old and a Dessauer; yet I felt extremely proud of him, and proud of Germany, and proud of myself as I saw the place where we fought under him and won. 'Oh blood and iron!' I cried, 'Glorious and potent mixture! Do you see that monument, Gertrud? It marks the spot where we Prussians won a mighty battle, led by the old, the heroic Dessauer.' And though Gertrud, I am positive, is even more vague about him than I am, at the mention of a Prussian victory her face immediately and mechanically took on the familiar expression of him who is secretly swelling.

Beyond Stresow the road was hilly and charming, with woods drawing sometimes to the edge of it and shading us, and sometimes drawing back to the other side of meadows; and there were the first fields of yellow lupins in flower, and I had the delight to which I look forward each year as July approaches of smelling that peculiarly exquisite scent. And so we came to the region of Baabe, passing first round the outskirts of Sellin, a place of villas built in the woods on the east coast of Rügen with the sea on one side and a big lake called the Selliner See on the other; and driving round the north end of this lake we got on to the dullest bit of road we had yet had, running beside a railway line and roughly paved with stones, pine-woods on our left shutting out the sea, and on our right across a marshy flat the lake, and bare and dreary hills.

These, then, were the woods of Baabe. Down the straight road, unpleasing even in the distance, I could see new houses standing aimlessly about, lodging-houses out of sight and sound of the sea waiting for chest-sufferers, the lodging-houses of the Lonely One. 'I will not stay at Baabe,' I called energetically to August, who had been told we were to stop there that night, 'go on to the next place.'

The next place is Göhren, and the guide-book's praise of it is hysterical. Filled with distrust of the guide-book I could only hope it would be possible to sleep in it, for the shadows had grown very long and there is nowhere to stop at beyond Göhren except Thiessow, the farthest southern point on the island. Accordingly we drove past the two Baabe hotels, little wooden houses built on the roadside facing the line, with the station immediately opposite their windows. A train was nearly due, and intending passengers were sitting in front of the hotels drinking beer while they waited, and various conveyances had stopped there on their way to Göhren or Sellin, and the Lonely One seemed a very noisy, busy one to me as we rattled by over the stones, and I was glad to turn off to the left at a sign-post pointing towards Göhren and get on to the deep, sandy, silent forest roads.

The forest, at first only pines and rather scrubby ones, stretches the whole way from Baabe to Göhren and grows more and more beautiful. We had to drive at a walking-pace because of the deep sand; but these sandy roads have the advantage of being so quiet that you can hear something besides the noise of wheels and hoofs. Not till we got to Göhren did we see the sea, but I heard it all the way, for outside the forest the breeze had freshened into a wind, and though we hardly felt it I could see it passing over the pine-tops and hear how they sighed. I suppose we must have been driving an hour among the pines before we got into a region of mixed forest—beeches and oaks and an undergrowth of whortleberries; and then tourists began to flutter among the trees, tourists with baskets searching for berries, so that it was certain Göhren could not be far off. We came quite suddenly upon its railway station, a small building alone in the woods, the terminus of the line whose other end is Putbus. Across the line were white dunes with young beeches bending in the wind, and beyond these dunes the sea roared. Beeches and dunes were in the full glow of the sunset. We, skirting the forest on the other side, were in deep shadow. The air was so fresh that it was almost cold. I stopped August and got out and crossed the deserted line and climbed up the dunes, and oh the glorious sight on the other side—the glorious, dashing, roaring sea! What was pale Lauterbach compared to this? A mere lake, a crystal pool, a looking- glass, a place in which to lie by the side of still waters and dream over your own and heaven's reflection. But here one could not dream; here was life, vigorous, stinging, blustering life; and standing on the top of the dune holding my hat on with both hands, banged and battered by the salt wind, my clothes flapping and straining like a flag in a gale on a swaying flagstaff, the weight of a generation was blown off my shoulders, and I was seized by a craving as unsuitable as it was terrific to run and fetch a spade and a bucket, and dig and dig till it was too dark to dig any longer, and then go indoors tired and joyful and have periwinkles or shrimps for tea. And behold Gertrud, cold reminder of realities, beside me cloak in hand; and she told me it was chilly, and she put the cloak round my unresisting shoulders, and it was heavy with the weight of hours and custom; and the sun dropped at that moment behind the forest, and all the radiance and colour went out together. 'Thank you, Gertrud,' I said as she wrapped me up; but though I shivered I was not grateful.

It was certainly not the moment to loiter on dunes. The horses had done enough for one day, nearly half their work having been over heavy sand, and we still had to look for our night quarters. Lauterbach had been empty; therefore, with the illuminating logic of women, I was sure Göhren would have plenty of room for us. It had not. The holidays had just begun, and the place swarmed with prudent families who had taken their rooms weeks before. Göhren is built on a very steep hill that drops straight down on to the sands. The hill is so steep that we got out, and August led or rather pulled the horses up it. Luckily the forest road we came by runs along the bottom of the hill, and when we came out of the trees and found ourselves without the least warning of stray houses or lamp-posts in the heart of Göhren, we had to climb up the road and not drive down it. Driving down it must be impossible, especially for horses which, like mine, never see a hill in their own home. When we had got safely to the top we left August and the horses to get their wind and set out to engage rooms in the hotel the guide-book says is the best. There is practically only that one street in Göhren, and it is lined with hotels and lodging-houses, and down at the bottom, between the over-arching trees, the leaden waves were dashing on the deserted sands. People were having supper. Whatever place we passed, at whatever hour during the entire tour, people were always having something. The hotel I had chosen was in a garden, and the windows evidently had lovely views over the green carpet of the level tree-tops. As I walked up to the door I pointed to the windows of the bedroom I thought must be the nicest, and told Gertrud it was the one I should take. It was a cold evening, and the bath-guests were supping indoors. There was no hall-porter or any one else whom I could ask for what I wanted, so we had to go into the restaurant, where the whole strength of the establishment was apparently concentrated. The room was crowded, and misty with the fumes of suppers. All the children of Germany seemed to be gathered in this one spot, putting knives into their artless mouths even when it was only sauce they wanted to eat, and devouring their soup with a passionate enthusiasm. I explained my wishes, grown suddenly less ardent, rather falteringly to the nearest waiter. All the children of Germany lifted their heads out of their soup-plates to listen. The waiter referred me to the head waiter. Embarrassed, I repeated my wishes, cooled down to the point where they almost cease to be wishes, to this person, and all the children of Germany sat with their knives suspended in the air and their mouths open while I did it. The head waiter told me I could have the rooms on the 15th of August—it was then the 17th of July—at which date the holidays ended and the families went home. 'Oh, thank you, thank you; that will do beautifully!' I cried, only too grateful that the families had left no corner unoccupied into which I might have felt obliged, by the lateness of the hour, to force my shrinking limbs; and hurrying to the door I could hear how all the children of Germany's heads seemed to splash back again into their soup-plates.

But my pleasure at not being doomed to stay there was foolish, as I quickly perceived, for stay somewhere I must, and the guide-book was right when it said this was the best hotel. Outside in the windy street August and the horses were waiting patiently. The stars were coming out in the pale green of the sky over Göhren, but from the east the night was dragging up a great curtain of chill black cloud. For the best part of an hour Gertrud and I went from one hotel to another, from one lodging-house to another. The hotels all promised rooms if I would call again in four weeks' time. The lodging-houses only laughed at our request for a night's shelter; they said they never took in people who were not going to stay the entire season, and who did not bring their own bedding. Their own bedding! What a complication of burdens to lay on the back of the patient father of a family. Did a holiday-maker with a wife and, say, four children have to bring six sets of bedding with him? Six sets of Teutonic bedding, stuffed with feathers? Six pillows, six of those wedge-like things to put under pillows called *Kielkissen*, and six quilted coverlets with insides of eider-down if there was a position to keep up, and of wadding if public opinion could afford to be defied? Yet the lodging-houses were full; and that there were small children in them was evident from the frequency with which the sounds that accompany the act of correction floated out into the street.

We found a room at last in the gloomiest hotel in the place. Only one room, under the roof in a kind of tower, with eight beds in it, and no space for anything else. August had no room at all, and slept with his horses in the stable. There was one small iron wash-stand, a thing of tiers with a basin at the top, a soap-dish beneath it, underneath that a water-bottle, and not an inch more space in which to put a sponge or a nail-brush. In the passage outside the door was a chest of drawers reserved for the use of the occupiers of this room. It was by the merest chance that we got even this, the arrival of the family who had taken it for six weeks having been delayed for a day or two. They were coming the very next day, eight of them, and were all going to spend six weeks in that one room. 'Which,' said the landlord, 'explains the presence of so many beds.'

'But it does not explain the presence of so many beds in one room,' I objected, gazing at them resentfully from the only corner where there were none.

'The *Herrschaften* are content,' he said shortly. 'They return every year.'

'And they are content, too, with only one of these?' I inquired, pointing to the extremely condensed wash-stand.

The landlord stared. 'There is the sea,' he said, not without impatience at being forced to state the obvious; and disliking, I suppose, the tone of my remarks, he hurried downstairs.

Now it is useless for me to describe Göhren for the benefit of possible travellers, because I am prejudiced. I was cold there, and hungry, and tired, and I lived in a garret. To me it will always be a place where there is a penetrating wind, a steep hill, and an iron wash-stand in tiers. Some day when the distinct vision of these things is blurred, I will order the best rooms in the best hotel several months beforehand to be kept for me till I come, wait for fair, windless weather and the passing of the holidays, and then go once more to Göhren. The place itself is, I believe, beautiful. No place with so much sea and forest could help being beautiful. That evening the beauties were hidden; and I abruptly left the table beneath some shabby little chestnuts in front of the hotel where I was trying, in gloom and wind, not to notice the wetness of the table-napkin, the stains on the cloth, and the mark on the edge of the plates where an unspeakable waiter had put his thumb, and went out into the street. At a baker's I bought some rusks—dry things that show no marks— and continued down the hill to the sea. There is no cold with quite so forlorn a chill in it as a sudden interruption of July heats; and there is no place with quite so forlorn a feeling about it as deserted sands on a leaden evening. Was it only the evening before that I had sailed away from Vilm in glory and in joy, leaving the form of the abstruse but beautiful youth standing in such a golden radiance that it was as the form of an angel? Down among the dunes, where the grey ribbons of the sea-grass were violently fluttering and indigo clouds lay in an unbroken level over leaden waves, I sat and ate my rusks and was wretched. My soul rebelled both at the wretchedness and at the rusks. Not for these had I come to Rügen. I looked at the waves and shuddered. I looked at the dunes and disliked them. I was haunted by the image of the eight beds waiting in my garret for me, and of certain portions of the wall from which the paper was torn—the summer before, probably, by one or more of the eight struggling in the first onslaughts of asphyxia—and had not been gummed on again. My thoughts drifted miserably into solemn channels, in the direction of what Carlyle calls the Immensities. I remembered how I was only a speck after all in uncomfortably limitless space, of no account whatever in the general scheme of things, but with a horrid private capacity for being often and easily hurt; and how specks have a trick of dying, which I in my turn would presently do, and a fresh speck, not nearly so nice, as I hoped and believed, would immediately start up and fill my vacancy, perhaps so exactly my vacancy that it would even wear my gloves and stockings. The last rusk, drier and drearier than any that had gone before, was being eaten by the time my thoughts emerged from the gloom that hangs about eternal verities to the desirable concreteness of gloves and stockings. What, I wondered, became of the gloves and stockings of the recently extinguished female speck? Its Gertrud would, I supposed, take possession of its dresses; but my Gertrud, for instance, could not wear my gloves, and I know believes only in those stockings she has knitted herself. Still, she has nieces, and I believe aunts. She would send them all the things she could not use herself, which would not be nice of Gertrud. It would not matter, I supposed, but it would not be nice. She would be letting herself down to being a kind of ghoul. I started up with the feeling that I must go and remonstrate with her before it was too late; and there, struggling in the wind and deep sand towards me, her arms full of warm things and her face of anxious solicitude, was the good Gertrud herself. 'I have prepared the gracious one's bed,' she called out breathlessly; 'will she not soon enter it?'

'Oh Gertrud,' I cried, remembering the garret and forgetting the ghoul, 'which bed?'

'With the aid of the chambermaid I have removed two of them into the passage,' said Gertrud, buttoning me into my coat.

'And the wash-stand?'

She shook her head. 'That I could not remove, for there is no other to be had in its place. The chambermaid said that in four weeks' time' —she stopped and scanned my face. 'The gracious one looks put out,' she said. 'Has anything happened?'

'Put out? My dear Gertrud, I have been thinking of very serious things. You cannot expect me to frolic along paths of thought that lead to mighty and unpleasant truths. Why should I always smile? I am not a Cheshire cat.'

'I trust the gracious one will come in now and enter her bed,' said Gertrud decidedly, who had never heard of Cheshire cats, and was sure that the mention of them indicated a brain in need of repose.

'Oh Gertrud,' I cried, intolerably stirred by the bare mention of that bed, 'this is a bleak and mischievous world, isn't it? Do you think we shall ever be warm and comfortable and happy again?'

THE FOURTH DAY

FROM GÖHREN TO THIESSOW

We left Göhren at seven the next morning and breakfasted outside it where the lodging-houses end and the woods begin. Gertrud had bought bread, and butter, and a bottle of milk, and we sat among the nightshades, whose flowers were everywhere, and ate in purity and cleanliness while August waited in the road. The charming little flowers with their one-half purple and other half yellow are those that have red berries later in the year and are called by Keats ruby grapes of Proserpine. Yet they are not poisonous, and there is no reason why you should not suffer your pale forehead to be kissed by them if you want to. They are as innocent as they are pretty, and the wood was full of them. Poison, death, and Proserpine seemed far enough away from that leafy place and the rude honesty of bread and butter. Still, lest I should feel too happy, and therefore be less able to bear any shocks that might be awaiting me at Thiessow, I repeated the melancholy and beautiful ode for my admonishment under my breath. It had no effect. Usually it is an unfailing antidote in its extraordinary depression to any excess of cheerfulness; but the wood and the morning sun and the bread and butter were more than a match for it. No incantation of verse could make me believe that Joy's hand was for ever at his lips bidding adieu. Joy seemed to be sitting contentedly beside me sharing my bread and butter; and when I drove away towards Thiessow he got into the carriage with me, and whispered that I was going to be very happy there.

Outside the wood the sandy road lay between cornfields gay with corncockles, bright reminders that the coming harvest will be poor. From here to Thiessow there are no trees except round the cottages of Philippshagen, a pretty village with a hoary church, beyond which the road became pure sand, dribbling off into mere uncertain tracks over the flat pasture land that stretches all the way to Thiessow.

The guide-book warmly recommends the seashore when the wind is in the east (which it was) as the quickest and firmest route from Göhren to Thiessow; but I chose rather to take the road over the plain because there was a poem in the guide-book about the way along the shore, and the guide-book said it described it extremely well, and I was sure that if that were so I would do better to go the other way. This is the poem—the translation is exact, the original being unrhymed, and the punctuation is the poet's—

Splashing waves

Rocking boat
Dipping gulls—
Dunes.

Raging winds
Floating froth.
Flashing lightning
Moon!

Fearful hearts
Morning grey—
Stormy nights
Faith!

I read it, marvelled, and went the other way.

Thiessow is a place that has to be gone to for its sake alone, as a glance at the map will show. If you make up your mind to journey the entire length of the plain that separates it from everywhere else you must also make up your mind to journey the entire length back again, to see Göhren once more, to pass through Baabe, and to make a closer acquaintance with Sellin which is on the way to the yet unvisited villages going north. It is a singular drive down to Thiessow, singular because it seems as though it would never leave off. You see the place far away in the distance the whole time, and you jolt on and on at a walking pace towards it, in and out of ruts, over grass-mounds, the sun beating on your head, sea on your left rolling up the beach in long waves, more sea on your right across the undulating greenness, a distant hill with a village by the water to the west, sails of fisher-boats, people in a curious costume mowing in a meadow a great way off, and tethered all over the plain solitary sheep and cows, whose nervousness at your approach is the nervousness begotten of a retired life. There are no trees; and if we had not seen Thiessow all the time we should have lost our way, for there is no road. As it is, you go on till you are stopped by the land coming to an end, and there you are at Thiessow. I believe in the summer you can get there by steamer from Göhren or Baabe; but if it is windy and the waves are too big for the boats that land you to put off, the steamer does not stop; so that the only way is over the plain or along the shore. I walked nearly all the time, the jolting was so intolerable. It was heavy work for the horses, and straining work for the carriage. Gertrud sat gripping the bandbox, for with every lurch it tried to roll out. August looked unhappy. His experiences at Göhren had been worse than ours, and Thiessow was right down at the end of all things, and had the drawback, obvious even to August, that whatever it was like we would have to endure it, for swelter back again over the broiling plain only to stay a second night at Göhren was as much out of the question for the horses as for ourselves. As for me, I was absolutely happy. The wide plain, the wide sea, the wide sky were so gloriously full of light and life. The very turf beneath my feet had an eager spring in it; the very daisies covering it looked sprightlier than anywhere else; and up among the great piled clouds the blessed little larks were fairly drunk with delight. I walked some way ahead of the carriage so as to feel alone. I could have walked for ever in that radiance and freshness. The black-faced sheep ran wildly round and round as I passed, tugging at their chains in frantic agitation. Even the cows seemed uneasy if I came too close; and in the far-off meadow the mowers stopped mowing to watch us dwindle into dots. In this part of Rügen the natives wear a peculiarly hideous dress, or rather the men do—the women's costume is not so ugly—and looking through my glasses to my astonishment I saw that the male mowers had on long baggy white things that were like nothing so much as a woman's white petticoat on either leg. But the mowers and their trousers were soon left far behind. The sun had climbed very high, was pouring down almost straight on to our heads, and still Thiessow seemed no nearer. Well, it did not matter. That is the chief beauty of a tour like mine, that nothing matters. As soon as there are no trains to catch a journey becomes magnificently simple. We might loiter as long as we liked on the road if only we got to some place, any place, by nightfall. This, of course, was my buoyant midday mood, before fatigue had weighed down my limbs and hunger gnawed holes in my cheerfulness. The wind, smelling of sea and freshly-cut grass, had quite blown away the memory of how tragic life had looked the night before when set about by too many beds and not enough wash-stand; and I walked along with what felt like all the brightness of heaven in my heart.

The end of this walk—I think of it as one of the happiest and most beautiful I have had—came about one o'clock. At that dull hour, when the glory of morning is gone and the serenity of afternoon has not begun, we arrived at a small grey wooden hotel, separated from the east sea by a belt of fir-wood, facing a common to the south, and about twenty minutes' walk from Thiessow proper, which lies on the sea on the western and southern shore of the point. It looked clean, and I went in. August and Gertrud sat broiling in the sun of the shelterless sandy road in front of the lily-grown garden. Somehow I had no doubts about being taken in here, and I was at once shown a spotless little bedroom by a spotless landlady. It was a corner room in the south-west corner of the house, and one window looked south on to the common and the other west on to the plain. The bed was drawn across this window, and lying on it I could see the western sea, the distant hill on the shore with its village, and grass, grass, nothing but grass, rolling away from the very wall of the house to infinity and the sunset. The room was tiny. If I had had more than a hold-all I should not have been able to get into it. It had a locked door leading into another bedroom which was occupied, said the chambermaid, by a quiet lady who would make no noise. Gertrud's room was opposite mine. August cheered up when I went out and told him he could go to the stables and put up, and Gertrud was visibly agreeably surprised by the cleanliness of both our rooms.

I lunched on a verandah overlooking the common, with the Madonna lilies of the little garden within reach of my hand; and the tablecloth and the spoons and the waiter were all in keeping with the clean landlady. The inn being small the visitors were few, and those I saw dining at the other little tables on the verandah appeared to be quiet, inoffensive people such as one would expect to find in a quiet, out-of-the-way place. The sea was not visible, but I could hear it on the other side of the belt of firs; and the verandah facing south and being hot and airless, a longing to get into the cool water took hold of me. The waiter said the bathing-huts were open in the afternoon from four to five, and I went upstairs to tell Gertrud to bring my things down to the beach at four, when she would find me lying in the sand. While I was talking, the quiet lady in the next room began to talk too, apparently to the chambermaid, for she talked of hot water. I broke off my own talk short. It was not that the partition was so thin that it seemed as if she were in the same room as myself, though that was sufficiently disturbing—it was that I thought for a moment I knew the voice. I looked at Gertrud. Gertrud's face was empty of all expression. The quiet lady, continuing, told the chambermaid to let down the sun-blinds, and the note in her voice that had struck me was no longer there. Feeling relieved, for I did not want to come across acquaintances, I put *The Prelude* in my pocket and went out. The fir-wood was stuffy, and suggested mosquitoes, but several bath-guests had slung up hammocks and were lying in them dozing, so that there could not have been mosquitoes; and coming suddenly out on to the sands all idea of stuffiness vanished, for there was the same glorious, heaving, sparkling, splashing blue that I had seen from the dunes of Göhren the evening before at sunset. The bathing-house, a modest place with only two cells and a long plank bridge running into deep water, was just opposite the end of the path through the firs. It was locked up and deserted. The sands were deserted too, for the tourists were all dozing in hammocks or in beds. I made a hollow in the clean dry sand beneath the last of the fir trees, and settled down to enjoy myself till Gertrud came. Oh, I was happy! Thiessow was so quiet and primitive, the afternoon so radiant, the colours of the sea and of the long line of silver sand, and of the soft green gloom of the background of firs so beautiful. Commendably far away to the north I saw the coastguard hill belonging to

Göhren. On my right the woods turned into beechwoods, and scrambled up high cliffs that seemed to form the end of the peninsula. I would go and look at all that later on after my bathe. If there is a thing I love it is exploring the little paths of an unknown wood, finding out the corners where it keeps its periwinkles and anemones, discovering its birds' nests, waiting motionless for its hedgehogs and squirrels, and even searching out those luscious recesses, oozy and green, where it keeps its happy slugs. They tell me slugs are not really happy, that Nature is cruel, and that you only have to scratch the pleasant surface of things to get at once to blood-curdling brutalities. Perhaps if you were to go on scratching you might get to consolations and beneficiencies again; but why scratch at all? Why not take the beauty and be grateful? I will not scratch. I will not criticise my own mother who has sheltered me so long in her broad bosom, and been so long my surest guide to all that is gentle and lovely. Whatever she does, from thunderbolts to headaches, I will not criticise; for if she gives me a headache, is there not pleasure when it leaves off? And if she hurls a thunderbolt at me and I am unexpectedly exterminated, my body shall serve as a basis for fresh life and growth, and shall blossom out presently into an immortality of daisies.

I think I must have slept, for the sound of the waves grew very far away, and I only seemed to have been watching the sun on them for a few minutes, when Gertrud's voice floated across space to my ears; and she was saying it was past four, and that one lady had already gone down to bathe, and that, as there were only two cells, if I did not go soon I might not get a bathe at all. I sat up in my hollow and looked across to the huts. The bathing woman in the usual white calico sunbonnet was there, waiting on the plank bridge. No one was in the sea yet. It was a great bore that there should be any one else bathing just then, for German female tourists are apt to be extraordinarily cordial in the water. On land, laced into suppressive whalebone, dressed, and with their hair dry and curled, they cannot but keep within the limits set by convention; but the more clothes they take off the more do they seem to consider the last barrier between human creature and human creature broken down, and they will behave towards you, meeting you on this common ground of wateriness, as though they had known you and extravagantly esteemed you for years. Their cordiality, too, becomes more pronounced in proportion to the coldness and roughness of the water; and the water that day looked cold and was certainly rough, and I felt that there being only two of us in it it would be impossible to escape the advances of the other one. Still, as the cells were shut at five, I could not wait till she had done, so I went down and began to undress.

While I was doing it I heard her leave her cell and anxiously ask the woman if the sea were very cold. Then she apparently put in one foot, for I heard her shriek. Then she apparently bent down, and scooping up water in her hand splashed her face with it, for I heard her gasp. Then she tried the other foot, and shrieked again. And then the bathing woman, fearful lest five o'clock should still find her on duty, began mellifluously to persuade. By this time I was ready, but I did not choose to meet the unknown emotional one on the plank bridge because the garments in which one bathes in German waters are regrettably scanty; so I waited, peeping through the little window. After much talk the eloquence of the bathing woman had its effect, and the bather with one wild scream leapt into the foam, which immediately engulfed her, and when she emerged the first thing she did on getting her breath was to clutch hold of the rope and shriek without stopping for at least a minute. 'Unwürdiges Benehmen,' I observed to Gertrud with a shrug. 'It must be very cold,' I added to myself, not without a secret shrinking. But to my surprise, when I ran along the planks above where the unfortunate clutched and shrieked, she looked up at me with a wet but beaming countenance, and interrupted her shrieks to gasp out, '*Prachtvoll!*'

'Really these bath-guests in the water——' I thought indignantly. What right had this one, only because my apparel was scanty, to smile at me and say *prachtvoll*? I was so much startled by the unexpected exclamation from a person who had the minute before been rending the air with her laments, that my foot slipped on the wet planks, I just heard the bathing woman advising me to take care, just had time to comment to myself on the foolishness of such advice to one already hurling through space, and then came a shock of all-engulfing coldness and wetness and suffocation, and the next moment there I was gasping and spluttering exactly as the other bath-guest had gasped and spluttered, but with this difference, that she had clutched the rope and shrieked, and I, with all the convulsive energy of panic, was shrieking and clutching the bath-guest.

'*Prachtvoll*, nicht?' I heard her say with an odious jollity through the singing in my ears. Every wave lifted me a little off my feet. My mouth was full of water. My eyes were blinded with spray. I continued to cling to her with one hand, miserably conscious that after this there would be no shaking her off, and rubbing my eyes with the other looked at her. My shrieks froze on my lips. Where had I seen her face before? Surely I knew it? She wore one of those grey india-rubber caps, drawn tightly down to her eyes, that keep the water out so well and are so hopelessly hideous. She smiled back at me with the utmost friendliness, and asked me again whether I did not think it glorious.

'*Ach ja-ja*,' I panted, letting her go and groping blindly for the rope. 'Thank you, thank you; pray pardon me for having seized you so rudely.'

'*Bitte, bitte,*' she cried, beginning to jump up and down again.

'Who in the world is she?' I asked myself, getting away as fast as I could. 'Where have I seen her before?'

Probably she was an undesirable acquaintance. Perhaps she was my dressmaker. I had not paid her last absurd bill, and that and a certain faint resemblance to what my dressmaker would look like in an india-rubber cap was what put her into my head; and no sooner had I thought it than I was sure of it, and the conviction was one of quite unprecedented disagreeableness. How profoundly unpleasant to meet this person in the water, to have come all the way to Rügen, to have suffered at Göhren, to have walked miles in the heat of the day to Thiessow, for the sole purpose of bathing tête-à-tête with my dressmaker. And to have tumbled in on top of her and clung about her neck! I climbed out and ran into my cell. My idea was to get dressed and away as speedily as possible; yet with all Gertrud's haste, just as I came out of my cell the other woman came out of hers in her clothes, and we met face to face. With one accord we stopped dead and our mouths fell open, 'What,' she cried, 'it is *you*?'

'What,' I cried, 'it is *you*?'

It was my cousin Charlotte whom I had not seen for ten years.

THE FOURTH DAY—*Continued*

AT THIESSOW

My cousin Charlotte was twenty when I saw her last. Now she was thirty, besides having had an india-rubber cap on. Both these things make a difference to a woman, though she did not seem aware of it, and was lost in amazement that I should not have recognised her at once. I told her it was because of the cap. Then I expressed the astonishment I felt that she had not at once recognised me, and after hesitating a moment she said that I had been making too many faces; and so with infinite delicacy did we avoid all allusion to those ten unhideable years.

Charlotte had had a chequered career; at least, beside my placid life it seemed to have bristled with events. In her early youth, and to the dismay of her parents, she insisted on being educated at one of the English colleges for women—it was at Oxford, but I forget its name—a most unusual course for a young German girl of her class to take. She was so determined, and made her relations so uncomfortable during their period of opposition, that they gave in with what appeared to more distant relatives who were not with Charlotte all day long a criminal weakness. At Oxford she took everything there was to take in the way of honours and prizes, and was the joy and pride of her college. In her last year, a German savant of sixty, an exceedingly bright light in the firmament of European learning, came to Oxford and was fêted. When Charlotte saw the great local beings she was accustomed to look upon as the most marvellous men of the age—the heads of colleges, professors, and other celebrities—vying with each other in honouring her countryman, her admiration for him was such that it took her breath away. At some function she was brought to his notice, and her family being well known in Germany and she herself then in the freshness of twenty-one, besides being very pretty, the great man was much interested, and beamed benevolently upon her, and chucked her under the chin. The head in whose house he was staying, a person equally exquisite in appearance and manners, who had had much to forgive that was less excellent in his guest and had done so freely for the sake of the known profundity of his knowledge, could not but remark this interest in Charlotte, and told him pleasantly of her promising career. The professor appeared to listen with attention, and looked pleased and approving; but when the head ceased, instead of commenting on her talents or the creditable manner in which she had developed them, what he said was, 'A nice, round little girl. A very nice, round little girl. *Colossal appetitlich.*' And this he repeated emphatically several times, to the distinct discomfort of the head, while his eyes followed her benignly into the distant corner placed at the disposal of the obscure.

Six months later she married the professor. Her family wept and implored in vain; told her in vain of the terrificness of marrying a widower with seven children all older than herself. Charlotte was blinded by the glory of having been chosen by the greatest man Oxford had ever seen. Oxford was everything to her. Her distant German home and its spiritless inhabitants were objects only of her good-natured shrugs. She wrote to me saying she was going to be the life companion of the finest thinker of the age; her people, so illiterate and so full of prejudices, could not, she supposed, be expected to appreciate the splendour of her prospects; she thanked heaven that her own education had saved her from such a laughable blindness; she could conceive nothing more glorious than marrying the man in all the world whom you most reverently admire, than being chosen as the sharer of his thoughts, and the partner of his intellectual joys. After that I seldom heard from her. She lived in the south of Germany, and her professor's fame waxed vaster every year. Every year, too, she brought a potential professor into a world already so full of them, and every year death cut short its career after a period varying from ten days to a fortnight, and the *Kreuzzeitung* seemed perpetually to be announcing that *Heute früh ist meine liebe Frau Charlotte von einem strammen Jungen leicht und glücklich entbunden worden*, and *Heute starb unser Sohn Bernhard im zarten Alter von zwei Wochen.* None of the children lived long enough to meet the next brother, and they were steadily christened Bernhard, after a father apparently thirsting to perpetuate his name. It became at last quite uncomfortable. Charlotte seemed never to be out of the *Kreuzzeitung.* For six years she and the poor little Bernhards went on in this manner, haunting its birth and death columns, and then abruptly disappeared from them; and the next I heard of her was that she was in England,—in London, Oxford, and other intellectual centres, lecturing in the cause of Woman. The *Kreuzzeitung* began about her again, but on another page. The *Kreuzzeitung* was shocked; for Charlotte was emancipated. Charlotte's family was so much shocked that it was hysterical. Charlotte, not content with lecturing, wrote pamphlets,—lofty documents of a deadly earnestness, in German and English, and they might be seen any day in the bookshop windows *Unter den Linden.* Charlotte's family nearly fainted when it had to walk *Unter den Linden.* The Radical papers, which were only read by Charlotte's family when nobody was looking and were never allowed openly to darken their doors, took her under their wing and wrote articles in her praise. It was, they said, surprising and refreshing to find views and intelligence of the sort emerging from the suffocating ancestral atmosphere that hangs about the *Landadel*. The paralysing effect of too many ancestors was not as a rule to be lightly shaken off, especially by the female descendants. When it did get shaken off, as in this instance, it should be the subject of rejoicing to every person who had the advancement of civilisation at heart. The civilisation of a state could never be great so long as its women, etc. etc.

My uncle and aunt nearly died of this praise. Her brothers and sisters stayed in the country and refused invitations. Only the professor seemed as pleased as ever. 'Charlotte is my cousin,' I said to him at a party in Berlin where he was being lionised. 'How proud you must be of such a clever wife!' I had not met him before, and a more pleasant, rosy, nice little old man I have never seen.

He beamed at me through his spectacles. Almost could I see the narrow line that separated me from a chin-chucking. 'Yes, yes,' he said, 'so they all tell me. The little Lotte is making a noise. Empty vessels do. But I daresay what she tells them is a very pretty little nonsense. One must not be too critical in these cases.' And, seizing upon the cousinship, he began to call me *Du*.

I inquired how it was she was wandering about the world alone. He said he could not imagine. I asked him what he thought of the pamphlets. He said he had no time for light reading. I was so unfortunate as to remark, no doubt with enthusiasm, that I had read some of his simpler works to my great benefit and unbounded admiration. He looked more benign than ever, and said he had had no idea that anything of his was taught in elementary schools.

In a word, I was routed by the professor. I withdrew, feeling crushed, and wondering if I had deserved it. He came after me, called me his *liebe kleine Cousine*, and sitting down beside me patted my hand and inquired with solicitude how it was he had never seen me before. Renewed attempts on my part to feed like a bee on the honey of his learning were met only by pats. He would pat, but he would not impart wisdom; and the longer he patted the more perfect did his serenity seem to become. When people approached us and showed a tendency to hang on the great man's lips, he looked up with a happy smile and said, 'This is my little cousin—we have much to say to each other,' and turned his back on them. And when I was asked whether I had not spent a memorable, an elevating evening, being talked to so much by the famous Nieberlein, I could only put on a solemn face and say that I should not soon forget it. 'It will be something to tell your children of, in the days to come when he is a splendid memory,' said the enthusiast.

'Oh won't it!' I ejaculated, with the turned-up eyes of rapture.

'Tell me one thing,' I said to Charlotte as we walked slowly along the sands towards the cliff and the beechwood; 'why, since you took me for a stranger, were you so—well, so gracious to me in the water?'

Gertrud had gone back to the hotel laden with both our bathing-things. 'She may as well take mine up at the same time,' Charlotte had remarked, piling them on Gertrud's passive arms. Undeniably she might; and accordingly she did. But her face was wry, and so had been the smile with which she returned Charlotte's careless greetings. 'You still keep that old fool, I see,' said Charlotte. 'It would send me mad to have a person of inferior intellect for ever fussing round me.'

'It would send me much madder to have a person of superior intellect buttoning my boots and scorning me while she does it,' I replied.

'Why was I so gracious to you in the water?' repeated Charlotte in answer to my inquiry, made not without anxiousness, for one likes to know one's own cousin above the practices of ordinary bath-guests. 'I'll tell you why. I detest the stiff, icy way women have of turning their backs if they don't know each other.'

'Oh they're not very stiff,' I remarked, thinking of past bathing experiences, 'and besides, in the water——'

'It is not only unkind, it is simply wicked. For how shall we ever be anything but tools and drudges if we don't co-operate, if we don't stand shoulder to shoulder? Oh my heart goes out to all women! I never see one without feeling I must do all in my power to get to know her, to help her, to show her what she must do, so that when her youth is gone there will still be something left, a so much nobler happiness, a so much truer joy.'

'Than what?' I asked, puzzled.

Charlotte was looking into my eyes as though she were reading my soul. She wasn't, whatever she might have thought she was doing. 'Than what she had before, of course,' she said with some asperity.

'But perhaps what she had before was just what she liked best.'

'But if it was only the sort of joy every woman who is young and pretty gets heaped on her, does it not take wings and fly away the moment she happens to look haggard, or is low-spirited, or ill?'

It was as I had feared. Charlotte was strenuous. There was not a doubt of it. And the strenuous woman is a form of the sex out of whose way I have hitherto kept. Of course I knew from the pamphlets and the lectures that she was not one to stay at home and see the point of purring over her husband's socks; but I had supposed one might lecture and write things without bringing the pamphlet manner to bear on one's own blood relations.

'You were very jolly in the water,' I said. 'Why are you suddenly so serious?'

'The water,' replied Charlotte, 'is the only place I am ever what you call jolly in. It is the only place where I can ever forget how terribly earnest life is.'

'My dear Charlotte, shall we sit down? The bathing has made me tired.'

We did sit down, and leaning my back against a rock, and pulling my hat over my eyes, I gazed out at the sunlit sea and at the flocks of little white clouds hanging over it to the point where they met the water, while Charlotte talked. Yes, she was right, nearly always right, in everything she said, and it was certainly meritorious to use one's strength, and health, and talents as she was doing, trying to get rid of mouldy prejudices. I gathered that what she was fighting for were equal rights and equal privileges for women and men alike. It is a story I have heard before, and up to now it has not had a satisfactory ending. And Charlotte was so small, and the world she defied was so big and so indifferent and had such an inconsequent habit of associating all such efforts—in themselves nothing less than heroic—with the ridiculousness of cropped hair and extremities clothed in bloomers. I protest that the thought of this brick wall of indifference with Charlotte hurling herself against it during all the years that might have been pleasant was so tragic to me that I was nearly tempted to try to please her by offering to come and hurl myself too. But I have no heroism. The hardness and coldness of bricks terrifies me. What, I wondered, could her experiences with her great thinker have been, to make her turn her back so absolutely on the fair and sheltered land of matrimony? I could not but agree with much that she was saying. That women, if they chose, need not do or endure any of the things against which those of them who find their voice cry out has long been clear to me. That they are, on the whole, not well-disposed towards each other is also a fact frequently to be observed. And that this secret antagonism must be got over before there can be any real co-operation may, I suppose, be regarded as certain. But when Charlotte spoke of co-operation she was apparently thinking only of the co-operation of those whom years, in place of the might of youth, have provided with the sad sensibleness that comes of repeated disappointments—the co-operation, that is, of the elderly; and the German elderly in the immense majority of cases remains obscurely in her kitchen and does not dream of co-operating. Has she not got over the conjugal quarrels of the first married years? Has she not filled her nurseries and become indefinite in outline? And do not these things make for content? If thoughts of rebellion enter her head, she need only look honestly at her image in the glass to be aware that it is not her kind that will ever wring concessions from the other sex. She is a *brave Frau*, and a *brave Frau* who should try to do anything beyond keeping her home tidy and feeding its inmates would be almost pathetically ridiculous.

'You shouldn't bother about the old ones,' I murmured, watching a little white steamer rounding the Göhren headland. 'Get the young to co-operate, my dear Charlotte. The young inherit the earth—Teutonic earth certainly they do. If you got all the pretty women between twenty and thirty on your side the thing's done. No wringing would be required. The concessions would simply shower down.'

'I detest the word concession,' said Charlotte.

'Do you? But there it is. We live on the concessions made us by those beings you would probably call the enemy. And, after all, most of us live fairly comfortably.'

'By the way,' she said, turning her head suddenly and looking at me, 'what have you been doing all these years?'

'Doing?' I repeated in some confusion. I don't know why there should have been any confusion, unless it was a note in Charlotte's voice that made her question sound like a stern inquiry after that one talent which is death to hide lodged with me useless. 'Now, as though you didn't very well know what I have been doing. I have had a row of babies and brought it up quite nicely.'

'*That* isn't anything to be proud of.'

'I didn't say it was.'

'Your cat achieves precisely the same thing.'

'My dear Charlotte, I haven't got a cat.'

'And now—what are you doing now?'

'You see what I am doing. Apparently exactly what you are.'

'I don't mean that. Of course you know I don't mean that. What are you doing now with your life?'

I turned my head and gazed reproachfully at Charlotte. How pretty she used to be. How prettily the corners of her mouth used to turn up, as though her soul were always smiling. And she had had the dearest chin with a dimple in it, and she had had clear, hopeful eyes, and all the lines of her body had been comely and gracious. These are solid advantages that should not lightly be allowed to go. Not a trace of them was left. Her face was thin, and its expression of determination made it look hard. There was a deep line straight down between her eyebrows, as though she frowned at life more than is needful. Angles had everywhere taken the place of curves. Her eyes were as bright and intelligent as ever, but seemed to have grown larger. Something had completely done for Charlotte as far as beauty of person goes; whether it was the six Bernhards, or her actual enthusiasms, or the unusual mixture of both, I could not at this stage discover; nor could I yet see if her soul had gained the beauty that her body had lost, which is undoubtedly what the rightly cared-for soul does do. Meanwhile anything more utterly unlike the wife of a famous professor I have never seen. The wife of an aged German celebrity should be, and is, calm, comfortable, large, and slow. She must be, and is, proud of her great man. She attends to his bodily wants, and does not presume to share his spiritual excitements. In their common life he is the brain, she the willing hands and feet. It is perfectly fair. If there are to be great men some one must be found to look after them—some one who shall be more patient, faithful, and admiring than a servant, and unable like a servant to throw up the situation on the least provocation. A wife is an admirable institution. She is the hedge set between the precious flowers of the male intellect and the sun and dust of sordid worries. She is the flannel that protects when the winds of routine are cold. She is the sheltering jam that makes the pills of life possible. She is buffer, comforter, and cook. And so long as she enjoys these various roles the arrangement is perfect. The difficulties begin when, defying Nature's teaching, which on this point is luminous, she refuses to be the hedge, flannel, jam, buffer, comforter, and cook; and when she goes so far on the sulphuric path of rebellion as to insist on being clever on her own account and publicly, she has, in Germany at least, set every law of religion and decency at defiance. Charlotte had been doing this, if all I had heard was true, for the last three years; therefore her stern inquiry addressed to a wife of my sobriety struck me as singularly out of place. What had I been doing with my life? Looking back into it in search of an answer it seemed very spacious, and sunny, and quiet. There were children in it, and there was a garden, and a spouse in whose eyes I was precious; but I had not done anything. And if I could point to no pamphlets or lectures, neither need I point to a furrow between my eyebrows.

'It is very odd,' Charlotte went on, as I sat silent, 'our meeting like this. I was on the verge of writing to ask if I might come and stay with you.'

'Oh were you?'

'So often lately I have thought just you might be such a help to me if only I could wake you up.'

'Wake me up, my dear Charlotte?'

'Oh, I've heard about you. I know you live stuffed away in the country in a sort of dream. You needn't try to answer my question about what you have done. You can't answer it. You have lived in a dream, entirely wrapped up in your family and your plants.'

'Plants, my dear Charlotte?'

'You do not see nor want to see farther than the ditch at the end of your garden. All that is going on outside, out in the great real world where people are in earnest, where they strive, and long, and suffer, where they unceasingly pursue their ideal of a wider life, a richer experience, a higher knowledge, is absolutely indifferent to you. Your existence—no one could call it life—is quite negative and unemotional. It is as negative and as unemotional as——' She paused and looked at me with a faint, compassionate smile.

'As what?' I asked, anxious to hear the worst.

'Frankly, as an oyster's.'

'Really, my dear Charlotte,' I exclaimed, naturally upset. How very unfortunate that I should have hurried away from Göhren. Why had I not stayed there two or three days, as I had at first intended? It was such a safe place; you could get out of it so easily and so quickly. If I were an oyster—curious how much the word disconcerted me—at least I was a happy oyster, which was surely better than being miserable and not an oyster at all. Charlotte was certainly nearer being miserable than happy. People who are happy do not have the look she had in her eyes, nor is their expression so uninterruptedly determined. And why should I be lectured? When I am in the mood for a lecture, my habit is to buy a ticket and go and listen; and when I have not bought a ticket, it is a sign that I do not want a lecture. I did not like to explain this beautifully simple position to Charlotte, yet felt that at all costs I must nip her eloquence in the bud or she would keep me out till it was dark; so I got up, cleared my throat, and said in the balmy tone in which people on platforms begin their orations, '*Geehrte Anwesende*.'

'Are you going to give me a lecture?' she inquired with a surprised smile.

'In return for yours.'

'My dear soul, may I not talk to you about anything except plants?'

'I really don't know why you should think plants are the only things that interest me. I have not yet mentioned them. And, as a matter of fact, you are the last person with whom I would share my vegetable griefs. But that isn't what I wished to say. I was going to offer you, *geehrte Anwesende*, a few remarks about husbands.'

Charlotte frowned.

'About husbands,' I repeated blandly, in a voice of milk and honey. '*Geehrte Anwesende*, in the course of an uneventful existence I have had much leisure for reflection, and my reflections have led me to the conclusion, erroneous perhaps, but fixed, that having got a husband, taken him of one's own free will, taken him sometimes even in the face of opposition, the least one can do is to stick to him. Now, Charlotte, where is yours? What have you done with him? Is he here? And if not, why is he not here, and where is he?'

Charlotte got up hastily and brushed the sand out of the folds of her dress. 'You haven't changed a bit,' she said with a slight laugh. 'You are just as ____,'

'Silly?' I suggested.

'Oh, I didn't say that. And as for Bernhard, he is where he always was, marching triumphantly along the road to undying fame. But you know that. You only ask because your ideas of the duties of woman are medieval, and you are shocked. Well, I'm afraid you must be shocked then. I haven't seen him for a whole year.'

Luckily at this moment, for I think we were going to quarrel, Gertrud came heaving through the sand towards us with a packet of letters. She had been to the post, and knowing I loved getting letters came out to look for me so that I might have them at once; and as I eagerly opened them and buried myself in them, Charlotte confined her occasional interjections to deprecating the obviously inferior shape of Gertrud's head.

THE FIFTH DAY

FROM THIESSOW TO SELLIN

Many a time have I wondered at the unworthy ways of Fate, at the pettiness of the pleasure it takes in frustrating plans that are small and innocent, at its entire want of dignity, at its singular spitefulness, at the resemblance of its manners to those of an evilly-disposed kitchen-maid; but never have I wondered more than I did that night at Thiessow.

We had been for a walk after tea through the beechwood, up a hill behind it to the signal station, along a footpath on the edge of the cliff with blue gleams of sea on one side through a waving fringe of blue and purple flowers, and the ryefields on the other. We had stood looking down at the village of Thiessow far below us, a cluster of picturesque roofs surrounded on three sides by sunlit water; had gazed across the vast plain to the distant hill and village of Gross Zickow; watched the shadows passing over meadows miles away; seen how the sea to the west had the calm colours of a pearl; how the sea beneath us through the parting stalks of scabious and harebells was quiet but very blue; and how behind us, over the beech-tops, there was the eastern sea where the wind was, as brilliant and busy and foam-flecked as before. It was all very wide, and open, and roomy. It was a place to bless God in and cease from vain words. And when the stars came out we went down into the plain, and wandered out across the dewy grass in the gathering night, our faces towards the red strip of sky where the sun had set.

Charlotte had not been silent all this time; she had been, on the contrary, passionately explanatory. She had passionately explained the intolerableness of her life with the famous Nieberlein; she had passionately justified her action in cutting it short. And listening in silence, I had soon located the real wound, the place she did not mention where all the bruises were; for talk and explain as she might it was clear that her chief grievance was that the great man had never taken her seriously. To be strenuous, to hold intense views on questions that seem to you to burn, and to be treated as an airy nothing, a charming nothing perhaps, but still a nothing, must be, on the whole, disconcerting. I do not know that I should call it more than disconcerting. You need not, after all, let your vision be blocked entirely by the person with whom you chance to live; however vast his intellectual bulk may be, you can look round him and see that the stars and the sky are still there, and you need not run away from him to do that. If the great Nieberlein had not taken Charlotte sufficiently seriously, she had manifestly taken him much too seriously. It is better to laugh at one's Nieberlein than to be angry with him, and it is infinitely more personally soothing. And presently you find you have grown old together, and that your Nieberlein has become unaccountably precious, and that you do not want to laugh at all,—or if you do, it is a very tender laughter, tender almost to tears.

And then, as we walked on over the wonderful starlit plain in the huge hush of the brooding night, the air, heavy with dew and the smell of grass cut that afternoon in distant meadows, so sweet and soft that it seemed as if it must smooth away every line of midday eagerness from our tired faces, Charlotte paused; and before I had done praising Providence for this refreshment, she not yet having paused at all, she began again in a new key of briskness, and said, 'By the way, I may as well come with you when you leave this. I have nothing particular to do. I came down here for a day or two to get away from some English people I was with at Binz who had rather got on to my nerves. And I have so much to say to you, and it will be a good opportunity. We can talk all day, while we are driving.'

Talk all day while we were driving! If Hazlitt saw no wit in talking and walking, I see less than none in talking and driving. It was this speech of Charlotte's that set me marvelling anew at the maliciousness of Fate. Here was I, the most harmless of women, engaged in the most harmless of little expeditions, asking and wanting nothing but to be left alone; a person so obscure as to be, one would think, altogether out of the reach of the blind Fury with the accursèd shears; a person with a plan so mild and humble that I was ashamed of the childishness of the Fate that could waste its energies spoiling it. Yet before the end of the fourth day I was confronted with the old familiar inexorableness, taking its stand this time on the impossibility of refusing the company of a cousin whom you have not seen for ten years.

'Oh Charlotte,' I cried, seized her arm convulsively, struggling in the very clutches of Fate, 'what—what a good idea! And what a thousand pities that it can't be managed! You see it is a victoria, and there are only two places because of all the luggage, so that we can't use the little seat, or Gertrud might have sat on that——'

'Gertrud? Send her home. What do you want with Gertrud if I am with you?'

I stared dismayed through the dusk at Charlotte's determined face. 'But she—packs,' I said.

'Don't be so helpless. As though two healthy women couldn't wrap up their own hair-brushes.'

'Oh it isn't only hair-brushes,' I went on, still struggling, 'it's everything. You can't think how much I loathe buttoning boots—I know I never would button them, but go about with them undone, and then I'd disgrace you, and I don't want to do that. But that isn't it really either,' I went on hurriedly, for Charlotte had opened her mouth to tell me, I felt certain, that she would button them for me, 'my husband never will let me go anywhere without Gertrud. You see she looked after his mother too, and he thinks awful things would happen if I hadn't got her. I'm very sorry, Charlotte. It is most unfortunate. I wish—I wish I had thought of bringing the omnibus.'

'But is your husband such an absurd tyrant?' asked Charlotte, a robust scorn for my flabby obedience in her voice.

'Oh—tyrant!' I ejaculated, casting up my eyes to the stars, and mentally begging the unconscious innocent's pardon.

'Well, then, we must get a luggage cart and put the things into that.'

'Oh,' I cried, seizing her arm again, my thoughts whirling round in search of a loophole of escape, 'what—what another good idea!'

'And Gertrud can go in the cart too.'

'So she can. What—what a trilogy of good ideas! Have you got any more, Charlotte? What a resourceful woman you are. I believe you like fighting and getting over difficulties.'

'I believe I do,' said Charlotte complacently.

I dropped her arm, ceased to struggle, walked on vanquished. Henceforth, if no more interesting difficulties presented themselves, Charlotte was going to spend her time overcoming me. And besides an eloquent Charlotte sitting next to me, there would be a cart rattling along behind me all day. I could have wept at the sudden end to the peace and perfect freedom of my journey. I went to bed, to a clean and pleasant bed that at another time would have pleased me, strongly of opinion that life was not worth while. Nor did it comfort me that from my pillow I looked out at the mysterious dark plain with its roof of stars and its faint red window in the north-west, because Charlotte had opened the door between our rooms and every now and then asked me if I were asleep. I lay making plans for the circumvention of Charlotte, and rejecting them one after the other as too uncousinly; and when I had made my head ache with the difficulty of uniting a becoming cousinliness with the cold-bloodedness necessary for shaking her off, I spent my time feebly deprecating the superabundance of cousins in the world. Surely there are too many? Surely almost everybody has more than he can manage comfortably? It must have been long after midnight that Charlotte, herself very restless, called out once more to know if I were asleep.

'Yes I am,' I answered; not quite kindly I fear, but indeed it is an irritating question.

We left Thiessow at ten the next morning under a grey sky, and drove, at the strong recommendation of the landlord, along the hard sands as far as a little fishing place called Lobberort, where we struck off to the left on to the plain again, and so came once more to Philippshagen and the high road that runs from there to Göhren, Baabe, and Sellin. I took the landlord's advice willingly, because I did not choose to drive on that grey morning in my altered circumstances over the plain along which I had walked so happily only the day before. The landlord, as obliging a person as his wife was a capable one, had provided a cart with two long-tailed, raw-boned horses who were to come with us as far as Binz, my next stopping-place. Gertrud sat next to the driver of this cart looking grim. Her prospects were gloomy, for the seat was hard, the driver was dirty, the cart had no springs, and she had had to pack Charlotte's clothes. She did not approve of the Frau Professor; how should she? Gertrud read her *Kreuzzeitung* as regularly as she did her Bible, and believed it as implicitly; she knew all about the pamphlets, and only from the *Kreuzzeitung's* point of view. And then Charlotte made the mistake clever people sometimes do of too readily supposing that others are stupid; and it did not need much shrewdness on Gertrud's part to see that the Frau Professor disliked the shape of her head.

The drive along the wet sands was uninteresting because of the prevailing greyness of sky and sea; but the waves made so much noise that Charlotte, unable to get anything out of me but head-shakings and pointings to my ears, gave up trying to talk and kept quiet. The luggage cart came on close behind, the lean horses showing an undesirable skittishness, and once, in an attempt to run away, swerved so close to the water that Gertrud's gloom became absolutely leaden. But we reached Lobberort safely, ploughed up through the deep sand on to the track again, and after Philippshagen the sky cleared, the sun came out, and the world began on a sudden to sparkle.

We did not see Göhren again. The road, very hilly just there, passes behind it between steep grassy banks blue with harebells and with a strip of brilliant sky above it between the tops of the beeches. But once more did I rattle over the stones of the Lonely One, pass the wooden inn where the same people seemed to be drinking the same beer and still waiting for the same train, and drive along the dull straight bit between Baabe and the first pines of Sellin. At Sellin we were going to lunch, rest the horses, and then, late in the afternoon, go on to Binz. Sellin from this side is a pine-forest with a very deep sandy road. Occasional villas appear between the trees, and becoming more frequent join into a string and form one side of the road. After passing them we came to a broad gravel road at right angles to the one we were on, with restaurants and villas on either side, trim rows of iron lamp-posts and stripling chestnut trees, and a wide gap at the end at the edge of the cliff below which lay the sea.

This was the real Sellin, this single wide hot road, with its glaring white houses, and at the back of them on either side the forest brushing against their windows. It was one o'clock. Dinner bells were ringing all down the street, visitors were streaming up from the sands into the different hotels, dishes clattered, and the air was full of food. On every balcony families were sitting round tables waiting for the servant who was fetching their dinner from a restaurant. Down at the foot of the cliff the sea lay in perfect quiet, a heavenly blue, out of reach in that bay of the wind that was blowing on Thiessow. There was no wind here, only intense heat and light and smells of cooking. 'Shall we leave August to put up, and get away into the forest and let Gertrud buy some lunch and bring it to us?' I asked Charlotte. 'Don't you think dinner in one of these places will be rather horrid?'

'What sort of lunch will Gertrud buy?' inquired Charlotte cautiously.

'Oh bread, and eggs, and fruit, and things. It is enough on a hot day like this.'

'My dear soul, it is not enough. Surely it is foolish to starve. I'll come with you if you like, of course, but I see no sense in not being properly nourished. And we don't know where and when we shall get another meal.'

So we drove on to the end hotel, from whose terrace we could look down at the deserted sands and the wonderful colour of the water. August and the driver of the luggage cart put up. Gertrud retired to a neighbouring cafe, and we sat and gasped under the glass roof of the verandah of the hotel while a hot waiter brought us boiling soup.

It is a barbarous custom, this of dining at one o'clock. Under the most favourable circumstances one o'clock is a difficult hour to manage profitably to the soul. There is something peculiarly base about it. It is the hour, I suppose, when the life of the spirit is at its lowest ebb, and one should be careful not to extinguish it altogether under the weight of a gigantic menu. I know my spirit fainted utterly away at the aspect of those plates of steaming soup and at the smell of all the other things we were going to be given after it. Charlotte ate her soup calmly and complacently. It did not seem to make her hotter. She also ate everything else with equal calmness, and remarked that full brains are never to be found united to an empty stomach.

'But a full stomach is often to be found united to empty brains,' I replied.

'No one asserted the contrary,' said Charlotte; and took some more *Rinderbrust.*

I thought that dinner would never be done. The hotel was full, and the big dining-room was crowded, as well as the verandah where we were. Everybody talked at once, and the noise was like the noise of the parrot house at the Zoological Gardens. It looked as if it were an expensive place; it had parquet floors and flowers on the tables and various other things I had not yet come across in Rügen; and when the bill came I found that it not only looked so but was so. All the more, then, was I astonished at the numbers of families with many children and the necessary Fräulein staying in it. How did they manage it? There was a visitors' list on the table, and turning it over I found that none of them, in the nature of things, could be well off. They all gave their occupations, and the majority were *Apotheker* and *Photographen*. There were two *Herren Pianofabrikanten*, several *Lehrer*, a *Herr Geheimcalculator* whatever that is, many *Bankbeamten* or clerks, and one surely who must have found the place beyond his means, a *Herr Schriftsteller*. All these had wives and children with them, 'I can't make it out,' I said to Charlotte.

'What can't you make out?'

'How these people contrive to stay weeks in a dear hotel like this.'

'Oh, it is quite simple. The *Badereise* is the great event of the year. They save up for it all the rest of the year. They live at home as frugally as possible so that for one magnificent month they can pretend to waiters and chambermaids and the other visitors that they are richer than they are. It is very foolish, sadly foolish. It is one of the things I am trying to persuade women to give up.'

'But you are doing it yourself.'

'But surely there is a difference in the method. Besides, I was run down.'

'Well, so I should think were the poor mothers of families by the time they have kept house frugally for a year. And if it makes them happy, why not?'

'Just that is another of the things I am working to persuade them to give up.'

'What, being happy?'

'No, being mothers of families.'

'My dear Charlotte,' I murmured; and mused in silence on the six Bernhards.

'Of unwieldily big ones, of course I mean.'

'And what do you understand by unwieldily big ones?' I asked, still musing on the Bernhards.

'Any number above three. And for most of these women even three is excessive.'

The images of the six Bernhards troubled me so much that I could not speak.

'Look,' said Charlotte, 'at the women here. All of them, or any of them. The one at the opposite table, for instance. Do you see the bulk of the poor soul? Do you see how difficult existence must be made for her by that circumstance alone? How life can be nothing to her but uninterrupted panting?'

'Perhaps she doesn't walk enough,' I suggested. 'She ought to walk round Rügen once a year instead of casting anchor in the flesh-pots of Sellin.'

'She looks fifty,' continued Charlotte. 'And why does she look fifty?'

'Perhaps because she is fifty.'

'Nonsense. She is quite young. But those four awful children are hers, and no doubt there is a baby, or perhaps two babies, upstairs, and they have finished her. How is such a woman to realise herself? How can she work out her own salvation? What energies she has must be spent on her children. And if ever she tries to think, she must fall asleep from sheer torpor of brain. Now why should she be deprived of the use of her soul?'

'Charlotte, are you not obscure? Here, take my pudding. I don't like it.'

I hoped the pudding would stem the stream of her eloquence. I feared an impending lecture. She had resumed the pamphlet manner of the previous afternoon, and I felt very helpless. She took the pudding, and I was dismayed, to find that though she ate it it had no effect whatever. She did not even seem to know she was eating it, and continued to address me with rapidly- increasing vehemence on the proper treatment of female souls. Now why could she not talk on this subject without being vehement? There is something about vehemence that freezes responsiveness out of me; I suppose it is what Charlotte would call the oyster characteristics coming out. Anyhow, by the time the waiter brought cheese and woolly radishes and those wicked black slabs of leather called *Pumpernickel*, I was sitting quite silent, and Charlotte was leaning across the little table hurling fiery words at me. And as for the stout lady who had set her ablaze, she ate almonds and raisins with a sublime placidity, throwing the almonds down on to the stone floor, cracking them with the heel of her boot, and exhibiting an unexpected nimbleness in picking them up again.

'Do you suppose that if she hadn't had those four children and heaven knows how many besides she wouldn't be different from what she is now?' asked Charlotte, leaning her elbows on the table and fixing me with eyes whose brightness dazzled me, 'As different as day is from night? As health from disease? As briskness from torpor? She'd have looked and felt ten years younger. She'd have had all her energies unimpaired. She'd have had the use of her soul, her time, her individuality. Now it is too late. All that has been choked out of her by the miserable daily drudgery. What would the man, her smug husband there, say if he were made to help in the soul-killing work a woman is expected to do as a matter of course? Yet why shouldn't he help her bear her burdens? Why shouldn't he take them on his stronger shoulders? Don't give me the trite answer that it is because he has his own work to do— we know his work, the man's work, at its hardest full of satisfactions and pleasures, and hopes and ambitions, besides coming to an end every day at a certain hour, while she grows old in hopeless, hideous, never-ending drudgery. There is a difference between the two that makes my blood boil.'

'Oh don't let it boil,' I cried, alarmed. 'We're so hot as it is.'

'I tell you I think that woman over there as tragic a spectacle as it would be possible to find. I could cry over her—poor dumb, half-conscious remnant of what was meant to be the image of God.'

'My dear Charlotte,' I murmured uneasily. There were actual tears in Charlotte's eyes. Where I saw only an ample lady serenely cracking almonds in a way condemned by the polite, Charlotte's earnest glance pierced the veil of flesh to the withered, stunted soul of her. And Charlotte was so sincere, was so honestly grieved by the hopeless dulness of the fulfilment of what had once been the blithe promise of young girlhood, that I began to feel distressed too, and cast glances of respectful sympathy at the poor lady. Very little more would have made me cry, but I was saved by something unexpected; for the waiter came round with newly-arrived letters for the visitors, and laying two by the almond-eating lady's plate he said quite distinctly, and we both heard him distinctly, *Zwei für Fräulein Schmidt*; and the eldest of the four children, a pert little girl with a pig-tail, cried out, *Ei, ei, hast Du heute Glück, Tante Marie*; and having finished our dinner we got up and went on our way in silence; and when we were at the door, I said with a suavity of voice and manner meant to be healing, 'Shall we go into the woods, Charlotte? There are a few remarks I should like to offer you on the Souls of Maiden Aunts;' and Charlotte said, with some petulance, that the principle was the same, and that her head ached, and would I mind being quiet.

THE FIFTH DAY—*Continued*

FROM SELLIN TO BINZ

Suppose a being who should be neither man nor woman, a creature wholly removed from the temptations that beset either sex, a person who could look on with absolute indifference at all our various ways of wasting life, untouched by the ambitions of man, and unstirred by the longings of woman, what would such a being think of the popular notion against which other uneasy women besides Charlotte raise their voices, that the man should never be bothered by the cares of the house and the babies, but rather go his daily round of business or pleasure precisely as he did before he had his house and his babies? I love to have the details of life arranged with fastidious justice, all its little burdens distributed with an exact fairness among those who have to carry them; and I imagine that this being, who should be rather more than man and less than god, who should understand everything and care nothing, would call it wrong to allot a double weight to the strong merely because he is strong, and would call it right that he should have his exact share, and use the strength he has left over not in carrying the burden of some weak friend who, burdenless, is still of no account in life, but in praising God, going first, and showing the others the way.

Thus did I meditate, walking in silence by Charlotte's side in the beech forest of Sellin. Not for anything would I have put my meditations into words, well aware that though they might be nourishing to me they would poison Charlotte. The maiden aunt and the dinner together had given Charlotte a headache, which I respected by keeping silent; and for two hours we wandered and sat about among the beeches, sometimes on the grassy edge of the cliffs, our backs against tree trunks, looking out over the brilliant blue water with its brilliant green shallows, or lying in the grass watching the fine weather clouds floating past between the shining beech-leaves.

Those were glorious hours, for Charlotte dozed most of the time, and it was almost as quiet as though she had not been there at all. No bath-guests parted the branches to stare at us; they were sleeping till the cool of the day. No pedestrians with field-glasses came to look at the view and ask each other, with one attentive eye on us, if it were not colossal. No warm students walked along wiping their foreheads as they sang of love and beer. Nothing that had dined at a *table d'hôte* could possibly move in such heat.

And so it came about that Charlotte and I shared the forest only with birds and squirrels.

This forest is extremely beautiful. It stretches for miles along the coast, and is full of paths and roads that lead you to unexpected lovelinesses—sudden glimpses of the sea between huge beech trunks on grassy plateaus; deep ravines, their sides clothed with moss, with water trickling down over green stones to the sea out in the sun at the bottom; silent glades of bracken, silvery in the afternoon light, where fallow deer examine you for one brief moment of curiosity before they spring away, panic-stricken, into the deeper shadows of the beeches. In that sun-flecked place, so exquisite whichever way I looked, so spacious, and so quiet, how could I be seriously interested in stuffy indoor questions such as the equality of the sexes, in anything but the beauty of the world and the joy of living in it? I was not seriously interested; I doubt if I have ever been. Destiny having decided that I shall walk through life petticoated, weighed down by the entire range of disabilities connected with German petticoats, I will waste no time arguing. There it is, the inexorable fact, and there it will remain; and one gets used to the disabilities, and finds, on looking at them closer, that they exclude nothing that is really worth having.

I glanced at the dozing Charlotte, half inclined to wake her up to tell her this, and exhort her to do as the dragons in the glorious verse of Doctor Watts, who

> Changed their fierce hissings into joyful songs.
> And praised their Maker with their forked tongues.

But I was afraid to stir her up lest her tongue should be too forked and split my arguments to pieces. So she dozed on undisturbed, and I enjoyed myself in silence, repeating gems from the pages of the immortal doctor, echoes of the days when I lisped in numbers that were not only infant but English at the knee of a pious nurse from the land of fogs.

At five o'clock, when I felt that a gentle shaking of Charlotte was no longer avoidable if we were to reach Binz that evening, and was preparing to apply it with cousinly gingerliness, an obliging bumble-bee who had been swinging deliciously for some minutes past in the purple flower of a foxglove on the very edge of the cliff, backed out of it and blundered so near Charlotte's face that he brushed it with his wings. Charlotte instantly sat up, opened her eyes, and stared hard at me. Such is the suspiciousness of cousins that though I was lying half a dozen yards away she was manifestly of opinion that I had tickled her. This annoyed me, for Charlotte was the last person in the world I would think of tickling. There was something about her that would make it impossible, however sportively disposed I might be; and besides, you must be very great friends before you begin to tickle. Charlotte and I were cousins, but we were as yet nowhere near being very great friends. I got up, put on my hat, and said rather stiffly, for she still sat staring, that it was time to go. We walked back in silence, each feeling resentful, and keeping along the cliff passed, just before we came to Sellin, a little restaurant of coloured glass, a round building of an atrocious ugliness, which we discovered was one of the prides of Sellin; for afterwards, driving through the forest to Binz, all the sign-posts had fingers pointing in its direction, and bore the inscription *Glas Pavilion, schönste Aussicht Sellins*. The *schöne Aussicht* was indisputable, but to choose the loveliest spot and blot its beauty with a coloured glass restaurant so close to a place full of restaurants is surely unusually profane. There it is, however, and all day long it industriously scents the forest round it with the smell of soup. People were beginning to gather about its tables, the people we had seen dining and who had slept since, and some of them were already drinking coffee and eating slabs of cherry cake with a pile of whipped cream on each slab, for all the world as though they had had nothing since breakfast. Conspicuous at one table sat the maiden aunt, still rosy from her sleep. She too had ordered cherry cake, and the waiter put it down before her as we came by, and she sat for a moment fondly regarding it, turning the plate round and round so as to take in all its beauties, and if ever a woman looked happy it was that one. 'Poor dumb, half-conscious remnant'—I murmured under my breath. Charlotte seemed to read my thoughts, for she turned her head impatiently away from the cake and the lady, and said once again and defiantly, 'The principle is the same, of course.'

'Of course,' said I.

The drive from Sellin to Binz was by far the most beautiful I had had. Up to that point no drive had been uninterruptedly beautiful, but this one was lovely from end to end. It took about an hour and a half, and we were the whole time in the glorious mixed forest belonging to Prince Putbus and called the Granitz. As we neared Binz the road runs down close to the sea, and through the overhanging branches we could see that we had rounded another headland and were in another bay. Also, after having met nothing but shy troops of deer, we began to pass increasing numbers of bath-guests, walking slowly, taking the gentlest of exercise before their evening meal. Charlotte had been fairly quiet. Her head, apparently, still ached; but suddenly she started and exclaimed 'There are the Harvey-Brownes.'

'And who, pray, are the Harvey-Brownes?' I inquired, following the direction of her eyes.

It was easy enough to see which of the groups of tourists were the Harvey-Brownes. They were going in the same direction as ourselves, a tall couple in clothes of surpassing simplicity and excellence. Immediately afterwards we drove past them; Charlotte bowed coldly; the Harvey-Brownes bowed cordially, and I saw that the young man was my philosophic friend of the afternoon at Vilm.

'And who, pray, are the Harvey-Brownes?' I asked again.

'The English people I told you about who had got on to my nerves. I thought they'd have left by now.'

'And why were they on your nerves?'

'Oh she's a bishop's wife, and is about the narrowest person I have met, so we're not likely to be anywhere but on each other's nerves. But she adores that son of hers and would do anything in the world that pleases him, and he pursues me.'

'Pursues you?' I cried, with an incredulousness that I immediately perceived was rude. I hastened to correct it by shaking my head in gentle reproof and saying: 'Dear me, Charlotte—dear, dear me.' Simultaneously I was conscious of feeling disappointed in young Harvey-Browne.

'What do you suppose he pursues me for?' Charlotte asked, turning her head and looking at me.

'I can't think,' I was going to say, but stopped in time.

'The most absurd reason. He torments me with attentions because I am Bernhard's wife. He is a hero-worshipper, and he says Bernhard is the greatest man living.'

'Well, but isn't he?'

'He can't get hold of him, so he hovers round me, and talks Bernhard to me for hours together. That's why I went to Thiessow. He was sending me mad.'

'He hasn't an idea, poor innocent, that you don't—that you no longer——'

'I have as much courage as other people, but I don't think there's enough of it for explaining things to the mother. You see, she's the wife of a bishop.'

Not being so well acquainted as Charlotte with the characteristics of the wives of bishops I did not see; but she seemed to think it explained everything.

'Doesn't she know about your writings?' I inquired.

'Oh yes, and she came to a lecture I gave at Oxford—the boy is at Balliol—and she read some of the pamphlets. He made her.'

'Well?'

'Oh she made a few conventional remarks that showed me her limitations, and then she began about Bernhard. To these people I have no individuality, no separate existence, no brains of my own, no opinions worth listening to—I am solely of interest as the wife of Bernhard. Oh, it's maddening! The boy has put I don't know what ideas into his mother's head. She has actually tried to read one of Bernhard's works, and she pretends she thought it sublime. She quotes it. I won't stay at Binz. Let us go on somewhere else to-morrow.'

'But I think Binz looks as if it were a lovely place, and the Harvey-Brownes look very nice. I am not at all sure that I want to go on somewhere else to-morrow.'

'Then I'll go on alone, and wait for you at Sassnitz.'

'Oh, don't wait. I mightn't come to Sassnitz.'

'Oh well, I'll be sure to pick you up again somewhere. It isn't a very big island, and you are a conspicuous object, driving round it.'

This was true. So long as I was on that island I could not hope to escape Charlotte. I entered Binz in a state of moody acquiescence.

Every hotel was full, and every room in the villas was taken. It was the Göhren experience over again. At last we found shelter by the merest chance in the prettiest house in the place—we had not dared inquire there, certain that its rooms would be taken first of all—a little house on the sands, overhung at the back by beechwoods, its windows garnished with bright yellow damask curtains, its roof very red, and its walls very white. A most cheerful, trim little house, with a nice tiled path up to the door, and pots of geraniums on its sills. A cleanly person of the usual decent widow type welcomed us with a cordiality contrasting pleasantly with the indifference of those widows whose rooms had been all engaged. The entire lower floor, she said, was at our disposal. We each had a bedroom opening on to a verandah that seemed to hang right over the sea; and there was a dining-room, and a beautiful blue- and-white kitchen if we wanted to cook, and a spacious chamber for Gertrud. The price was low. Even when I said that we should probably only stay one or two nights it did not go up. The widow explained that the rooms were engaged for the entire season, but that the Berlin gentleman who had taken them was unavoidably prevented coming, which was the reason why we might have them, for it was not her habit to take in the passing stranger.

I asked whether it were likely that the Berlin gentleman might yet appear and turn us out. She stared at me a moment as though struck by my question, and then shook her head. 'No, no,' she said decidedly; 'he will not appear.'

A very pretty little maidservant who was bringing in our luggage was so much perturbed by my innocent inquiry that she let the things drop.

'Hedwig, do not be a fool,' said the widow sternly. 'The gentleman,' she went on, turning to me, 'cannot come, because he is dead.'

'Oh,' I said, silenced by the excellence of the reason.

Charlotte, being readier of speech, said 'Indeed.'

The reason was a good one; but when I heard it it seemed as if the pleasant rooms with the beds all ready and everything set out for the expected one took on a look of awfulness. It is true it was now past eight o'clock, and the sun had gone, and across the bay the dusk was creeping. I went out through the long windows to the little verandah. It had white pillars of great apparent massiveness, which looked as though they were meant to support vast weights of masonry; and through them I watched the water rippling in slow, steely ripples along the sand just beneath me, and the ripples had the peculiar lonely sound that slight waves have in the evening when they lick a deserted shore.

'When was he expected?' I heard Charlotte, within the room, ask in a depressed voice.

'To-day,' said the widow.

'To-day?' echoed Charlotte.

'That is why the beds are made. It is lucky for you ladies.'

'Very,' agreed Charlotte; and her voice was hollow.

'He died yesterday—an accident. I received the telegram only this morning. It is a great misfortune for me. Will the ladies sup? I have some provisions in the house sent on by the gentleman for his supper to-night. He, poor soul, will never sup again.'

The widow, more moved by this last reflection than she had yet been, sighed heavily. She then made the observation usual on such occasions that it is a strange world, and that one is here to-day and gone to-morrow—or rather, correcting herself, here yesterday and gone to-day—and that the one thing certain was the *schönes Essen* at that moment on the shelves of the larder. Would the ladies not seize the splendid opportunity and sup?

'No, no, we will not sup,' Charlotte cried with great decision. 'You won't eat here to-night, will you?' she asked through the yellow window-curtains, which made her look very pale. 'It is always horrid in lodgings. Shall we go to that nice red-brick hotel we passed, where the people were sitting under the big tree looking so happy?'

We went in silence to the red-brick hotel; and threading our way among the crowded tables set out under a huge beech tree a few yards from the water to the only empty one, we found ourselves sitting next to the Harvey-Brownes.

'Dear Frau Nieberlein, how delightful to have you here again!' cried the bishop's wife in tones of utmost cordiality, leaning across the little space between the tables to press Charlotte's hand. 'Brosy has been scouring the country on his bicycle trying to discover your retreat, and was quite disconsolate at not finding you.'

Scouring the country in search of Charlotte! Heavens. And I who had dropped straight on top of her in the waters of Thiessow without any effort at all! Thus does Fortune withhold blessings from those who clamour, and piles them unasked on the shrinking heads of the meek.

Brosy Harvey-Browne meanwhile, like a polite young man acquainted with German customs, had got out of his chair and was waiting for Charlotte to present him to me. 'Oh yes, my young philosopher,' I thought, not without a faint regret, 'you are now to find out that your promising and intellectual Fräulein isn't anything of the sort.'

'Pray present me,' said Brosy.

Charlotte did.

'Pray present me,' I said in my turn, bowing in the direction of the bishop's wife.

Charlotte did.

At this ceremony the bishop's wife's face took on the look of one who thinks there is really no need to make fresh acquaintances in breathless hurries. It also wore the look of one who, while admitting a Nieberlein within the range of her cordiality on account of the prestige of that Nieberlein's famous husband, does not see why the Nieberlein's obscure female relatives should be admitted too. So I was not admitted; and I sat outside and studied the menu.

'How very strange,' observed Brosy in his beautifully correct German as he dropped into a vacant chair at our table, 'that you should be related to the Nieberleins.'

'One is always related to somebody,' I replied; and marvelled at my own intelligence.

'And how odd that we should meet again here.'

'One is always meeting again on an island if it is small enough.'

This is a sample of my conversation with Brosy, weighty on my part with solid truths, while our supper was being prepared and while Charlotte answered his mother's questions as to where she had been, where she had met me, how we were related, and who my husband was.

'Her husband is a farmer,' I heard Charlotte say in the dreary voice of hopeless boredom.

'Oh, really. How interesting,' said Mrs. Harvey-Browne; and immediately ceased to be interested.

The lights of Sassnitz twinkled on the other side of the bay. A steamer came across the calm grey water, gaily decked out in coloured lights, the throbbing of her paddle-wheels heard almost from the time she left Sassnitz in the still evening air. Up and down the road between our tables and the sea groups of bath-guests strolled—artless family groups, papa and mamma arm in arm, and in front the daughter and the admirer; knots of girls in the *backfisch* stage, tittering and pushing each other about; quiet maiden-ladies, placid after their supper, gently praising, as they passed, the delights of a few weeks spent in the very bosom of Nature, expatiating on her peace, her restfulness, and the freshness of her vegetables. And with us, while the stars flashed through the stirring beech leaves, Mrs. Harvey-Browne rhapsodised about the great Nieberlein to the blank Charlotte, and Brosy tried to carry on a reasonable conversation about things like souls with a woman who was eating an omelette.

I was in an entirely different mood from the one of the afternoon at Vilm, and it was a mood in which I like to be left alone. When it is on me not all the beautiful young men in the world, looking like archangels and wearing the loveliest linen, would be able to shake me out of it. Brosy was apparently in exactly the same mood as he had been then. Was it his perennially? Did he always want to talk about the Unknowable, and the Unthinkable, and the Unspeakable? I am positive I did not look intelligent this time, not only because I did not try to, but because I was feeling profoundly stupid. And still he went on. There was only one thing I really wanted to know, and that was why he was called Brosy. While I ate my supper, and he talked, and his mother listened during the pauses of her fitful conversation with Charlotte, I turned this over in my mind. Why Brosy? His mother kept on saying it. To Charlotte her talk, having done with Nieberlein, was all of Brosy. Was it in itself a perfect name, or was it the short of something long, or did it come under the heading Pet? Was he perhaps a twin, and his twin sister was Rosy? In which case, if his parents were lovers of the neat, his own name would be almost inevitable.

It was when our supper had been cleared away and he was remarking for the second time—the first time he remarked it I had said 'What?',—that ultimate religious ideas are merely symbols of the actual, not cognitions of it, and his mother not well knowing what he meant but afraid it must be something a bishop's son ought not to mean said with gentle reproach, 'My dear Brosy,' that I took courage to inquire of him 'Why Brosy?'

'It is short for Ambrose,' he answered.

'He was christened after Ambrose,' said his mother,—' one of the Early Fathers, as no doubt you know.'

But I did not know, because she spoke in German, for the sake, I suppose, of making things easier for me, and she called the Early Fathers *frühzeitige Väter*, so how could I know?

'*Frühzeitige Väter?*' I repeated dully; 'Who are they?'

The bishop's wife took the kindest view of it. 'Perhaps you do not have them in the Lutheran Church,' she said; but she did not speak to me again at all, turning her back on me quite this time, and wholly concentrating her attention on the monosyllabic Charlotte.

'My mother,' Ambrose explained in subdued tones, 'meant to say *Kirchenväter.*'

'I am sorry,' said I politely, 'that I was so dull.'

And then he went on with the paragraph—for to me it seemed as though he spoke always in entire paragraphs instead of sentences—he had been engaged upon when I interrupted him; and, for my refreshment, I caught fragments of Mrs. Harvey-Browne's conversation in between.

'I have a message for you, dear Frau Nieberlein,' I heard her say,—'a message from the bishop.'

'Yes?' said Charlotte, without warmth.

'We had letters from home to-day, and in his he mentions you.'

'Yes?' said Charlotte, ungratefully cold.

'"Tell her," he writes,—"tell her I have been reading her pamphlets."'

'Indeed?' said Charlotte, beginning to warm.

'It is not often that the bishop has time for reading, and it is quite unusual for him to look at anything written by a woman, so that it is really an honour he has paid you.'

'Of course it is,' said Charlotte, quite warmly.

'And he is an old man, dear Frau Nieberlein, of ripe experience, and admirable wisdom, as no doubt you have heard, and I am sure you will take what he says in good part.'

This sounded ominous, so Charlotte said nothing.

'"Tell her," he writes,—"tell her that I grieve for her."'

There was a pause. Then Charlotte said loftily, 'It is very good of him.'

'And I can assure you the bishop never grieves without reason, or else in such a large diocese he would always be doing it.'

Charlotte was silent.

'He begged me to tell you that he will pray for you.'

There was another pause. Then Charlotte said, 'Thank you.'

What else was she to say? What does one say in such a case? Our governesses teach us how pleasant and amiable an adornment is politeness, but not one of mine ever told me what I was to say when confronted by an announcement that I was to be included in somebody's prayers. If Charlotte, anxious to be polite, had said, 'Oh, please don't let him trouble,' the bishop's wife would have been shocked. If she had said what she felt, and wholly declined to be prayed for at all by strange bishops, Mrs. Harvey-Browne would have been horrified. It is a nice question; and it preoccupied me for the rest of the time we sat there, and we sat there a very long time; for although Charlotte was manifestly sorely tried by Mrs. Harvey-Browne I had great difficulty in getting her away. Each time I suggested going back to our lodgings to bed she made some excuse for staying where she was. Everybody else seemed to have gone to bed, and even Ambrose, who had been bicycling all day, had begun visibly to droop before I could persuade her to come home. Slowly she walked along the silent sands, slowly she went into the house, still more slowly into her bedroom; and then, just as Gertrud had blessed me and blown out my candle in one breath, in she came with a light, and remarking that she did not feel sleepy sat down on the foot of my bed and began to talk.

She had on a white dressing-gown, and her hair fell loose about her face, and she was very pale.

'I can't talk; I am much too sleepy,' I said, 'and you look dreadfully tired.'

'My soul is tired—tired out utterly by that woman. I wanted to ask you if you won't come away with me to-morrow.'

'I can't go away till I have explored these heavenly forests.'

'I can't stay here if I am to spend my time with that woman.'

'That woman? Oh Charlotte, don't call her such awful names. Try and imagine her sensations if she heard you.'

'Why, I shouldn't care.'

'Oh hush,' I whispered, 'the windows are open—she might be just outside on the beach. It gives me shivers only to think of it. Don't say it again. Don't be such an audacious German. Think of Oxford—think of venerable things like cathedral closes and bishops' palaces. Think of the dignity and deference that surround Mrs. Harvey-Browne at home. And won't you go to bed? You can't think how sleepy I am.'

'Will you come away with me to-morrow?'

'We'll talk it over in the morning. I'm not nearly awake enough now.'

Charlotte got up reluctantly and went to the door leading into her bedroom. Then she came back and crossed over to the windows and peeped out between the yellow curtains. 'It's bright moonlight,' she said, 'and so quiet. The sea is like a pond. How clear the Sassnitz lights are.'

'Are they?' I murmured drowsily.

'Are you really going to leave your windows open? Any one can get in. We are almost on a level with the beach.'

To this I made no answer; and my little travelling-clock on the table gave point to my silence by chiming twelve.

Charlotte went away slowly, candle in hand. At her door she stopped and looked back. 'It seems,' she said, 'that I have got that unfortunate man's bed.'

So it was the Berlin gentleman who was making her restless.

'And you,' she went on, 'have got the one his daughter was to have had.'

'Is she alive?' I asked sleepily.

'Oh yes, she's alive.'

'Well, that was nice, anyway.'

'I believe you are frightened,' I murmured, as she still lingered.

'Frightened? What of?'

'The Berlin gentleman.'

'Absurd,' said Charlotte, and went away.

I was having a most cheerful dream in which I tried hard to remember the exact words Herbert Spencer uses about effete beliefs that, in the stole, still cling about the necks of priests, and, in gaiters, linger round the legs of bishops, and was repeating the words about the bishops in a rapture of enjoyment—and indeed it is a lovely sentence—when a sudden pause of fear came into my dream, and I felt that some one beside myself was in the room.

The dark to me has always been full of terrors. I can look back through my memories and find past years studded with horrible black nights on which I woke up and was afraid. Till I have lit a candle, how can I remember that I do not believe in ghosts, and in nameless hideousnesses infinitely more frightful than ghosts? But what courage is needed to sit up in all the solid, pressing blackness, and stretch out one defenceless hand into it to feel about for the matches, appalled by the echoing noises the search produces, cold with fear that the hand may touch something unknown and terrible. And so at Binz, dragged out of my pleasant dream to night and loneliness, I could not move for a moment for sheer extremity of fright. When I did, when I did put out a shaking hand to feel for the matches, the dread of years became a reality—I touched another hand. Now I think it was very wonderful of me not to scream. I suppose I did not dare. I don't know how I managed it, petrified as I was with terror, but the next thing that happened was that I found myself under the bedclothes thinking things over. Whose hand had I touched? And what was it doing on my table? It was a nasty, cold hand, and it had clutched at mine as I tore it away. Oh—there it was, coming after me—it was feeling its way along the bedclothes—surely it was not real—it must be a nightmare

—and that was why no sound came when I tried to shriek for Charlotte—but what a horrible nightmare—so very, very real—I could hear the hand sliding along the sheet to the corner where I was huddling—oh, why had I come to this frightful island? A gasp of helpless horror did get out, and instantly Charlotte's voice whispered, 'Be quiet. Don't make a sound. There's a man outside your window.'

At this my senses came back to me with a rush. 'You've nearly killed me,' I whispered, filling the whisper with as much hot indignation as it would hold. 'If my heart had had anything the matter with it I would have died. Let me go —I want to light the candle. What does a man, a real living man, matter?'

Charlotte held me tighter. 'Be quiet,' she whispered, in an agony, it seemed, of fear. 'Be quiet—he isn't—he doesn't look—I don't think he is alive.'

'*What?*' I whispered.

'Sh—sh—your window's open—he only need put his leg over the sill to get in.'

'But if he isn't alive he can't put his leg over sills,' I whispered back incredulously. 'He's some poor drowned sailor washed ashore.'

'Oh be *quiet!*' implored Charlotte, burying her face on my shoulder; and having got over my own fright I marvelled at the abjectness of hers.

'Let me go. I want to look at him,' I said, trying to get away.

'Sh—sh—don't move—he'd hear—he is just outside——' And she clung to me in terror.

'But how can he hear if he isn't alive? Let me go——'

'No—no—he's sitting there—just outside—he's been sitting there for hours —and never moves—oh, it's that man!—I know it is—I knew he'd come ——'

'What man?'

'Oh the dreadful, dreadful Berlin man who died——'

'My dear Charlotte,' I expostulated, feeling now perfectly calm in the presence of such a collapse. 'Let me go. I'll look through the curtains so that he shall not see me, and I'll soon tell you if he's alive or not. Do you suppose I don't know a live man when I see one?'

I wriggled out of her arms and crept with bare, silent feet to the window, and cautiously moving the curtains a slit apart peeped through. There certainly was a man outside, sitting on a rock exactly in front of my window, with his face to the sea. Clouds were passing slowly across the moon, and I waited for them to pass to see him more clearly. He never moved. And when the light did fall on him it fell on a well-clothed back with two shining buttons on it,— not the back of a burglar, and surely not the back of a ghost. In all my varied imaginings I had never yet imagined a ghost in buttons, and I refused to believe that I saw one then.

Back I crept to the cowering Charlotte. 'It isn't anybody who's dead,' I whispered cheerfully, 'and I think he wants to paddle.'

'Paddle?' echoed Charlotte sitting up, the word seeming to restore her to her senses. 'Why should he want to paddle in the middle of the night?'

'Well, why not? It's the only thing I can think of that makes you sit on rocks.'

Charlotte was so much recovered and so much relieved at finding herself recovered, that she gave a hysterical giggle. Instantly there was a slight noise outside, and the shadow of a man appeared on the curtains. We clung to each other in consternation.

'Hedwig,' whispered the man, pushing the curtains a little aside, and peering into the darkness of the room; '*kleiner Schatz—endlich da? Lässt mich so lange warten——*'

He waited, uncertain, trying to see in. Charlotte grasped the situation quickest. 'Hedwig is not here,' she said with immense dignity, 'and you should be ashamed of yourself, disturbing ladies in this manner. I must request you to go away at once, and to give me your name and address so that I may report you to the proper authorities. I shall not fail in my duty, which will be to make an example of you.'

'That was admirably put,' I remarked, going across to the window and shutting it, 'only he didn't stay to listen. Now we'll light the candle.'

And looking out as I drew the curtains I saw the moonlight flash on flying buttons.

'Who would have thought,' I observed to Charlotte, who was standing in the middle of the room shaking with indignation,—'who would have thought that that very demure little Hedwig would be the cause of a night of terror for us?'

'Who could have imagined her so depraved?' said Charlotte wrathfully.

'Well, we don't know that she is.'

'Doesn't it look like it?'

'Poor little thing.'

'Poor little thing! What drivel is this?'

'Oh I don't know—we all want forgiving very badly, it seems to me— Hedwig not more than you and I. And we want it so much more badly than we want punishing, yet we are always getting punished and hardly ever getting forgiven.'

'I don't know what you mean,' said Charlotte.

'It isn't very clear,' I admitted.

THE SIXTH DAY

THE JAGDSCHLOSS

She was asleep next morning when I looked into her bedroom, so I shut the door softly, and charging Gertrud not to disturb her, went out for a walk. It was not quite eight and people had not got away from their coffee yet, so I had it to myself, the walk along the shore beneath the beeches, beside the flashing morning sea. The path runs along for a little close to the water at the foot of the steep beech-grown hill that shuts the west winds out of Binz—a hill steep enough and high enough to make him pant grievously who goes up it after dinner; then on the right comes a deep narrow cutting running up into the woods, cut, it seems, entirely out of smoothest, greenest moss, so completely are its sides covered with it. Standing midway up this cutting in the soft gloom of its green walls, with the branches of the beeches meeting far away above, and down at the bottom the sheet of shining water, I found absolutely the most silent bit of the world I have ever been in. The silence was wonderful. There seemed positively to be no sound at all. No sound came down from the beech leaves, and yet they were stirring; no sound came up from the water, not a ripple, not a splash; I heard no birds while I stood there, nor any hum of insects. It might have been the entrance to some holy place, so strange and solemn was the quiet; and looking from out of its shadows to the brightness shining at the upper end where the sun was flooding the bracken with happy morning radiance, I felt suddenly that my walk had ceased to be a common thing, and that I was going up into the temple of God to pray.

I know no surer way of shaking off the dreary crust formed about the soul by the trying to do one's duty or the patient enduring of having somebody else's duty done to one, than going out alone, either at the bright beginning of the day, when the earth is still unsoiled by the feet of the strenuous and only God is abroad; or in the evening, when the hush has come, out to the blessed stars, and looking up at them wonder at the meanness of the day just past, at the worthlessness of the things one has struggled for, at the folly of having been so angry, and so restless, and so much afraid. Nothing focusses life more exactly than a little while alone at night with the stars. What are perfunctory bedroom prayers hurried through in an atmosphere of blankets, to this deep abasement of the spirit before the majesty of heaven? And as a consecration of what should be yet one more happy day, of what value are those hasty morning devotions, disturbed by fears lest the coffee should be getting cold and that person, present in every household, whose property is always to reprove, be more than usually provoked, compared to going out into the freshness of the new day and thanking God deliberately under His own wide sky for having been so good to us? I know that when I had done my open-air *Te Deum* up there in the sun-flooded space among the shimmering bracken I went on my way with a lightheartedness never mine after indoor religious exercises. The forest was so gay that morning, so sparkling, so full of busy, happy creatures, it would have been a sorry heart that did not feel jolly in such society. In that all-pervading wholesomeness there was no room for repentance, no place for conscience-stricken beating of the breast; and indeed I think we waste a terrible amount of time repenting. The healthy attitude, the only reasonable one towards a fault made or a sin committed is surely a vigorous shake of one's moral shoulders, vigorous enough to shake it off and out of remembrance. The sin itself was a sad waste of time and happiness, and absolutely no more should be wasted in lugubriously reflecting on it. Shall we, poor human beings at such a disadvantage from the first in the fight with Fate through the many weaknesses and ailments of our bodies, load our souls as well with an ever-growing burden of regret and penitence? Shall we let a weight of vivid memories break our hearts? How are we to get on with our living if we are continually dropping into sloughs of bitter and often unjust self-reproach? Every morning comes the light, and a fresh chance of doing better. Is it not the sheerest folly and ingratitude to let yesterday spoil the God-given to-day?

There had been a heavy dew, and the moss along the wayside was soaked with it, and the leaves of the slender young beeches sparkled with it, and the bracken bending over the path on either side left its wetness on my dress as I passed. Nowhere was there a single bit of gloom where you could sit down and be wretched. The very jays would have laughed you out of countenance if you had sat there looking sorrowful. Sometimes the path was narrow, and the trees shut out the sky; sometimes it led me into the hot sunshine of an open, forest-fringed space; once it took me along the side of a meadow sloping up on its distant side to more forest, with only a single row of great beeches between me and the heat and light dancing over the grass; and all the way I had squirrels for company, chattering and enjoying themselves as sensible squirrels living only in the present do; and larks over my head singing in careless ecstasy just because they had no idea they were probably bad larks with pasts; and lizards, down at my feet, motionless in the hot sun, quite unaware of how wicked it becomes to lie in the sun doing nothing directly you wear clothes and have consciences. As for the scent of the forest, he who has been in it early after a dewy night knows that, and the effect it has on the spirits of him who smells it; so I need not explain how happy I was and how invigorated as I climbed up a long hill where the wood was thick and cool, and coming out at the top found I had reached a place of turf and sunshine, with tables in the shade at the farther side, and in the middle, coffee-pot in hand, a waiter.

This waiter came as a shock. My thoughts had wandered quite into the opposite channel to the one that ends in waiters. There he stood, however, solitary and suggestive, in the middle of the sunny green, a crumpled waiter in regard to shirt-front, and not a waiter, I should say, of more than bi-weekly washings; but his eye was persuasive, steam came out of the spout of his coffee-pot, and out of his mouth as I walked towards him issued appropriate words about the weather. I had meant to go back to breakfast with Charlotte, and there was no reason at all why I should cross the green and walk straight up to the waiter; but there was that in his eye which made me feel that if I did not drink his coffee not only had I no business on the top of the hill but I was unspeakably base besides. So I sat down at one of the tables beneath the beeches—there were at least twelve tables, and only one other visitor, a man in spectacles— and the waiter produced a tablecloth that made me shiver, and poured me out a cup of coffee and brought me a roll of immense resistance— one of yesterday's, I imagined, the roll cart from Binz not having had time yet to get up the hill. He fetched this roll from a pretty house with latticed windows standing on the side of the green, and he fixed me with his hungry eye and told me the house was an inn, and that it was not only ready but anxious to take me as a lodger for any period I might choose. I excused myself on the plea of its distance from the water. He said that precisely this distance was its charm. 'The lady,' he continued, with a wave of his coffee- pot that immediately caused a thin streak of steam to rise from the grass—'the lady can see for herself how idyllic is the situation.'

The lady murmured assent; and in order to avoid his hungry eye busied herself dividing her roll among some expectant fowls who, plainly used to the business, were crowding round her; so that the roll's staleness, perhaps intentional, ended by being entirely to the good of the inn.

By the time the fowls were ready for more the waiter, who had nothing pressing on hand, had become a nuisance too great to be borne. I would have liked to sit there and rest in the shade, watching the clouds slowly appear above the tree-tops opposite and sail over my head and out of sight, but I could not because of the waiter. So I paid him, got up, once more firmly declined either to take or look at rooms at the inn, and wished him a good morning instinct with dignity and chill.

'The lady will now of course visit the Jagdschloss,' said the waiter, whipping out a bundle of tickets of admission.

'The Jagdschloss?' I repeated; and following the direction of his eyes I saw a building through the trees just behind where I had been sitting, on the top of a sharp ascent.

So that was where my walk had led me to. The guide-book devotes several animated pages to this Jagdschloss, or shooting lodge. It belongs to Prince Putbus. Its round tower, rising out of a green sea of wood, was a landmark with which I had soon grown familiar. Whenever you climb up a hill in Rügen to see the view, you see the Jagdschloss. Whichever way you drive, it is always the central feature of the landscape. If it isn't anywhere else it is sure to be on the horizon. Only in some northern parts of the island does one get away from it, and even there probably a telescope used with skill would produce it at once. And here I was beneath its walls. Well, I had not intended going over it, and all I wanted at that moment was to get rid of the waiter and go on with my walk. But it was easier to take a ticket than to refuse and hear him exclaim and protest; so I paid fifty *pfennings*, was given a slip of paper, and started climbing the extremely steep ascent.

The site was obviously chosen without the least reference to the legs or lungs of tourists. They arrive at the top warm and speechless, and sinking down on the steps between two wolves made of copper the first thing they do is to spend several minutes gasping. Then they ring a bell, give up their tickets and umbrellas, and are taken round in batches by an elderly person who manifestly thinks them poor things.

When I got to the top I found the other visitor, the man in spectacles, sitting on the steps getting his gasping done. Having finished mine before him, he being a man of bulk, I rang the bell. The elderly official, who had a singular talent for making one feel by a mere look what a worm one really is, appeared. 'I cannot take each of you round separately,' he said, pointing at the man still fighting for air on the bottom step, 'or does your husband not intend to see the Schloss?'

'My husband?' I echoed, astonished.

'Now, sir,' he continued impatiently, addressing the back below, 'are you coming or not?'

The man in spectacles made a great effort, caught hold of the convenient leg of one of the copper wolves, pulled himself on to his feet with its aid, and climbed slowly up the steps.

'The public is requested not to touch the objects of art,' snapped the custodian, glancing at the wolf's leg to see if it had suffered.

The man in spectacles looked properly ashamed of his conduct; I felt ashamed of myself too, but only on the more general grounds of being such a worm;

and together we silently followed the guide into the house, together gave up our tickets, and together laid our stick and sunshade side by side on a table.

A number was given to the man in spectacles.

'And my number?' I inquired politely.

'Surely one suffices?' said the guide, eyeing me with disapproval; for taking me for the wife of the man in spectacles he regarded my desire to have a number all to myself as only one more instance of the lengths to which the modern woman in her struggle for emancipation will go.

The stick and sunshade were accordingly tied together.

'Do you wish to ascend the tower?' he asked my companion, showing us the open-work iron staircase winding round and round inside the tower up to the top.

'Gott Du Allmächtiger, nein,' was the hasty reply after a glance and a shudder.

Taking for granted that without my husband I would not want to go up towers he did not ask me, but at once led the way through a very charming hall decorated with what are known as trophies of the chase, to a locked door, before which stood a row of enormous grey felt slippers.

'The public is not allowed to enter the princely apartments unless it has previously drawn these slippers over its boots,' said the guide as though he were quoting.

'All of them?' I asked, faintly facetious.

Again he eyed me, but this time in silence.

The man in spectacles thrust his feet into the nearest pair. They were generously roomy even for him, and he was a big man with boots to match. I looked down the row hoping to see something smaller, and perhaps newer, but they were all the same size, and all had been worn repeatedly by other tourists.

'The next time I come to the Jagdschloss,' I observed thoughtfully, as I saw my feet disappear into the gaping mouths of two of these woolly monsters, 'I shall bring my own slippers. This arrangement may be useful, but no one could call it select.'

Neither of my companions took the least notice of me. The guide looked disgusted. Judging from his face, though he still thought me a worm he now suspected me of belonging to that highly objectionable class known as turned.

Having seen us safely into our slippers he was about to unlock the door when the bell rang. He left us standing mute before the shut door, and leaning over the balustrade—for, Reader, as Charlotte Brontë would say, he had come upstairs—he called down to the Fräulein who had taken our stick and sunshade to let in the visitors. She did so; and as she flung open the door I saw, through the pillars of the balustrade, Brosy on the threshold, and at the bottom of the steps, leaning against one of the copper wolves, her arm, indeed, flung over its valuable shoulder, the bishop's wife gasping.

At this sight the custodian rushed downstairs. The man in spectacles and myself, mute, meek, and motionless in our felt slippers, held our breaths.

'The public is requested not to touch the objects of art!' shouted the custodian as he rushed.

'Is he speaking to me, dear?' asked Mrs. Harvey-Browne, looking up at her son.

'I think he is, mother,' said Ambrose. 'I don't think you may lean on that wolf.'

'Wolf?' said his mother in surprise, standing upright and examining the animal through her eyeglasses with interest. 'So it is. I thought they were Prussian eagles.'

'Anyhow you mustn't touch it, mother,' said Ambrose, a slight impatience in his voice. 'He says the public are not to touch things.'

'Does he really call me the public? Do you think he is a rude person, dear?'

'Does the lady intend to see the Schloss or not?' interrupted the custodian. 'I have another party inside waiting.'

'Come on, mother—you want to, don't you?'

'Yes—but not if he's a rude man, dear,' said Mrs. Harvey-Browne, slowly ascending the steps. 'Perhaps you had better tell him who father is.'

'I don't think it would impress him much,' said Brosy, smiling. 'Parsons come here too often for that.'

'Parsons! Yes; but not bishops,' said his mother, coming into the echoing hall, through whose emptiness her last words rang like a trumpet.

'He wouldn't know what a bishop is. They don't have them.'

'No bishops?' exclaimed his mother, stopping short and staring at her son with a face of concern.

'*Bitte um die Eintrittskarten,*' interrupted the custodian, slamming the door; and he pulled the tickets out of Brosy's hand.

'No bishops?' continued Mrs. Harvey-Browne, 'and no Early Fathers, as that smashed-looking person, that cousin of Frau Nieberlein's, told us last night? My dear Brosy, what a very strange state of things.'

'I don't think she quite said that, did she? They have Early Fathers right enough. She didn't understand what you meant.'

'Stick and umbrella, please,' interrupted the custodian, snatching them out of their passive hands. 'Take the number, please. Now this way, please.'

He hurried, or tried to hurry, them under the tower, but the bishop's wife had not hurried for years, and would not have dreamed of doing so; and when he had got them under it he asked if they wished to make the ascent. They looked up, shuddered, and declined.

'Then we will at once join the other party,' said the custodian, bustling on.

'The other party?' exclaimed Mrs. Harvey-Browne in German. 'Oh, I hope no objectionable tourists? I quite thought coming so early we would avoid them.'

'Only two,' said the custodian: 'a respectable gentleman and his wife.'

The man in spectacles and I, up to then mute, meek, and motionless in our grey slippers, started simultaneously. I looked at him cautiously out of the corners of my eyes, and found to my confusion that he was looking at me cautiously out of the corners of his. In another moment the Harvey-Brownes stood before us.

After one slight look of faintest surprise at my companion the pleasant Ambrose greeted me as though I were an old friend; and then bowing with a politeness acquired during his long stay in the Fatherland to the person he supposed was my husband, introduced himself in German fashion by mentioning his name, and observed that he was exceedingly pleased to make his acquaintance. *'Es freut mich sehr Ihre Bekanntschaft zu machen,'* said the pleasant Ambrose.

'Gleichfalls, gleichfalls,' murmured the man in spectacles, bowing repeatedly, and obviously astonished. To the bishop's wife he also made rapid and bewildered bows until he saw she was gazing over his head, and then he stopped. She had recognised my presence by the merest shadow of a nod, which I returned with an indifference that was icy; but, oddly enough, what offended me more than her nod was the glance she had bestowed on the man in spectacles before she began to gaze over his head. He certainly did not belong to me, and yet I was offended. This seemed to me so subtle that it set me off pondering.

'The public is not allowed to enter the princely apartments unless it has previously drawn these slippers over its boots,' said the custodian.

Mrs. Harvey-Browne looked at him critically. 'He has a very crude way of expressing himself, hasn't he, dear?' she remarked to Ambrose.

'He is only quoting official regulations. He must, you know, mother. And we are undoubtedly the public.'

Ambrose looked at my feet, then at the feet of my companion, and then without more ado got into a pair of slippers. He wore knickerbockers and stockings, and his legs had a classic refinement that erred, if at all, on the side of over-slenderness. The effect of the enormous grey slippers at the end of these Attic legs made me, for one awful moment, feel as though I were going to shriek with laughter. An immense effort strangled the shriek and left me unnaturally solemn.

Mrs. Harvey-Browne had now caught sight of the row of slippers. She put up her eyeglasses and examined them carefully. 'How very German,' she remarked.

'Put them on, mother,' said Ambrose; 'we are all waiting for you.'

'Are they new, Brosy?' she asked, hesitating.

'The lady must put on the slippers, or she cannot enter the princely apartments,' said the custodian severely.

'Must I really, Brosy?' she inquired, looking extremely unhappy. 'I am so terribly afraid of infection, or—or other things. Do they think we shall spoil their carpets?'

'The floors are polished, I imagine,' said Ambrose, 'and the owner is probably afraid the visitors might slip and hurt themselves.'

'Really quite nice and considerate of him—if only they were new.'

Ambrose shuffled to the end of the row in his and took up two.' Look here, mother,' he said, bringing them to her, 'here's quite a new pair. Never been worn before. Put them on—they can't possibly do any harm.'

They were not new, but Mrs. Harvey-Browne thought they were and consented to put them on. The instant they were on her feet, stretching out in all their hugeness far beyond the frills of her skirt and obliging her to slide instead of walk, she became gracious. The smile with which she slid past me was amiable as well as deprecatory. They had apparently reduced her at once to the level of other sinful mortals. This effect seemed to me so subtle that again I fell a-pondering.

'Frau Nieberlein is not with you this morning?' she asked pleasantly, as we shuffled side by side into the princely apartments.

'She is resting. She had rather a bad night.'

'Nerves, of course.'

'No, ghosts.'

'Ghosts?'

'It's the same thing,' said Ambrose. 'Is it not, sir?' he asked amiably of the man in spectacles.

'Perhaps,' said the man in spectacles cautiously.

'But not a real ghost?' asked Mrs. Harvey-Browne, interested.

'I believe the great point about a ghost is that it never is real.'

'The bishop doesn't believe in them either. But I—I really hardly know. One hears such strange tales. The wife of one of the clergy of our diocese believes quite firmly in them. She is a vegetarian, and of course she eats a great many vegetables, and then she sees ghosts.'

'The chimney-piece,' said the guide, 'is constructed entirely of Roman marble.'

'Really?' said Mrs. Harvey-Browne, examining it abstractedly through her eyeglasses. 'She declares their vicarage is haunted; and what in the world do you think by? The strangest thing. It is haunted by the ghost of a cat.'

'The statue on the right is by Thorwaldsen,' said the guide.

'By the ghost of a cat,' repeated Mrs. Harvey-Browne impressively.

She seemed to expect me to say something, so I said Indeed.

'That on the left is by Rauch,' said the guide.

'And this cat does not do anything. I mean, it is not prophetic of impending family disaster. It simply walks across a certain room—the drawing-room, I believe—quite like a real cat, and nothing happens.'

'But perhaps it is a real cat?'

'Oh no, it is supernatural. No one sees it but herself. It walks quite slowly with its tail up in the air, and once when she went up to it to try to pull its tail so as to convince herself of its existence, she only clutched empty air.'

'The frescoes with which this apartment is adorned are by Kolbe and Eybel,' said the guide.

'You mean it ran away?'

'No, it walked on quite deliberately. But the tail not being made of human flesh and blood there was naturally nothing to pull.'

'Beginning from left to right, we have in the first a representation of the entry of King Waldemar I. into Rügen,' said the guide.

'But the most extraordinary thing about it happened one day when she put a saucer of cream on the floor for it. She had thought it all over in the night, and had come to the conclusion that as no ghost would lap cream and no real cat be able to help lapping it this would provide her with a decisive proof one way or the other. The cat came, saw the cream, and immediately lapped it up. My friend was so pleased, because of course one likes real cats best——'

'The second represents the introduction of Christianity into the island,' said the guide.

'—and when it had done, and the saucer was empty, she went over to it——'

'The third represents the laying of the foundation stone of the church at Vilmnitz,' said the guide.

'—and what do you think happened? *She walked straight through it.*'

'Through what?' I asked, profoundly interested. 'The cream, or the cat?'

'Ah, that was what was so marvellous. She walked right through the body of the cat. Now what had become of the cream?'

I confess this story impressed me more than any ghost story I have ever heard; the disappearance of the cream was so extraordinary.

'And there was nothing—nothing at all left on her dress?' I asked eagerly. 'I mean, after walking through the cat? One would have thought that some, at least, of the cream——'

'Not a vestige.'

I stood gazing at the bishop's wife absorbed in reflection. 'How truly strange,' I murmured at length, after having vainly endeavoured to account for the missing cream.

'*Wasn't* it?' said Mrs. Harvey-Browne, much pleased with the effect of her story. Indeed the amiability awakened in her bosom by the grey felt slippers had increased rapidly, and the unaccountable conduct of the cream seemed about to cement our friendship when, at this point, she having remarked that there are more things in heaven and earth than are dreamt of in our philosophy, and I, in order to show my acquaintance with the classics of other countries, having added 'As Chaucer justly observes,' to which she said, 'Ah, yes—so beautiful, isn't he?' a voice behind us made us both jump; and turning round we beheld, at our elbows, the man in spectacles. Ambrose, aided by the guide, was on the other side of the room studying the works of Kolbe and Eybel, The man in spectacles had evidently heard the whole story of the cat, for this is what he said:—

'The apparition, madam, if it has any meaning at all, which I doubt, being myself inclined to locate its origin in the faulty digestion of the lady, seems to point to a life beyond the grave for the spirits of cats. Considered as a proof of such a life for the human soul, which is the one claim to our interest phenomena of the kind can possess, it is, of course, valueless.'

Mrs. Harvey-Browne stared at him a moment through her eyeglasses. 'Christians,' she then said distantly, 'need no further proof of that.'

'May I ask, madam, what, precisely, you mean by Christians?' inquired the man in spectacles briskly. 'Define them, if you please.'

Now the bishop's wife was not used to being asked to define things, and disliked it as much as anybody else. Besides, though rays of intelligent interest darted through his spectacles, the wearer of them also wore clothes that were not only old but peculiar, and his whole appearance cried aloud of much work and small reward. She therefore looked not only helpless but indignant. 'Sir,' she said icily, 'this is not the moment to define Christians.'

'I hear the name repeatedly,' said the man in spectacles, bowing but undaunted; 'and looking round me I ask myself where are they?'

'Sir,' said Mrs. Harvey-Browne, 'they are in every Christian country.'

'And which, pray, madam, would you call the Christian countries? I look around me, and I see nations armed to the teeth, ready and sometimes even anxious to fly at each other's throats. Their attitude may be patriotic, virile, perhaps necessary, conceivably estimable; but, madam, would you call it Christian?'

'Sir——' said Mrs. Harvey-Browne.

'Having noticed by your accent, madam, that the excellent German you speak was not originally acquired in our Fatherland, but must be the result of a commendable diligence practised in the schoolrooms of your youth and native land, and having further observed, from certain unmistakable signs, that the native land in question must be England, it would have a peculiar interest for me to be favoured with the exact meaning the inhabitants of that enlightened country attach to the term. My income having hitherto not been sufficient to enable me to visit its hospitable shores, I hail this opportunity with pleasure of discussing questions that are of importance to us all with one of its, no doubt, most distinguished daughters.'

'Sir——' said Mrs. Harvey-Browne.

'At first sight,' went on the man in spectacles, 'one would be disposed to say that a Christian is a person who believes in the tenets of the Christian faith. But belief, if it is genuine, must necessarily find its practical expression in works. How then, madam, would you account for the fact that when I look round me in the provincial town in which I pursue the honourable calling of a pedagogue, I see numerous Christians but no works?'

'Sir, I do not account for it,' said Mrs. Harvey-Browne angrily.

'For consider, madam, the lively faith inspired by other creeds. Place against this inertia the activity of other believers. Observe the dervish, how he dances; observe the fakir, hanging from his hook——'

'I will not, sir,' said Mrs. Harvey-Browne, roused now beyond endurance; 'and I do not know why you should choose this place and time to thrust your opinions on sacred subjects on a stranger and a lady.'

With which she turned her back on him, and shuffled away with all the dignity the felt slippers allowed.

The man in spectacles stood confounded.

'The lady,' I said, desirous of applying balm, 'is the wife of a clergyman'— (Heavens, if she had heard me!)—'and is therefore afraid of talking about things that must lead her on to sacred ground. I think you will find the son very intelligent and ready to talk.'

But I regret to say the man in spectacles seemed extremely shy of me; whether it was because the custodian had taken me for his wife, or because I was an apparently unattached female wandering about and drinking coffee by myself contrary to all decent custom, I do not know. Anyhow he met my well- meant attempt to explain Mrs. Harvey-Browne to him with suspicion, and murmuring something about the English being indeed very strangely mannered, he edged cautiously away.

We now straggled through the rooms separately,—Ambrose in front with the guide, his mother by herself, I by myself, and a good way behind us, the mortified man in spectacles. He made no effort to take my advice and talk to Ambrose, but kept carefully as far away from the rest of us as possible; and when we presently found ourselves once more outside the princely apartments, on the opposite side to the door by which we had gone into them, he slid forward, shook off his felt slippers with the finality of one who shakes off dust from his feet, made three rapid bows, one to each of us, and hurried down the stairs. Arrived at the bottom we saw him take his stick from the Fräulein, shake his head with indignant vigour when she tried to make him take my sunshade too, pull open the heavy door, and almost run through it. He slammed it with an energy that made the Jagdschloss tremble.

The Fräulein looked first at the slammed door, then at the sunshade, and then up at me. 'Quarrelled,' said the Fräulein's look as plainly as speech.

Ambrose looked at me too, and in his eyes was an interrogation.

Mrs. Harvey-Browne looked at me too, and in her eyes was coldest condemnation. 'Is it possible,' said Mrs. Harvey-Browne's eyes, 'that any one can really marry such a person?'

As for me, I walked downstairs, my face bland with innocence and unconcern. 'How delightful,' I said enthusiastically, 'how truly delightful these walls look, with all the antlers and things on them.'

'Very,' said Ambrose.

Mrs. Harvey-Browne was silent. Probably she had resolved never to speak to me again; but when we were at the bottom, and Ambrose was bestowing fees on the Fräulein and the custodian, she said, 'I did not know your husband was travelling with you.'

'My husband?' I repeated inquiringly. 'But he isn't. He's at home. Minding, I hope, my neglected children.'

'At home? Then who—then whose husband was that?'

'Was what?' I asked, following her eyes which were fixed on the door so lately slammed.

'Why, that man in spectacles?'

'Really, how can I tell? Perhaps nobody's. Certainly not mine.'

Mrs. Harvey-Browne stared at me in immense surprise. 'How very extraordinary,' she said.

THE SIXTH DAY—*Continued*

THE GRANITZ WOODS, SCHWARZER SEE, AND KIEKÖWER

In the woods behind Binz, alone in the heart of them, near a clearing where in past days somebody must have lived, for ancient fruit trees still mark the place that used to be a garden, there is a single grave on which the dead beech leaves slowly dropping down through the days and nights of many autumns, have heaped a sober cover. On the headstone is a rusty iron plate with this inscription—

> Hier ruht ein Finnischer Krieger
> 1806.

There is no fence round it, and no name on it. Every autumn the beech leaves make the unknown soldier a new brown pall, and through the sparkling frozen winters, except for the thin shadows of naked branches, he lies in sunshine. In the spring the blue hepaticas, children of those that were there the first day, gather about his sodden mound in little flocks of loveliness. Then, after a warm rain, the shadows broaden and draw together, for overhead the leaves are bursting; the wind blowing on to him from the clearing is scented, for the grass out there has violets in it; the pear trees in the deserted garden put on their white robes of promise; and then comes summer, and in the long days there are wanderers in the woods, and the chance passer-by, moved perhaps by some vague sentiment of pity for so much loneliness, throws him a few flowers or a bunch of ferns as he goes his way. There was a cross of bracken lying on the grave when I came upon it, still fresh and tied together with bits of grass, and a wreath of sea-holly hung round the headstone.

Sitting down by the side of the nameless one to rest, for the sun was high and I began to be tired, it seemed to me as I leaned my face against his cool covering of leaves, still wet with the last rain, that he was very cosily tucked away down there, away from worries and the chill fingers of fear, with everything over so far as he was concerned, and each of the hours destined for him in which hard things were to happen lived through and done with. A curiosity to know how he came to be in the Granitz woods at a time when Rügen, belonging to the French, had nothing to do with Finland, made me pull out my guide-book. But it was blank. The whole time I was journeying round Rügen it was invariably blank when it ought to have been illuminating. What had this man done or left undone that he should have been shut out from the company of those who are buried in churchyards? Why should he, because he was nameless, be outcast as well? Why should his body be held unworthy of a place by the side of persons who, though they were as dead as himself, still went on being respectable? I took off my hat and leaned against the Finnish warrior's grave and stared up along the smooth beech trunks to the point where the leaves, getting out of the shade, flashed in the sun at the top, and marvelled greatly at the ways of men, who pursue each other with conventions and disapproval even when their object, ceasing to be a man, is nothing but a poor, unresentful, indifferent corpse.

It is—certainly with me it is—a symptom of fatigue and want of food to marvel at the ways of men. My spirit grows more and more inclined to carp as my body grows more tired and hungry. When I am not too weary and have not given my breakfast to fowls, my thoughts have a cheerful way of fixing themselves entirely on the happy side of things, and life seems extraordinarily charming. But I see nothing happy and my soul is lost in blackness if, for many hours, I have had no food. How useless to talk to a person of the charities if you have not first fed him. How useless to explain that they are scattered at his feet like flowers if you have fed him too much. Both these states, of being over-fed and not fed enough, are equally fatal to the exquisitely sensitive life of the soul. And so it came about that because it was long past luncheon-time, and I had walked far, and it was hot, I found myself growing sentimental over the poor dead Finn; inclined to envy him because he could go on resting there while I had to find a way back to Binz in the heat and excuse my absence to an offended cousin; launching, indignant at his having been denied Christian burial, into a whole sea of woful reflections on the spites and follies of mankind, from which a single piece of bread would have rescued me. And as I was very tired, and it was very hot, and very silent, and very drowsy, my grumblings and disapprovals grew gradually vaguer, grew milder, grew confused, grew intermittent, and I went to sleep.

Now to go to sleep out of doors on a fine summer afternoon is an extremely pleasant thing to do if nobody comes and looks at you and you are comfortable. I was not exactly comfortable, for the ground round the grave was mossless and hard; and when the wind caught it the bracken cross tickled my ear and jerked my mind dismally on to earwigs. Also some spiders with frail long legs which they seemed to leave lying about at the least and gentlest attempt to persuade them to go away, walked about on me and would not walk anywhere else. But presently I left off feeling them or caring and sank away deliciously into dreams, the last thing I heard being the rustling of leaves, and the last thing I felt the cool wind lifting my hair.

And now the truly literary, if he did not here digress into a description of what he dreamed, which is a form of digression skipped by the truly judicious, would certainly write 'How long I had slept I know not,' and would then tell the reader that, waking with a start, he immediately proceeded to shiver. I cannot do better than imitate him, leaving out the start and the shiver, since I did neither, and altering his method to suit my greater homeliness, remark that I don't know how long I had been asleep because I had not looked at a watch when I began, but opening my eyes in due season I found that they stared straight into the eyes of Mrs. Harvey-Browne, and that she and Brosy were standing side by side looking down at me.

Being a woman, my first thought was a fervent hope that I had not been sleeping with my mouth wide open. Being a human creature torn by ungovernable passions, my second was to cry out inwardly and historically, 'Will no one rid me of this troublesome prelatess?' Then I sat up and feverishly patted my hair.

'I am not in the guide-book,' I said with some asperity.

'We came to look at the grave,' smilingly answered Mrs. Harvey-Browne.

'May I help you up?' asked Ambrose.

'Thanks, no.'

'Brosy, fetch me my camp-stool out of the fly—I will sit here a few minutes with Frau X. You were having a little post-prandial nap?' she added, turning to me still smiling.

'Ante-prandial.'

'What, you have been in the woods ever since we parted this morning at the Jagdschloss? Brosy,' she called after him, 'bring the tea-basket out as well. My dear Frau X., you must be absolutely faint. Do you not think it injudicious to go so many hours without nourishment? We will make tea now instead of a little later, and I insist on your eating something.'

Really this was very obliging. What had happened to the bishop's wife? Her urbanity was so marked that I thought it could only be a beautiful dream, and I rubbed my eyes before answering. But it was undoubtedly Mrs. Harvey-Browne. She had been home since I saw her last, rested, lunched, put on fresh garments, perhaps bathed; but all these things, soothing as they are, could not by themselves account for the change. Also she spoke to me in English for the first time. 'You are very kind,' I murmured, staring.

'Just imagine,' she said to Ambrose, who approached across the crackling leaves with the camp-stool, tea-basket, and cushions from the seats of the fly waiting in the forest road a few yards away, 'this little lady has had nothing to eat all day.'

'Oh I say!' said Brosy sympathetically.

'Little lady?' I repeated to myself, more and more puzzled.

'If you must lean against a hard grave,' said Brosy; 'at least, let me put this cushion behind your back. And I can make you much more comfortable if you will stand up a moment.'

'Oh I am so stiff,' I exclaimed as he helped me up; 'I must have been here hours. What time is it?'

'Past four,' said Brosy.

'*Most* injudicious,' said his mother. 'Dear Frau X., you must promise me never to do such a thing again. What would happen to those sweet children of yours if their little mother were to be laid up?'

Dear, dear me. What was all this? Sweet children? Little mother? I could only sit on my cushions and stare.

'This,' she explained, noticing I suppose that I looked astonished, and thinking it was because Brosy was spreading out cups and lighting the spirit- lamp so very close to the deceased Finn, 'is not desecration. It is not as though we were having tea in a churchyard, which of course we never would have. This is unconsecrated ground. One cannot desecrate that which has never been consecrated. Desecration can only begin after consecration has taken place.'

I bowed my head and then, cheered into speech by the sight of an approaching rusk, I added, 'I know a family with a mausoleum, and on fine days they go and have coffee at it.'

'Germans, of course,' said Mrs. Harvey-Browne, smiling, but with an effort. 'One can hardly imagine English——'

'Oh yes, Germans. When any one goes to see them, if it is fine they say, "Let us drink coffee at the mausoleum." And then they do.'

'Is it a special treat?' asked Brosy.

'The view there is very lovely.'

'Oh I see,' said Mrs. Harvey-Browne, relieved. 'They only sit outside. I was afraid for a moment that they actually——'

'Oh no,' I said, eating what seemed to be the most perfect rusk ever produced by German baker, 'not actually.'

'What a sweet spot this is to be buried in,' remarked Mrs. Harvey-Browne, while Brosy, with the skill of one used to doing it, made the tea; and then according to the wont of good women when they speak of being buried, she sighed. 'I wonder,' she went on, 'how he came to be put here.'

'That is what I have been wondering ever since I found him,' I said.

'He was wounded in some battle and was trying to get home,' said Brosy. 'You know Finland was Swedish in those days, and so was Rügen.'

As I did not know I said nothing, but looked exceedingly bright.

'He had been fighting for Sweden against the French. I met a forester yesterday, and he told me there used to be a forester's house where those fruit trees are, and the people in it took him in and nursed him till he died. Then they buried him here.'

'But why was he not buried in a churchyard?' asked his mother.

'I don't know. Poor chap, I don't suppose he would have cared. The great point I should say under such circumstances would be the being dead.'

'My dear Brosy,' murmured his mother; which was what she always murmured when he said things that she disapproved without quite knowing why.

'Or a still greater point,' I remarked, moved again to cheerful speech by the excellent tea Brosy had made, and his mother, justly suspicious of the tea of Teutons, had smuggled through the customs, as she afterwards told me with pride,—'a still greater point if those are the circumstances that lie in wait for one, would be the never being born.'

'Oh but that is pessimism!' cried Mrs. Harvey-Browne, shaking a finger at me. 'What have you, of all people in the world, to do with pessimism?'

'Oh I don't know—I suppose I have my days, like everybody else,' I said, slightly puzzled again by this remark. 'Once I was told of two aged Germans,' I continued, for by this time I had had three rusks and was feeling very pleasant,—'of two aged Germans whose digestive machinery was fragile.'

'Oh, poor things,' said Mrs. Harvey-Browne sympathetically.

'And in spite of that they drank beer all their lives persistently and excessively.'

'How very injudicious,' said Mrs. Harvey-Browne.

'They drank such a fearful lot and for so long that at last they became philosophers.'

'My dear Frau X.,' said Mrs. Harvey-Browne incredulously, 'what an unexpected result.'

'Oh but indeed there is hardly anything you may not at last become,' I insisted, 'if besides being German your diet is indiscreet enough.'

'Yes, I quite think *that*,' said Mrs. Harvey-Browne.

'Well, and what happened?' asked Brosy with smiling eyes.

'Well, they were naturally profoundly pessimistic, both of them. You are, you know, if your diet——'

'Oh yes, yes indeed,' agreed Mrs. Harvey-Browne, with the conviction of one who has been through it.

'They were absolutely sick of things. They loathed everything anybody said or did. And they were disciples of Nietzsche.'

'Was that the cause or the effect of the excessive beer-drinking?' asked Brosy.

'Oh, I can't *endure* Nietzsche,' cried Mrs. Harvey-Browne. 'Don't ever read him, Brosy. I saw some things he says about women—he is too dreadful.'

'And one said to the other over their despairing potations: "Only those can be considered truly happy who are destined never to be born."'

'There!' cried Mrs. Harvey-Browne. 'That is Nietzsche all over—*rank* pessimism.'

'I never heard ranker,' said Brosy smiling.

'And the other thought it over, and then said drearily: "But to how few falls that happy lot."'

There was a pause. Brosy was laughing behind his teacup. His mother, on the contrary, looked solemn, and gazed at me thoughtfully. 'There is a great want of simple faith about Germans,' she said. 'The bishop thinks it so sad. A story like that would quite upset him. He has been very anxious lest Brosy—our only child, dear Frau X., so you may imagine how precious—should become tainted by it.'

'I dislike beer,' said Brosy.

'That man this morning, for instance—did you ever hear anything like it? He was just the type of man, quite apart from his insolence, that most grieves the bishop.'

'Really?' I said; and wondered respectfully at the amount of grieving the bishop got through.

'An educated man, I suppose—did he not say he was a schoolmaster? A teacher of the young, without a vestige himself of the simple faith he ought to inculcate. For if he had had a vestige, would it not have prevented his launching into an irreverent conversation with a lady who was not only a stranger, but the wife of a prelate of the Church of England?'

'He couldn't know that, mother,' said Brosy; 'and from what you told me it wasn't a conversation he launched into but a monologue. And I must beg your pardon,' he added, turning to me with a smile, 'for the absurd mistake we made. It was the guide's fault.'

'Oh yes, my dear Frau X., you must forgive me—it was really too silly of me —I might have known—I was completely taken aback, I assure you, but the guide was so very positive——' And there followed such a number of apologies that again I was bewildered, only retaining the one clear impression that the bishop's wife desired exceedingly to be agreeable.

Well, a woman bent on being agreeable is better than a woman bent on being disagreeable, though, being the soul of caution in my statements, I must add, Not always; for I suppose few of us have walked any distance along the path of life without having had to go at least some part of the way in the company of persons who, filled with the praiseworthy wish to be very pleasant, succeeded only in drenching our spirits with the depressing torrents of effusion. And effusiveness applied to myself has precisely the effect of a finger applied to the horns of a snail who shall be innocently airing himself in the sun: he gets back without more ado into his shell, and so do I.

That is what happened on this occasion. For some reason, which I could only faintly guess, the bishop's wife after disapproving of me in the morning was petting me in the afternoon. She had been lunching, she told me, with Charlotte, and they had had a nice talk, she said, about me. About me? Instantly I scrambled back into my shell. There is surely nothing in the world so tiresome as being questioned, as I now was, on one's household arrangements and personal habits. I will talk about anything but that. I will talk with the courage of ignorance about all high matters, of which I know nothing. I am ready to discourse on all or any of the great Abstractions with the glibness of the shallow mind. I will listen sympathetically to descriptions of diseases suffered and operations survived, of the brilliance of sons and the beauty of daughters. I will lend an attentive ear to an enumeration of social successes and family difficulties, of woes and triumphs of every sort, including those connected with kitchens; but I will not answer questions about myself. And indeed, what is there to talk about? No one is interested in my soul, and as for my body I long ago got tired of that.

One cannot, however, eat a person's rusks without assuming a certain amount of subsequent blandness; so I did my best to behave nicely. Brosy smoked cigarettes. Whatever it was that had sent me up in his mother's estimation had apparently sent me down in his. He no longer, it seemed, looked upon me as a good specimen of the intelligent German female. I might be as eloquently silent as I liked, and it did not impress him in the least. The few remarks he made showed me that. This was grievous, for Brosy was, in person, a very charming young man, and the good opinion of charming young men is quite a nice thing to possess. Now I began to regret, now that he was merely interjectional, those earnest paragraphs in which he had talked the night before at supper and during the sunset walk on the island of Vilm. Observing him sideways and cautiously I saw that the pretty speeches his mother was making me *apropos* of everything and nothing were objectionable to him; and I silently agreed with him that pretty speeches are unpleasant things, especially when made by one woman to another. You can forgive a man perhaps, because in your heart in spite of all experience lurks the comfortable belief that he means what he says; but how shall you forgive a woman for mistaking you for a fool?

They persuaded me to drive with them to the place in the woods they were bound for called Kieköwer, where the view over the bay was said to be very beautiful; and when I got on to my feet I found I was so stiff that driving seemed the only thing possible. Ambrose was very kind and careful of my bodily comfort, but did not bother about me spiritually. Whenever there was a hill, and there kept on being hills, he got out and walked, leaving me wholly to his mother. But it did not matter any more, for the forest was so exquisite that way, the afternoon so serene, so mellow with lovely light, that I could not look round me without being happy. Oh blessed state, when mere quiet weather, trees and grass, sea and clouds, can make you forget that life has anything in it but rapture, can make you drink in heaven with every breath! How long will it last, this joy of living, this splendid ecstasy of the soul? I am more afraid of losing this, of losing even a little of this, of having so much as the edge of its radiance dimmed, than of parting with any other earthly possession. And I think of Wordsworth, its divine singer, who yet lost it so soon and could no longer see the splendour in the grass, the glory in the flower, and I ask myself with a sinking heart if it faded so quickly for him who saw it and sang it by God's grace to such perfection, how long, oh how long does the common soul, half blind, half dead, half dumb, keep its little, precious share?

My intention when I began this book was to write a useful Guide to Rügen, one that should point out its best parts and least uncomfortable inns to any English or American traveller whose energy lands him on its shores. With every page I write it grows more plain that I shall not fulfil that intention. What, for instance, have Charlotte and the bishop's wife of illuminating for the tourist who wants to be shown the way? As I cannot conscientiously praise the inns I will not give their names, and what is the use of that to a tourist who wishes to know where to sleep and dine? I meant to describe the Jagdschloss, and find I only repeated a ghost story. It is true I said the rolls at the inn there were hard, but the information was so deeply embedded in superfluities that no tourist will discover it in time to save him from ordering one. Still anxious to be of use, I will now tell the traveller that he must on no account miss going from Binz to Kieköwer, but that he must go there on his feet, and not allow himself to be driven over the roots and stones by the wives of bishops; and that shortly before he reaches Kieköwer (Low German for look, or peep over), he will come to four cross-roads with a sign-post in the middle, and he is to follow the one to the right, which will lead him to the Schwarze See or Black Lake, and having got there let him sit down quietly, and take out the volume of poetry he ought to have in his pocket, and bless God who made this little lovely hollow on the top of the hills, and drew it round with a girdle of forest, and filled its reedy curves with white water- lilies, and set it about with silence, and gave him eyes to see its beauty.

I am afraid I could not have heard Mrs. Harvey-Browne's questions for quite a long time, for presently I found she had sauntered round this enchanted spot to the side where Brosy was taking photographs, and I was sitting alone on the moss looking down through the trees at the lilies, and listening only to frogs. I looked down between the slender stems of some silver birches that hung over the water; every now and then a tiny gust of wind came along and rippled their clear reflections, ruffling up half of each water-lily leaf, and losing itself somewhere among the reeds. Then when it had gone, the lily leaves dropped back one after the other on to the calm water, each with a little thud. On the west side the lake ends in a reedy marsh, very froggy that afternoon, and starred with the snowy cotton flower. A peculiarly fragrant smell like exceedingly delicate Russian leather hangs round the place, or did that afternoon. It was, I suppose, the hot sun bringing out the scent of some hidden herb, and it would not always be there; but I like to think of the beautiful little lake as for ever fragrant, all the year round lying alone and sweet-smelling and enchanted, tucked away in the bosom of the solitary hills.

When the traveller has spent some time lying on the moss with his poet—and he should lie there long enough for his soul to grow as quiet and clear as the water, and the poet, I think, should be Milton—he can go back to the cross-roads, five minutes' walk over beech leaves, and so to Kieköwer, about half a mile farther on. The contrast between the Schwarze See and Kieköwer is striking. Coming from that sheltered place of suspended breath you climb up a steep hill and find yourself suddenly on the edge of high cliffs where the air is always moving and the wind blows freshly on to you across the bay. Far down below, the blue water heaves and glitters. In the distance lies the headland beyond Sassnitz, hazy in the afternoon light. The beech trees, motionless round the lake, here keep up a ceaseless rustle. You who have been so hot all day find you are growing almost too cool.

'Sie ist schön, unsere Ostsee, was?' said a hearty male voice behind us.

We were all three leaning against the wooden rail put up for our protection on the edge of the cliff. A few yards off is a shed where a waiter, battered by the sea breezes he is forced daily to endure, supplies the thirsty with beer and coffee. The hearty owner of the voice, brown with the sun, damp and jolly with exercise and beer-drinking, stood looking over Mrs. Harvey-Browne's shoulder at the view with an air of proud proprietorship, his hands in his pockets, his legs wide apart, his cap pushed well off an extremely heated brow.

He addressed this remark to Mrs. Harvey-Browne, to whom, I suppose, she being a matron of years and patent sobriety, he thought cheery remarks might safely be addressed. But if there was a thing the bishop's wife disliked it was a cheery stranger. The pedagogue that morning, so artlessly interested in her conversation with me as to forget he had not met her before, had manifestly revolted her. I myself the previous evening, though not cheery still a stranger, had been objectionable to her. How much more offensive, then, was a warm man speaking to her with a familiarity so sudden and jolly as to resemble nothing so much as a slap on the back. She, of course, took no notice of him after the first slight start and glance round, but stared out to sea with eyes grown stony.

'In England you do not see such blue water, what?' shouted the jolly man, who was plainly in the happy mood the French call *déboutonné*.

His wife and daughters, ladies clothed in dust-cloaks sitting at a rough wooden table with empty beer-glasses before them, laughed hilariously. The mere fact of the Harvey-Brownes being so obviously English appeared to amuse them enormously. They too were in the mood *déboutonné*.

Ambrose, as ready to talk as his mother to turn her back, answered for her, and assured the jolly man that he had indeed never seen such blue water in England.

This seemed to give the whole family intense delight. *'Ja, ja,'* shouted the father, *'Deutschland, Deutschland, über Alles!'* And he trolled out that famous song in the sort of voice known as rich.

'Quite so,' said Ambrose politely, when he had done.

'Oh come, we must drink together,' cried the jolly man, 'drink in the best beer in the world to the health of Old England, what?' And he called the waiter, and in another moment he and Ambrose stood clinking glasses and praising each other's countries, while the hilarious family laughed and applauded in the background.

The bishop's wife had not moved. She stood staring out to sea, and her stare grew ever stonier.

'I wish——' she began; but did not go on. Then, there being plainly no means of stopping Ambrose's cordiality, she wisely resolved to pass the time while we waited for him in exchanging luminous thoughts with me. And we did exchange them for some minutes, until my luminousness was clouded and put out by the following short conversation:—

'I must say I cannot see what there is about Germans that so fascinates Ambrose. Do you hear that empty laughter? "The loud laugh that betrays the empty mind"?'

'As Shakespeare says.'

'Dear Frau X., you are so beautifully read.'

'So nice of you.'

'I know you are a woman of a liberal mind, so you will not object to my saying that I am much disappointed in the Germans.'

'Not a bit.'

'Ambrose has always been so enthusiastic about them that I expected quite wonders. What do I find? I pass over in silence many things, including the ill-bred mirth—just listen to those people—but I cannot help lamenting their complete want of common sense.'

'Indeed?'

'How sensible English people are compared to them!'

'Do you think so?'

'Why, of course, in everything.'

'But are you not judging the whole nation by the few?'

'Oh, one can always tell. What could be more supremely senseless for instance'—and she waved a hand over the bay—'than calling the Baltic the Ostsee?'

'Well, but why shouldn't they if they want to?'

'But dear Frau X., it is so foolish. East sea? Of what is it the east? One is always the east of something, but one doesn't talk about it. The name has no meaning whatever. Now "Baltic" exactly describes it.'

THE SEVENTH DAY

FROM BINZ TO STUBBENKAMMER

We left Binz at ten o'clock the next morning for Sassnitz and Stubbenkammer. Sassnitz is the principal bathing-place on the island, and I had meant to stay there a night; but as neither of us liked the glare of chalk roads and white houses we went on that day to Stubbenkammer, where everything is in the shade.

Charlotte had not gone away as she said she would, and when I got back to our lodgings the evening before, penitent and apologetic after my wanderings in the forest, besides being rather frightened, for I was afraid I was going to be scolded and was not sure that I did not deserve it, I found her sitting on the pillared verandah indulgently watching the sunset sky, with *The Prelude* lying open on her lap. She did not ask me where I had been all day; she only pointed to *The Prelude* and said, 'This is great rubbish; 'to which I only answered 'Oh?'

Later in the evening I discovered that the reason of her want of interest in my movements and absence of reproachfulness was that she herself had had a busy and a successful day. Judgment, hurried on by Charlotte, had overtaken the erring Hedwig; and the widow, expressing horror and disgust, had turned her out. Charlotte praised the widow. 'She is an intelligent and a right-minded woman,' she said. 'She assured me she would rather do all the work herself and be left without a servant altogether than keep a wicked girl like that. I was prepared to leave at once if she had not dismissed her then and there.'

Still later in the evening I gathered from certain remarks Charlotte made that she had lent the most lurid of her works, a pamphlet called *The Beast of Prey*, to the widow, who to judge from Charlotte's satisfaction was quite carried away by it. Its nature was certainly sufficiently startling to carry any ordinary widow away.

We left the next morning, pursued by the widow's blessings,—blessings of great potency, I suppose, of the same degree of potency exactly as the curses of orphans, and we all know the peculiar efficaciousness of those. 'Good creature,' said Charlotte, touched by the number of them as we drove away; 'I am so glad I was able to help her a little by opening her eyes.'

'The operation,' I observed, 'is not always pleasant.'

'But invariably necessary,' said Charlotte with decision.

What then was my astonishment on looking back, as we were turning the corner by the red-brick hotel, to take a last farewell of the pretty white house on the shore, to see Hedwig hanging out of an upper window waving a duster to Gertrud who was following us in the luggage cart, and chatting and laughing while she did it with the widow standing at the gate below. 'That house is certainly haunted,' I exclaimed. 'There's a fresh ghost looking out of the window at this very moment.'

Charlotte turned her head with an incredulous face. Having seen the apparition she turned it back again.

'It can't be Hedwig,' I hastened to assure her, 'because you told me she had been sent to her mother in the country. It can only, then, be Hedwig's ghost. She is very young to have one, isn't she?'

But Charlotte said nothing at all; and so we left Binz in silence, and got into the sandy road and pine forest that takes you the first part of your way towards the north and Sassnitz.

The road I had meant to take goes straight from Binz along the narrow tongue of land, marked Schmale Heide on the map, separating the Baltic Sea from the inland sea called Jasmunder Bodden; but outside the village I saw a sheet of calm water shining through pine trunks on the left, and I got out to go and look at it, and August, always nervous when I got out, drove off the beaten track after me, and so we missed our way.

The water was the Schmachter See, a real lake in size, not a pond like the exquisite little Schwarze See, and I stood on the edge admiring its morning loveliness as it lay without a ripple in the sun, the noise of the sea on the other side of the belt of pines sounding unreal as the waves of a dream on that still shore. And while I was standing among its reeds August was busy thinking out a short cut that would strike the road we had left higher up. The result was that we very soon went astray, and emerging from the woods at the farm of Dollahn found ourselves heading straight for the Jasmunder Bodden. But it did not matter where we went so long as we were pleased, and when everything is fresh and new how can you help being pleased? So we drove on looking for a road to the right that should bring us back again to the Schmale Heide, and enjoyed the open fields and the bright morning, and pretended to ourselves that it was not dusty. At least that is what I pretended to myself. Charlotte pretended nothing of the sort; on the contrary, she declared at intervals that grew shorter that she was being suffocated.

And that is one of the many points on which the walker has the advantage of him who drives—he can walk on the grass at the side of the road, or over moss or whortleberries, and need not endure the dust kicked up by eight hoofs. But where has he not the advantage? The only one of driving is that you can take a great many clean clothes with you; for the rest, there is no comparing the two pleasures. And, after all, what does it matter if for one fortnight out of all the fortnights there are in a year you are not so clean as usual? Indeed, I think there must be a quite peculiar charm for the habitually well-washed in being for a short time deliberately dirty.

At Lubkow, a small village on the Jasmunder Bodden, we got on to the high road to Bergen, and turning up it to the right faced northwards once more. Soon after passing a forestry in the woods we reached the Schmale Heide again, and then for four miles drove along a white road between young pines, the bluest of skies overhead, and on our right, level with the road, the violet sea. This was the first time I saw the Baltic really violet. On other days it had been a deep blue or a brilliant green, but here it was a wonderful, dazzling violet.

At Neu Mucran—all these places are on the map—we left the high road to go on by itself up to the inland town of Sagard, and plunged into sandy, shadeless country roads, trying to keep as near the shore as possible. The rest of the way to Sassnitz was too unmitigatedly glaring and dusty to be pleasant. There were no trees at all; and as it was uphill nearly the whole way we had time to be thoroughly scorched and blinded. Nor could we keep near the sea. The road took us farther and farther away from it as we toiled slowly up between cornfields, crammed on that poor soil with poppies and marguerites and chickory. Earth and sky were one blaze of brightness. Our eyes, filled with dust, were smarting long before we got to the yet fiercer blaze of Sassnitz; and it was when we found that the place is all chalk and white houses, built in the open with the forest pushed well back behind, that with one accord we decided not to stay in it.

I would advise the intending tourist to use Sassnitz only as a place to make excursions to from Binz on one side or Stubbenkammer on the other; though, aware of my peculiarities, I advise it with diffidence. For out of every thousand Germans nine hundred and ninety-nine would give, with emphasis, a contrary advice, and the remaining one would not agree with me. But I have nothing to do with the enthusiasms of other people, and can only repeat that it is a dusty, glaring place—quaint enough on a fine day, with its steep streets leading down to the water, and on wet days dreary beyond words, for its houses all look as though they were built of cardboard and were only meant, as indeed is the case, to be used during a few weeks in summer.

August, Gertrud, and the horses were sent to an inn for a three hours' rest, and we walked down the little street, lined with stalls covered with amber ornaments and photographs, to the sea. As it was dinner-time the place was empty, and from the different hotels came such a hum and clatter of voices and dishes that, remembering Sellin, we decided not to go in. Down on the beach we found a confectioner's shop directly overlooking the sea, with sun- blinds and open windows, and no one in it. It looked cool, so we went in and sat at a marble table in a draught, and the sea splashed refreshingly on the shingle just outside, and we ate a great many cakes and sardines and vanilla ices, and then began to feel wretched.

'What shall we do till four o'clock?' I inquired disconsolately, leaning my elbows on the window-sill and watching the heat dancing outside over the shingle.

'Do?' said somebody, stopping beneath the window; 'why, walk with us to Stubbenkammer, of course.'

It was Ambrose, clad from head to foot in white linen, a cool and beautiful vision.

'You here? I thought you were going to stay in Binz?'

'We came across for the day in a steamer. My mother is waiting for me in the shade. She sent me to get some biscuits, and then we are going to Stubbenkammer. Come too.'

'Oh but the heat!'

'Wait a minute. I'm coming in there to get the biscuits.'

He disappeared round the corner of the house, the door being behind.

'He is good-looking, isn't he?' I said to Charlotte.

'I dislike that type of healthy, successful, self-satisfied young animal.'

'That's because you have eaten so many cakes and sardines,' I said soothingly.

'Are you never serious?'

'But invariably.'

'Frankly, I find nothing more tiring than talking to a person who is persistently playful.'

'That's only those three vanilla ices,' I assured her encouragingly.

'You here, too, Frau Nieberlein?' exclaimed Ambrose, coming in. 'Oh good. You will come with us, won't you? It's a beautiful walk—shade the whole way. And I have just got that work of the Professor's about the Phrygians, and want to talk about it frightfully badly. I've been reading it all night. It's the most marvellous book. No wonder it revolutionised European thought.

117

Absolutely epoch-making.' He bought his biscuits as one in a dream, so greatly did he glow with rapture.

'Come on Charlotte,' I said; 'a walk will do us both good. I'll send word to August to meet us at Stubbenkammer.'

But Charlotte would not come on. She would sit there quietly, she said; bathe perhaps, later, and then drive to Stubbenkammer.

'I tell you what, Frau Nieberlein,' cried Ambrose from the counter, 'I never envied a woman before, but I must say I envy you. What a marvellously glorious fate to be the wife of such an extraordinary thinker!'

'Very well then,' I said quickly, not knowing what Charlotte's reply might be, 'you'll come on with August and meet us there. *Auf Wiedersehen*, Lottchen.' And I hurried Ambrose and his biscuits out.

Looking up as we passed beneath the window, we saw Charlotte still sitting at the marble table gazing into space.

'Your cousin is wonderful about the Professor,' said Ambrose as we crossed a scorching bit of chalky promenade to the trees where Mrs. Harvey-Browne was waiting.

'In what way wonderful?' I asked uneasily, for I had no wish to discuss the Nieberlein conjugalities with him.

'Oh, so self-controlled, so quiet, so modest; never trots him out, never puts on airs because she's his wife—oh, quite wonderful.'

'Ah, yes. About those Phrygians——'

And so I got his thoughts away from Charlotte, and by the time we had found his mother I knew far more about Phrygians than I should have thought possible.

The walk along the coast from Sassnitz to Stubbenkammer is alone worth a journey to Rügen. I suppose there are few walks in the world more wholly beautiful from beginning to end. On no account, therefore, should the traveller, all unsuspecting of so much beauty so near at hand, be persuaded to go to Stubbenkammer by road. The road will give him merely a pretty country drive, taking him the shortest way, quite out of sight of the sea; the path keeps close to the edge of the cliffs, and is a series of exquisite surprises. But only the lusty and the spare must undertake it, for it is not to be done under three hours, and is an almost continual going down countless steps into deep ravines, and up countless steps out of them again. You are, however, in the shade of beeches the whole time; and who shall describe, as you climb higher and higher, the lovely sparkle and colour of the sea as it curls, far below you, in and out among the folds of the cliffs?

Mrs. Harvey-Browne was sufficiently spare to enjoy the walk. Ambrose was perfectly content telling us about Nieberlein's new work. I was perfectly content too, because only one ear was wanted for Nieberlein, and I still had one over for the larks and the lapping of the water, besides both my happy eyes. We did not hurry, but lingered over each beauty, resting on little sunny plateaus high up on the very edge of the cliffs, where, sitting on the hot sweet grass, we saw the colour of the sea shine through the colour of the fringing scabious—a divine meeting of colours often to be seen along the Rügen coast in July; or, in the deep shade at the bottom of a ravine, we rested on the moss by water trickling down over slimy green stones to the sea which looked, from those dark places, like a great wall of light.

Mrs. Harvey-Browne listened with a placid pride to her son's explanations of the scope and nature of Nieberlein's book. His enthusiasm made him talk so much that she, perforce, was silent; and her love for him written so plainly on her face showed what she must have been like in her best days, the younger days before her husband got his gaiters and began to grieve. Besides, during the last and steepest part of the walk we were beyond the range of other tourists, for they had all dropped off at the Waldhalle, a place half-way where you drink, so that there was nothing at all to offend her. We arrived, therefore, at Stubbenkammer about six o'clock in a state of perfect concord, pleasantly tired, and hot enough to be glad we had got there. On the plateau in front of the restaurant—there is, of course, a restaurant at the climax of the walk— there were tables under the trees and people eating and drinking. One table, at a little distance from the others, with the best view over the cliff, had a white cloth on it, and was spread for what looked like tea. There were nice thin cups, and strawberries, and a teapot, and a jug in the middle with roses in it; and while I was wondering who were the privileged persons for whom it had been laid Gertrud came out of the restaurant, followed by a waiter carrying thin bread and butter, and then I knew that the privileged persons were ourselves.

'I had tea with you yesterday,' I said to Mrs. Harvey-Browne. 'Now it is your turn to have tea with me.'

'How charming,' said Mrs. Harvey-Browne with a sigh of satisfaction, sinking into a chair and smelling the roses. 'Your maid seems to be one of those rare treasures who like doing extra things for their mistresses.'

Well, Gertrud is a rare treasure, and it did look clean and dainty next to the beer-stained tables at which coffee was being drunk and spilt by tourists who had left their Gertruds at home. Then the place was so wonderful, the white cliffs cutting out sheer and sharp into the sea, their huge folds filled with every sort of greenery—masses of shrubby trees, masses of ferns, masses of wild-flowers. Down at the bottom there was a steamer anchored, the one by which the Harvey-Brownes were going back later to Binz, quite a big, two-funnelled steamer, and it looked from where we were like a tiny white toy.

'I fear the gracious one will not enjoy sleeping here,' whispered Gertrud as she put a pot of milk on the table. 'I made inquiries on arrival, and the hotel is entirely full, and only one small bedroom in a pavilion, detached, among trees, can be placed at the gracious one's disposal.'

'And my cousin?'

'The room has two beds, and the cousin of the gracious one is sitting on one of them. We have been here already an hour. August is installed. The horses are well accommodated here. I have an attic of sufficient comfort. Only the ladies will suffer.'

'I will go to my cousin. Show me, I pray thee, the way.'

Excusing myself to Mrs. Harvey-Browne I followed Gertrud. At the back of the restaurant there is an open space where a great many feather-beds in red covers were being aired on the grass, while fowls and the waiting drivers of the Sassnitz waggonettes wandered about among them. In the middle of this space is a big, bare, yellow house, the only hotel in Stubbenkammer, the only house in fact that I saw at all, and some distance to the left of this in the shade of the forest, one-storied, dank, dark, and mosquito-y, the pavilion.

'Gertrud,' I said, scanning it with a sinking heart, 'never yet did I sleep in a pavilion.'

'I know it, gracious one.'

'With shutterless windows on a level with the elbows of the passers-by.'

'What the gracious one says is but too true.'

'I will enter and speak with my cousin Charlotte.'

Charlotte was, as Gertrud had said, sitting on one of the two beds that nearly filled the room. She was feverishly writing something in pencil on the margin of *The Beast of Prey*, and looked up with an eager, worried expression when I opened the door. 'Is it not terrible,' she said, 'that one should not be able to do more than one's best, and that one's best is never enough?'

'Why, what's the matter?'

'Oh everything's the matter! You are all dull, indifferent, deadened to everything that is vital. You don't care—you let things slide—and if any one tries to wake you up and tell you the truth you never, never listen.'

'Who—me?' I asked, confused into this sad grammar by her outburst.

She threw the pamphlet down and jumped up, 'Oh, I am sick of all your sins and stupidities!' she cried, pulling her hat straight and sticking violent pins into it.

'Whose—mine?' I asked in great perplexity.

'It would almost seem,' said Charlotte, fixing me with angry eyes,—'it would really almost seem that there is no use whatever in devoting one's life to one's fellow-creatures.'

'Well, one naturally likes to be left alone,' I murmured.

'What I try to do is to pull them out of the mud when they are in it, to warn them when they are going in it, and to help them when they have been in it.'

'Well, that sounds very noble. Being full of noble intentions, why on earth, my dear Charlotte, can't you be placid? You are never placid. Come and have some tea.'

'Tea! What, with those wretched people? Those leathern souls? Those Harvey-Brownes?'

'Come along—it isn't only tea—it's strawberries and roses, and looks lovely.'

'Oh, those people half kill me! They are so pleased with themselves, so satisfied with life, such prigs, such toadies. What have I in common with them?'

'Nonsense. Ambrose is not a toady at all—he's nothing but a dear. And his mother has her points. Why not try to do them good? You'd be interested in them at once if you'd look upon them as patients.'

I put my arm through hers and drew her out of the room. 'This stuffy room is enough to depress anybody,' I said. 'And I know what's worrying you—it's that widow.'

'I know what's an irritating trick of yours,' exclaimed Charlotte, turning on me, 'it's always explaining the reason why I say or feel what I do say or feel.'

'What, and isn't there any reason?'

'That widow has no power to worry me. Her hypocrisy will bear its own fruit, and she will have to eat it. Then, when the catastrophe comes, the sure consequence of folly and weakness, she'll do what you all do in face of the inevitable—sit and lament and say it was somebody else's fault. And of course every single thing that happens to you is never anybody's fault but your own miserable self's.'

'I wish you would teach me to dodge what you call the inevitable,' I said.

'As though it wanted any teaching,' said Charlotte stopping short in the middle of the open space before our table to look into my eyes. 'You've only not got to be silly.'

'But what am I to do if I am silly—naturally silly—born it?'

'The tea is getting very cold,' called out Mrs. Harvey-Browne plaintively. She had been watching us with impatience, and seemed perturbed. The moment we got near enough she informed us that the tourists were such that no decent woman could stand it. 'Ambrose has gone off with one of them,' she said,—'a most terrible old man—to look at some view over there. Would you believe it, while we were quietly sitting here not harming anybody, this person came up the hill and immediately began to talk to us as if we knew each other? He actually had the audacity to ask if he might sit with us at this table, as there was no room elsewhere. He was *most* objectionable. Of course I refused. The most pushing person I have met at all.'

'But there is ample room,' said Charlotte, to whom everything the bishop's wife said and did appeared bad.

'But, my dear Frau Nieberlein, a complete stranger! And such an unpleasantly jocular old man. And I think it so very ill-bred to be jocular in the wrong places.'

'I always think it a pity to cold-shoulder people,' said Charlotte sternly. She was not, it seemed, going to stand any nonsense from the bishop's wife.

'You must be dying for some tea,' I interposed, pouring it out as one who should pour oil on troubled waters.

'And you should consider,' continued Charlotte, 'that in fifty years we shall all be dead, and our opportunities for being kind will be over.'

'My dear Frau Nieberlein!' ejaculated the astonished bishop's wife.

'Why, it isn't certain,' I said. 'You'll only be eighty then, Charlotte, and what is eighty? When I am eighty I hope to be a gay granddame skilled in gestic lore, frisking beneath the burthen of fourscore.'

But the bishop's wife did not like being told she would be dead in fifty years, and no artless quotations of mine could make her like it; so she drank her tea with an offended face. 'Perhaps, then,' she remarked, 'you will tell me I ought to have accepted the proposal one of the other tourists, a woman, made me a moment ago. She suggested that I should drive back to Sassnitz with her and her party, and halve the expense of the fly.'

'Well, and why should you not?' said Charlotte.

'Why should I not? There were two excellent reasons why I should not. First, because it was an impertinence; and secondly, because I am going back in the boat.'

'The second reason is good, but you must pardon my seeing no excellence whatever in the first.'

'Your son's tea will be undrinkable,' I said, feebly interrupting. I can never see two people contradicting each other without feeling wretched. Why contradict? Why argue at all? Only one's Best-Beloved, one's Closest and Most Understanding should be contradicted and argued with. How simple to keep quiet with all the rest and agree to everything they say. Charlotte up to this had kept very quiet in the presence of Mrs. Harvey-Browne, had said yes in the right places, and had only been listless and bored. Now, after reading her own explosive pamphlet for an hour, stirred besides by the widow's base behaviour and by the failure of her effort to induce penitence in Hedwig by means of punishment, she was in the strenuous mood again, and inclined to see all manner of horrid truths and fates hovering round the harmless tea- table, where denser eyes like mine, and no doubt Mrs. Harvey-Browne's, only saw a pleasant flicker of beech leaves over cups and saucers, and bland strawberries in a nest of green.

'If women did not regard each other's advances with so much suspicion,' Charlotte proceeded emphatically, 'if they did not look upon every one of a slightly different class as an impossible person to be avoided, they would make a much better show in the fight for independent existence. The value of co-operation is so gigantic——'

'Ah yes, I fancy I remember your saying something like this at that lecture in Oxford last winter,' interrupted Mrs. Harvey-Browne with an immense plaintiveness.

'It cannot be said too often.'

'Oh yes dear Frau Nieberlein, believe me it can. What, for instance, has it to do with my being asked to drive back to Sassnitz with a strange family in a fly?'

'Why, with that it has very much to do,' I interposed, smiling pleasantly on them both. 'You would have paid half. And what is co-operation if it is not paying half? Indeed, I've been told by people who have done it that it sometimes even means paying all. In which case you don't see its point.'

'What I mean, of course,' said Charlotte, 'is moral co-operation. A ceaseless working together of its members for the welfare of the sex. No opportunity should ever be lost. One should always be ready to talk to, to get to know, to encourage. One must cultivate a large love for humanity to whatever class it belongs, and however individually objectionable it is. You, no doubt,' she continued, waving her teaspoon at the staring bishop's wife, 'curtly refused the very innocent invitation of your fellow-creature because she was badly dressed and had manners of a type with which you are not acquainted. You considered it an impertinence—nay, more than an impertinence, an insult, to be approached in such a manner. Now, how can you tell'—(here she leaned across the table, and in her earnestness pointed the teaspoon straight at Mrs. Harvey-Browne, who stared harder than ever)—'how will you ever know that the woman did not happen to be full, full to the brim, of that good soil in which the seed of a few encouraging words dropped during your drive would have produced a splendid harvest of energy and freedom?'

'But my dear Frau Nieberlein,' said the bishop's wife, much taken aback by this striking image, 'I do not think she was full of anything of the kind. She did not look so, anyhow. And I myself, to pursue your metaphor, am hardly fitted for the office of an agricultural implement. I believe all these things are done nowadays by machinery, are they not?' she asked, turning to me in a well-meant effort to get away from the subject. 'The old-fashioned and picturesque sower has been quite superseded, has he not?'

'Why are you talking about farming?' asked Ambrose, who came up at this moment.

'We are talking of the farming of souls,' replied Charlotte.

'Oh,' said Ambrose, in his turn taken aback. He pretended to be so busy sitting down that he couldn't say more than just Oh. We watched him in silence fussing into his chair. 'How pleasant it is here,' he went on when he was settled. 'No, I don't mind cold tea a bit, really. Mother, why wouldn't you let the old man sit with us? He's a frightfully good sort.'

'Because there are certain limits beyond which I decline to go,' replied his mother, visibly annoyed that he should thus unconsciously side with Charlotte.

'Oh but it was rough on him—don't you think so, Frau Nieberlein? We have the biggest table and only half-fill it, and there isn't another place to be had. It is so characteristically British for us to sit here and keep other people out. He'll have to wait heaven knows how long for his coffee, and he has walked miles.'

'I think,' said Charlotte slowly, loudly, and weightily, 'that he might very well have joined us.'

'But you did not see him,' protested Mrs. Harvey-Browne. 'I assure you he really was impossible. *Much* worse than the woman we were talking about.'

'I can only say,' said Charlotte, even slower, louder, and more weightily, 'that one should, before all things, be human, and that one has no right whatever to turn one's back on the smallest request of a fellow-creature.'

Hardly had she said it, hardly had the bishop's wife had time to open her mouth and stare in stoniest astonishment, hardly had I had time to follow her petrified gaze, than an old man in a long waterproof garment with a green felt hat set askew on his venerable head, came nimbly up behind Charlotte, and bending down to her unsuspecting ear shouted into it the amazing monosyllable 'Bo!'

THE SEVENTH DAY—*Continued*

AT STUBBENKAMMER

I believe I have somewhere remarked that Charlotte was not the kind of person one could ever tickle. She was also the last person in the world to whom most people would want to say Bo. The effect on her of this Bo was alarming. She started up as though she had been struck, and then stood as one turned to stone.

Brosy jumped up as if to protect her.

Mrs. Harvey-Browne looked really frightened, and gasped 'It is the old man again—an escaped lunatic—how very unpleasant!'

'No, no,' I hurriedly explained, 'it is the Professor.'

'*The Professor?* What, never the *Professor?* What, *the* Professor? Brosy—Brosy'—she leaned over and seized his coat in an agony of haste—'never breathe it's the old man I've been talking about—never breathe it—it's Professor Nieberlein himself!'

'*What?*' exclaimed Brosy, flushing all over his face.

But the Professor took no notice of any of us, for he was diligently kissing Charlotte. He kissed her first on one cheek, then he kissed her on the other cheek, then he pulled her ears, then he tickled her under the chin, and he beamed upon her all the while with such an uninterrupted radiance that the coldest heart must have glowed only to see it.

'So here I meet thee, little treasure?' he cried. 'Here once more thy twitter falls upon my ears? I knew at once thy little chirp. I heard it above all the drinking noises. "Come, come," I said to myself, "if that is not the little Lot!" And chirping the self-same tune I know of old, in the beautiful English tongue: Turn not your back on a creature, turn not your back. Only on the old husband one turns the pretty back—what? Fie, fie, the naughty little Lot!'

I protest I never saw a stranger sight than this of Charlotte being toyed with. And the rigidity of her!

'How *charming* the simple German ways are,' cried Mrs. Harvey-Browne in a great flutter to me while the toying was going on. She was so torn by horror at what she had said and by rapture at meeting the Professor, that she hardly knew what she was doing. 'It really does one good to be given a peep at genuine family emotions. Delightful Professor. You heard what he said to the

Duke after he had gone all the way to Bonn on purpose to see him? And my dear Frau X., *such* a Duke!' And she whispered the name in my ear as though it were altogether too great to be said aloud.

I conceded by a nod that he was a very superior duke; but what the Professor said to him I never heard, for at that moment Charlotte dropped back into her chair and the Professor immediately scrambled (I fear there is no other word, he did scramble) into the next one to her, which was Brosy's.

'Will you kindly present me?' said Brosy to Charlotte, standing reverential and bare-headed before the great man.

'Ah, I know you, my young friend, already,' said the Professor genially. 'We have just been admiring Nature together.'

At this the bishop's wife blushed, deeply, thoroughly, a thing I suppose she had not done for years, and cast a supplicating look at Charlotte, who sat rigid with her eyes on her plate. Brosy blushed too and bowed profoundly. 'I cannot tell you, sir, how greatly honoured I feel at being allowed to make your acquaintance,' he said.

'Tut, tut,' said the Professor. 'Lottchen, present me to these ladies.'

What, he did not remember me? What, after the memorable evening in Berlin? I know of few things more wholly grievous than to have a celebrated connection who forgets he has ever seen you.

'I must apologise to you, madam,' he said to the bishop's wife, for taking a seat at your table after all.'

'Oh, Professor——' murmured Mrs. Harvey-Browne.

'But you will perhaps forgive my joining a party of which my wife is a member.'

'Oh, Professor, do pray believe——'

'I know a Brown,' he continued; 'in England there is a Brown I know. He is of a great skill in card-tricks. Hold—I know another Brown—nay, I know several. Relations, no doubt, of yours, madam?'

'No, sir, our name is *Harvey*-Browne.'

'*Ach so.* I understood Brown. So it is Harvey. Yes, yes; Harvey made the excellent sauce. I eat it daily with my fish. Madam, a public benefactor.'

'Sir, we are not related. We are the Harvey-Brownes.'

'What, you are both Harveys and Browns, and yet not related to either Browns or Harveys? Nay, but that is a problem to split the head.'

'My husband is the Bishop of Babbacombe. Perhaps you have heard of him. Professor. He too is literary. He annotates.'

'In any case, madam, his wife speaks admirable German,' said the Professor, with a little bow. 'And this lady?' he asked, turning to me.

'Why, I am Charlotte's cousin,' I said, no longer able to hide my affliction at the rapid way in which he had forgotten me, 'and accordingly yours. Do you not remember I met you last winter in Berlin at a party at the Hofmeyers?'

'Of course—of course. That is to say, I fear, of course not. I have no memory at all for things of importance. But one can never have too many little cousins, can one, young man? Sit thee down next to me—then shall I be indeed a happy man, with my little wife on one side and my little cousin on the other. So— now we are comfortable; and when my coffee comes I shall ask for nothing more. Young man, when you marry, see to it that your wife has many nice little cousins. It is very important. As for my not remembering thee,' he went on, putting one arm round the back of my chair, while the other was round the back of Charlotte's, 'be not offended, for I tell thee that the day after I married my Lot here, I fell into so great an abstraction that I started for a walking tour in the Alps with some friends I met, and for an entire week she passed from my mind. It was at Lucerne. So completely did she pass from it that I omitted to tell her I was going or bid her farewell. I went. Dost thou remember, Lottchen? I came to myself on the top of Pilatus a week after our wedding day. "What ails thee, man?" said my comrades, for I was disturbed. "I must go down at once," I cried; "I have forgotten something." "Bah! you do not need your umbrella up here," they said, for they knew I forget it much. "It is not my umbrella that I have left behind," I cried, "it is my wife." They were surprised, for I had forgotten to tell them I had a wife. And when I got down to Lucerne, there was the poor Lot quite offended.' And he pulled her nearest ear and laughed till his spectacles grew dim.

'Delightful,' whispered Mrs. Harvey-Browne to her son. 'So natural.'

Her son never took his eyes off the Professor, ready to pounce on the first word of wisdom and assimilate it, as a hungry cat might sit ready for the mouse that unaccountably delays.

'Ah yes,' sighed the Professor, stretching out his legs under the table and stirring the coffee the waiter had set before him, 'never forget, young man, that the only truly important thing in life is women. Little round, soft women. Little purring pussy-cats. Eh, Lot? Some of them will not always purr, will they, little Lot? Some of them mew much, some of them scratch, some of them have days when they will only wave their naughty little tails in anger. But all are soft and pleasant, and add much grace to the fireside.'

'How true,' murmured Mrs. Harvey-Browne in a rapture, 'how very, very true. So, so different from Nietzsche.'

'What, thou art silent, little treasure?' he continued, pinching Charlotte's cheek.' Thou lovest not the image of the little cats?'

'No,' said Charlotte; and the word was jerked up red-hot from an interior manifestly molten.

'Well, then, pass me those strawberries that blink so pleasantly from their bed of green, and while I eat pour out of thy dear heart all that it contains concerning pussies, which interest thee greatly as I well know, and all else that it contains and has contained since last I saw thee. For it is long since I heard thy voice, and I have missed thee much. Art thou not my dearest wife?'

Clearly it was time for me to get up and remove the Harvey-Brownes out of earshot. I prepared to do so, but at the first movement the arm along the back of the chair slid down and gripped hold of me.

'Not so restless, not so restless, little cousin,' said the Professor, smiling rosily. 'Did I not tell thee I am happy so? And wilt thou mar the happiness of a good old man?'

'But you have Charlotte, and you must wish to talk to her——'

'Certainly do I wish it. But talking to Charlotte excludeth not the encircling of Elizabeth. And have I not two arms?'

'I want to go and show Mrs. Harvey-Browne the view from the cliff,' I said, appalled at the thought of what Charlotte, when she did begin to speak, would probably say.

'Tut, tut,' said the Professor, gripping me tighter, 'we are very well so. The contemplation of virtuous happiness is at least as edifying for this lady as the contemplation of water from a cliff.'

'Delightful originality,' murmured Mrs. Harvey-Browne.

'Madam, you flatter me,' said the Professor, whose ears were quick.

'Oh no. Professor, indeed, it is not flattery.'

'Madam, I am the more obliged.'

'We have so long wished we could meet you. My son spent the whole of last summer in Bonn trying to do so——'

'Waste of time, waste of time, madam.'

'—and all in vain. And this year we were both there before coming up here and did all we could, but also unfortunately in vain. It really seems as if

Providence had expressly led us to this place to-day.'

'Providence, madam, is continually leading people to places, and then leading them away again. I, for instance, am to be led away again from this one with great rapidity, for I am on foot and must reach a bed by nightfall. Here there is nothing to be had.'

'Oh you must come back to Binz with us,' cried Mrs. Harvey-Browne. 'The steamer leaves in an hour, and I am sure room could be found for you in our hotel. My son would gladly give you his, if necessary; he would feel only too proud if you would take it, would you not, Brosy?'

'Madam, I am overwhelmed by your amiability. You will, however, understand that I cannot leave my wife. Where I go she comes too—is it not so, little treasure? I am only waiting to hear her plans to arrange mine accordingly. I have no luggage. I am very movable. My night attire is on my person, beneath the attire appropriate to the day. In one pocket of my mantle I carry an extra pair of socks. In another my handkerchiefs, of which there are two. And my sponge, damp and cool, is embedded in the crown of my hat. Thus, madam, I am of a remarkable independence. Its one restriction is the necessity of finding a shelter daily before dark. Tell me, little Lot, is there no room for the old husband here with thee?' And there was something so sweet in his smile as he turned to her that I think if she had seen it she must have followed him wherever he went.

But she did not raise her eyes. 'I go to Berlin this evening,' she said. 'I have important engagements, and must leave at once.'

'My dear Frau Nieberlein,' exclaimed the bishop's wife, 'is not this very sudden?'

Brosy, who had been looking uncomfortable for some minutes quite apart from not having got his mouse, pulled out his watch and stood up. 'If we are to catch that steamer, mother, I think it would be wise to start,' he said.

'Nonsense, Brosy, it doesn't go for an hour,' said Mrs. Harvey-Browne, revolted at the notion of being torn from her celebrity in the very moment of finding him.

'I am afraid we must,' insisted Brosy. 'It takes much longer to get down the cliff than one would suppose. And it is slippery—I want to take you down an easier and rather longer way.'

And he carried her off, ruthlessly cutting short her parting entreaties that the Professor would come too, come to-morrow, then, come without fail the next day, then, to Binz; and he took her, as I observed, straight in the direction of the Hertha See as a beginning of the easy descent, and the Hertha See, as everybody knows, is in the exactly contrary direction to the one he ought to have gone; but no doubt he filled up the hour instructively with stories of the ancient heathen rites performed on those mystic shores, and so left Charlotte free to behave to her husband as she chose.

How she did behave I can easily guess, for hurrying off into the pavilion, desirous of nothing except to get out of the way, I had hardly had time to marvel that she should be able to dislike such an old dear, when she burst in. 'Quick, quick—help me to get my things!' she cried, flying up and down the slit of a room and pouncing on the bags stowed away by Gertrud in corners. 'I can just catch the night train at Sassnitz—I'm off to Berlin—I'll write to you from there. Why, if that fool Gertrud hasn't emptied everything out! What a terrible fate yours is, always at the mercy of an overfed underling—a person who empties bags without being asked. Give me those brushes—and the papers. Well, you've seen me dragged down into the depths to-day, haven't you?' And she straightened herself from bending over the bag, a brush in each hand, and looking at me with a most bitter and defiant smile incontinently began to cry.

'Don't cry, Charlotte,' I said, who had been dumbly staring, 'don't cry, my dear. I didn't see any depths. I only saw nice things. Don't go to Berlin—stay here and let us be happy together.'

'Stay here? Never!' And she feverishly crammed things into her bag, and the bag must have been at least as full of tears as of other things, for she cried bitterly the whole time.

Well, women have always been a source of wonderment to me, myself included, who am for ever hurled in the direction of foolishness, for ever unable to stop; and never are they so mysterious, so wholly unaccountable, as in their relations to their husbands. But who shall judge them? The paths of fate are all so narrow that two people bound together, forced to walk abreast, cannot, except they keep perfect step, but push each other against the rocks on either side. So that it behoves the weaker and the lighter, if he would remain unbruised, to be very attentive, very adaptable, very deft.

I saw Charlotte off in one of the waiting waggonettes that was to take her to Sassnitz where the railway begins. 'I'll let you know where I am,' she called out as she was rattled away down the hill; and with a wave of the hand she turned the corner and vanished from my sight, gone once more into those frozen regions where noble and forlorn persons pursue ideals.

Walking back slowly through the trees towards the cliffs I met the Professor looking everywhere for his wife. 'What time does Lot leave?' he cried when he saw me. 'Must she really go?'

'She is gone.'

'No! How long since?'

'About ten minutes.'

'Then I too take that train.'

And he hurried off, clambering with the nimbleness that was all his own into a second waggonette, and disappeared in his turn down the hill. 'Dearest little cousin,' he shouted just before being whisked round the corner, 'permit me to bid thee farewell and wish thee good luck. I shall seriously endeavour to remember thee this time.'

'Do,' I called back, smiling; but he could not have heard.

Once again I slowly walked through the trees to the cliffs. The highest of these cliffs, the Königsstuhl, jutting out into the sea forms a plateau where a few trees that have weathered the winter storms of many years stand in little groups. For a long while I sat on the knotted roots of one of them, listening to the slow wash of the waves on the shingle far below. I saw the ribbon of smoke left by the Harvey-Browne's steamer get thinner and disappear. I watched the sunset-red fade out of the sky and sea, and all the world grow grey and full of secrets. Once, after I had sat there a very long time, I thought I heard the faint departing whistle of a far-distant train, and my heart leapt up with exultation. Oh the gloriousness of freedom and silence, of being alone with my own soul once more! I drew a long, long breath, and stood up and stretched myself in the supreme comfort of complete relaxation.

'You look very happy,' said a rather grudging voice close to me.

It belonged to a Fräulein of uncertain age, come up to the plateau in galoshes to commune in her turn with night and Nature; and I suppose I must have been smiling foolishly all over my face, after the manner of those whose thoughts are pleasant.

A Harvey-Browne impulse seized me to stare at her and turn my back, but I strangled it. 'Do you know why I look happy?' I inquired instead; and my voice was as the voice of turtle-doves.

'No—why?' was the eagerly inquisitive answer.

'Because I am.'

And nodding sweetly I walked away.

THE EIGHTH DAY

FROM STUBBENKAMMER TO GLOWE

When Reason lecturing us on certain actions explains that they are best avoided, and Experience with her sledge-hammers drives the lesson home, why do we, convinced and battered, repeat the actions every time we get the chance? I have known from my youth the opinion of Solomon that he that passeth by and meddleth with strife belonging not to him, is like one that taketh a dog by the ears; and I have a wise relative—not a blood-relation, but still very wise—who at suitable intervals addresses me in the following manner:— 'Don't meddle.' Yet now I have to relate how, on the eighth day of my journey round Rügen, in defiance of Reason, Experience, Solomon, and the wise relative, I began to meddle.

The first desire came upon me in the night, when I could not sleep because of the mosquitoes and the constant coming into the pavilion of late and jovial tourists. The tourists came in in jolly batches till well on towards morning, singing about things like the Rhine and the Fatherland's frontiers, glorious songs and very gory, as they passed my hastily-shut window on their way round to the door. After each batch had gone I got out and cautiously opened the window again, and then waited for the next ones, slaying mosquitoes while I waited; and it was while I lay there sleepless and tormented that the longing to help reunite Charlotte and her husband first entered my head.

It is true that I was bothered for some time trying to arrive at a clear comprehension of what constitutes selfishness, but I gave that up for it only made my head ache. Surely Charlotte, for instance, was intensely selfish to leave her home and, heedless of her husband's unhappiness, live the life she preferred? But was not he equally selfish in wanting to have her back again? For whose happiness would that be? He could not suppose for hers. If she, determined to be unselfish, went home, she would only be pandering to his selfishness. The more she destroyed her individuality and laid its broken remains at his feet, the more she would be developing evil qualities in the acceptor of such a gift. We are taught that our duty is to make each other good and happy, not bad and happy; Charlotte, therefore, would be doing wrong if, making the Professor happy, she also made him bad. Because he had a sweet way with him and she had not, he got all the sympathy, including mine; and of course the whole of that windy mass of biassed superficiality called Public Opinion was on his side. But how can one, if one truly loves a woman, wish her to live a life that must make her wretched? Such love can only be selfish;

accordingly the Professor was selfish. They were both selfish; and if one were not so the other would be more so. And if to be unselfish meant making those about you the opposite, then it must be wrong; and were it conceivable that a whole family should determine to be unselfish and actually carry out the dreadful plan, life in that doomed house would become a perpetual *combat de générosité*, not in any way to be borne. Here it was that my head began to ache. 'What stuff is this?' I thought, veering round suddenly to the easeful simplicity of the old conventions. 'Just to think of it gives me a headache. The only thing I know of that does not give a woman a headache is to live the life for which she was intended—the comfortable life with a brain at rest and a body wholly occupied with benevolences; and if her meekness makes her husband bad, what does that matter in the end to any one but him? Charlotte ought to be very happy with that kind old man. Any woman would be. Her leaving him must have been owing to some trifling misunderstanding. I am sure it would be for her happiness to go back to him. She would grow quite round and mellow. Could I not do something, say something, to get her to give him another trial? I wish—oh, I wish I could!'

Now from time to time the wise relative quoted above amplifies his advice in the following manner:—'Of all forms of meddling that which deals with man and wife is, to the meddler, the most immediately fatal.'

But where are the persons who take advice? I never yet met them. When the first shaft of sunshine slanted through my window it fell on me in my dressing-gown feverishly writing to Charlotte. The eloquence of that letter! I really think it had all the words in it I know, except those about growing round and mellow. Something told me that they would not appeal to her. I put it in an envelope and locked it in my dressing-case till, unconscious of what was in store for her, she should send me her address; and then, full of the glow that warms the doer of good actions equally with the officious, I put on my bathing things, a decent skirt and cloak over them, got out of the window, and went down the cliff to the beach to bathe.

The water was icily cold in the shadow of the cliffs, but it was a wonderful feeling getting all the closeness of the night dashed off me in that vast and splendid morning solitude. Dripping I hurried up again, my skirt and cloak over the soaked bathing dress, my wet feet thrust into shoes I could never afterwards wear, a trickle of salt water marking the way I took. It was just five o'clock as I got in at the window. In another quarter of an hour I was dry and dressed and out of the window a second time—getting in and out of that window had a singular fascination for me—and on my way for an early exploring of the woods.

But those Stubbenkammer woods were destined never to be explored by me;

for I had hardly walked ten minutes along their beechen ways listening to the birds and stopping every few steps to look up at the blue of the sky between the branches, before I came to the Hertha See, a mysterious silent pond of black water with reeds round it and solemn forest paths, and on the moss by the shore of the Hertha See, his eyes fixed on its sullen waters, deep in thought, sat the Professor.

'Don't tell me you have forgotten me again,' I exclaimed anxiously; for his eyes turned from the lake to me as I came over the moss to him in an unchanged abstraction. What was he doing there? He looked exceedingly untidy, and his boots were white with dust.

'Good morning,' I said cheerfully, as he continued to gaze straight through me.

'I have no doubt whatever that this was the place,' he remarked, 'and Klüver was correct in his conjecture.'

'Now what is the use,' I said, sitting down on the moss beside him, 'of talking to me like that when I don't know the beginning? Who is Klüver? And what did he conjecture?'

His eyes suddenly flashed out of their dream, and he smiled and patted my hand. 'Why, it is the little cousin,' he said, looking pleased.

'It is. May I ask what you are doing here?'

'Doing? Agreeing with Klüver that this is undoubtedly the spot.'

'What spot?'

'Tacitus describes it so accurately that there can be no reasonable doubt.'

'Oh—Tacitus. I thought Klüver had something to do with Charlotte. Where is Charlotte?'

'Conceive the procession of the goddess Nerthus, or Hertha, mother of the earth, passing through these sacred groves on the way to bless her children. Her car is covered, so that no eye shall behold her. The priest alone, walking by the side, is permitted to touch it. Wherever she passes holyday is kept. Arms are laid aside. Peace reigns absolute. No man may seek to slay his brother while she who blesses all alike is passing among her children. Then, when she has once more been carried to her temple, in this water thou here seest, in this very lake, her car and its draperies are cleansed by slaves, who, after performing their office, are themselves thrown into the water and left to perish; for they had laid hands on that which was holy, and even to-day, when we are half-hearted in the defence of our adorations and rarely set up altars in our souls, that is a dangerous thing to do.'

'Dear Professor,' I said, 'it is perfectly sweet of you to tell me about the goddess Nerthus, but would you mind, before you go any further, telling me where Charlotte is? When I last saw you you were whirling after her in a waggonette. Did you ever catch her?'

He looked at me a moment, then gave the bulging pocket of his waterproof a sounding slap. 'Little cousin,' he said, 'in me thou beholdest a dreamer of dreams, an unpractical greybeard, a venerable sheep's-head. Never, I suppose, shall I learn to remember, unaided, those occurrences that I fain would not forget. Therefore I assist myself by making notes of them to which I can refer. Unfortunately it seldom happens that I remember to refer. Thou, however, hast reminded me of them. I will now seek them out.' And he dragged different articles from the bulging pocket, laying them carefully on the moss beside him in tidy rows. But the fact of only one of the two handkerchiefs being there nearly put him off the track, so much and so long did he marvel where its fellow could be; also the sight of his extra pair of socks reminded him of the urgent need they were in of mending, and he broke off his search for the note-book to hold each up in turn to me and eloquently lament. *'Nein, nein, was fur Socken!'* he moaned, with a final shake of the head as he spread them out too on the moss.

'Yes, they are very bad,' I agreed for the tenth time.

'Bad! They are emblematic.'

'Will you let me mend them? Or rather,' I hastily added, 'cause them to be mended?' For my aversion to needles is at least as great as Charlotte's.

'No, no—what is the use? There are cupboards full of socks like them in Bonn, skeletons of that which once was socks, mere outlines filled in with holes.'

'And all are emblematic?'

'Every single one.' But this time he looked at me with a twinkle in his eye.

'I don't think,' I said, 'that I'd let my soul be ruffled by a sock. If it offended me I'd throw it away and buy some more.'

'Behold wisdom,' cried the Professor gaily, 'proceeding from the mouth of an intellectual suckling!' And without more ado he flung both the socks into the Hertha See. There they lay, like strange flowers of yellow wool, motionless on the face of the mystic waters.

'And now the note-book?' I asked; for he had relapsed into immobility, and was watching the socks with abstracted eyes.

'Ach yes—the note-book.'

Being heavy, it was at the very bottom of what was more like a sack in size than a pocket; but once he had run his glance over the latest entries he began very volubly to tell me what he had been doing all night. It had been an even busier night than mine. Charlotte, he explained, had left Sassnitz by the Berlin train, and had taken a ticket for Berlin, as he ascertained at the booking-office, a few minutes before he took his. He arrived at the very last moment, yet as he jumped into the just departing train he caught sight of her sitting in a ladies' compartment. She also caught sight of him. 'I therefore gave a sigh of satisfaction,' he continued, 'lit my pipe, and, contemplating the evening heavens from the window, happy in the thought of being so near my little wife, I fell into an abstraction.'

I shook my head. 'These abstractions. Professor,' I observed, 'are inconvenient things to fall into. What had happened by the time you fell out again?'

'I found that I had emerged from my compartment and was standing on the ferry that takes the train across the water to Stralsund. The ancient city rose in venerable majesty——'

'Never mind the ancient city, dearest Professor. Look at your notes again— what was Charlotte doing?'

'Charlotte? She had entirely escaped my memory, so great was the pleasure excited in my breast by the contemplation of the starlit scene before me. But glancing away from the massive towers of Stralsund, my eye fell on the word *"Frauen"* on the window of the ladies' carriage. Instantly remembering Charlotte, I clambered up eager to speak to her. The compartment was empty.'

'She too was contemplating the starlit scene from the deck of the ferry?'

'She was not.'

'Were there no bags in the carriage?'

'Not a bag.'

'What had become of her?'

'She had left the train; and I'll tell thee how. At Bergen, our only stopping-place, we crossed a train returning to Sassnitz. Plentiful applications of drink-money to officials revealed the fact that she had changed into this train.'

'Not very clever,' I thought.

'No, no,' said the Professor, as if he had heard me thinking. 'The little Lot's cleverness invariably falls just short of the demands made upon it. At critical moments, when the choice lies between the substance and the shadow, I have observed she unfailingly chooses the shadow. This comical life she leads, what is it but a pursuit of shadows? However——' And he stopped short, not caring, I suppose, to discuss his wife.

'Where do you think she is now?'

'I conjecture not far from here. I arrived at Sassnitz at one o'clock this morning by the Swedish boat-train. I was told that a lady answering her description had got out there at eleven, taken a fly, and driven into the town. I walked out here to speak with thee, and was only waiting for the breakfast- hour to seek thee out, for she will not, being so near thee, omit to join thee.'

'You must be perfectly exhausted.'

'What I most wish for is breakfast.'

'Then let us go and see if we can't get some. Gertrud will be up by now, and can produce coffee at the shortest notice.'

'Who is Gertrud? Another dear little cousin? If it be so, lead me, I pray thee, at once to Gertrud.'

I laughed, and explaining Gertrud to him helped him pack his pocket again. Then we started for the hotel full of hope, each thinking that if Charlotte were not already there she would very soon turn up.

But Charlotte was not there, nor did she, though we loitered over our coffee till we ended by being as late as the latest tourist, turn up. 'She is certain to come during the day,' said the Professor.

I told him I had arranged to go to Glowe that day, a little place farther along the coast; and he said he would, in that case, engage my vacant pavilion-bedroom for himself and stay that night at Stubbenkammer. 'She is certain to come here,' he repeated; 'and I will not lose her a second time.'

'You won't like the pavilion,' I remarked.

About eleven, there being still no signs of Charlotte, I set out on foot on the first stage of my journey to Glowe, sending the carriage round by road to meet me at Lohme, the place where I meant to stop for lunch, and going myself along the footpath down on the shore. The Professor, who was a great walker and extraordinarily active for his years, came with me part of the way. He intended, he said, to go into Sassnitz that afternoon if Charlotte did not appear before then and make inquiries, and meanwhile he would walk a little with me; so we started very gaily down the same zigzag path up which I had crawled dripping a few hours before. At the bottom of the ravine the shore- path from Stubbenkammer to Lohme begins. It is a continuation of the lovely path from Sassnitz, but, less steep, it keeps closer to the beach. It is a white chalk path running along the foot of cliffs clothed with moss and every kind of wild-flower and fern. Masses of the leaves of lilies of the valley show what it must look like in May, and on the day we walked there the space between the twisted beech trunks—twisted into the strangest contortions under the lash of winter storms—was blue with wild campanula.

What a walk that was. The sea lay close to our feet in great green and blue streaks; the leaves of the beeches on our left seemed carved in gold, they shone so motionless against the sky; and the Professor was so gay, so certain that he was going to find Charlotte, that he almost danced instead of walking. He talked to me, there is no doubt, as he might have talked to quite a little child— of erudition there was not a sign, of wisdom in Brosy's sense not a word; but what of that? The happy result was that I understood him, and I know we were very merry. If I were Charlotte nothing would induce me to stir from the side of a good-natured man who could make me laugh. Why, what a quality in a husband, how precious and how rare. Think of living with a person who looks at the world with the kindliest amused eyes. Imagine having a perpetual spring of pleasant mirth in one's own house, babbling coolly of refreshing things on days when life is dusty. Must not wholesomeness pervade the very cellars and lumber-rooms of such a home? Well, I meant to do all in my power to persuade Charlotte to go into the home again. How delightful to be the means of doing the dear old man beside me a good turn! Meanwhile he walked along happily, all unconscious that I was meditating good turns, perhaps happy for that very reason, and full of confidence in his ability to catch and to keep Charlotte. 'Where she goes I go with her,' he said. 'I now have my summer leisure and can devote myself entirely to her.'

'Do not fall into abstractions then, dear Professor, at important moments,' I said; and inwardly rehearsed the eloquent pleadings with which I meant to shake Charlotte's soul when next I saw her.

We said good-bye where the wood ends and the white path goes out into the sun. 'Be sure you let me know when you meet Charlotte,' I said. 'I want particularly to speak to her. Something really important. Tell her so. And I have a letter for her if I can't see her. Don't forget I sleep at Glowe to-night. I'll telegraph where I stay to-morrow. Don't forget. Won't you be very nice and make notes of it?'

He promised, wished me Godspeed, kissed my hand, and turned back into the wood swinging his stick and humming gay little tunes; and I went on in the sun to Lohme.

There I bathed again, a delicious solitary bathe just as the woman was locking up for the day; and afterwards, when she had gone away up the cliff to her dinner, I sat on the empty beach in the sun and thought of all I was going to say to Charlotte. It interested me so much that I forgot I had meant to lunch at

Lohme, and when I remembered it it was already time to go up and meet the carriage. It did not matter, as the midday meal is the best one to leave out, and Lohme is not the kind of place I would ever want to lunch in. The beach at the foot of the cliffs is quiet and pleasant, and from it you can see the misty headland of Arkona with its lighthouse, the northernmost point of the island, far away on the left. Lohme itself is a small group of hotels and lodging- houses on the top of low cliffs, very small and modest compared even to Binz and Sassnitz, which are not very big themselves, and much more difficult to get at. There is no railway nearer than Sassnitz, and the few steamers that stop there disgorge the tourist who wants to get out into a small boat and steam away leaving him to his fate, which is only a nice one on quite calm days. Safely on land he climbs up a shadeless zigzag path which must be beautiful in June, for the cliffs are thickly covered with wild-rose bushes, and at the top finds himself among the lodging-houses of Lohme. The only thing I saw when I got to the top that made me linger was a row of tubs filled with nasturtiums along the little terrace in front of the first hotel I passed. The way those nasturtiums blazed against the vast blue curtain of sea and sky that hung behind them, with no tree or bush anywhere near to shadow their fierce splendour, was a sight well worth coming to Lohme for. There is no shade anywhere at Lohme. It stands entirely exposed out in the open beyond the Stubbenkammer forest, and on a dull day must be dreary. It is, I imagine, a convenient place for quiet persons who do not wish to spend much, and the air is beautiful. In spite of the heat I felt as if it were the most bracing air I had yet come across on my journey.

The carriage was waiting just outside the empty, sunny little place, in a road that winds chalkily between undulating fields in the direction of Glowe. Gertrud's face wore a look of satisfaction as she got into her old seat beside me and took out her knitting. She had not been able to knit during those few dreadful days in which her place had been usurped, and she had bumped after us ignominiously in a cart; and how pleasant it was not to have the ceaseless rattle just behind. Yes; it became more and more clear that Charlotte ought to be in her own home with her husband. Her being there would undoubtedly promote the general peace. And why should she go about stirring people up and forcing them to be dogged by luggage carts?

The road wound higher through the cornfields, dwindling at last into a stony track. The country heaved away in ample undulations on either side. There were no trees, but so many flowers that even the ruts were blue with chickory. On the right, over the cornfields, lay the Baltic. I could still see Arkona in front of me on the dim edge of the world. Down at our feet stretched the calm silver of the Jasmunder Bodden, the biggest of those inland seas that hollow out the island into a mere frame; and a tongue of pine-forest, black and narrow, curved northwards between its pale waters and the vigorous blue of the sea. I stopped the carriage as I love to do in lonely places, and there was no sound but a faint whispering in the corn.

We drove down over stones between grassy banks to a tiny village with a very ancient church and the pleasing name of Bobbin. I looked wistfully up at the church on its mound as we passed below it. It was very old—six centuries the guide-book said—and fain would I have gone into it; but I knew it would be locked, and did not like to disturb the parson for the key. The parson himself came along the road at that moment, and he looked so kind, and his eye was so mild that I got out and inquired of him with what I hope was an engaging modesty whether the guide-book were correct about the six centuries. He was amiability itself. Not only, he said, was the church ancient, but interesting. Would I like to see it? 'Oh please.' Then would I come to the parsonage while he got the key? 'Oh thank you.'

The Bobbin parsonage is a delightful little house of the kind that I dream of for my declining years, with latticed windows and a vine. It stands in a garden so pretty, so full of narrow paths disappearing round corners, that I longed far more to be shown where they led to than to be shown the inside of the church. Several times I said things that ought to have resulted in my being taken along them, but the parson heeded not; his talk was and remained wholly church. A friendly dog lay among croquet hoops on the lawn, a pleasant, silent dog, who wagged his tail when I came round the corner and saw no reason why he should bark and sniff. No one else was to be seen. The house was so quiet it seemed asleep while I waited in the parlour. The parson took me down a little path to the church, talking amiably on the way. He was proud, he said, of his church, very proud on week-days; on Sundays so few people came to the services that his pride was quenched by the aspect of the empty seats. A bell began to toll as we reached the door. In answer to my inquiring look he said it was the *Gebetglocke*, the prayer-bell, and was rung three times a day, at eight, and twelve, and four, so that the scattered inhabitants of the lonely country- side, the sower in the field, the housewife among her pots, the fisherman on the Bodden, or over there, in quiet weather, on the sea, might hear it and join together spiritually at those hours in a common prayer. 'And do they?' I asked. He shrugged his shoulders and murmured of hopes.

It is the quaintest church. The vaulted chancel is the oldest part, and there is an altarpiece put there by the Swedish Field-Marshal Wrangel, who in the seventeenth century lived in a turreted Schloss near by that I had seen from the hills. A closed-in seat high up on the side of the chancel was where he sat; it has latticed windows and curiously-painted panels, with his arms in the middle panel and those of Prince Putbus, to whom the Schloss now belongs, on either side. The parson took me up into the gallery and showed me a picture of John the Baptist's head, just off, with Herodias trying to pull out its tongue. I said I thought it nasty, and he told me it had been moved up there because the lady downstairs over whose head it used to hang was made ill by it every Sunday. Had the parishioners up in the gallery thicker skins, I asked? But there was no question of skins, because the congregation never overflowed into the galleries. There is another picture up there, the Supper at Emmaus, with the Scripture account written underneath in Latin. The parson read this aloud, and his eyes, otherwise so mild, woke into gleams of enthusiasm. It sounded very dignified and compressed to ears accustomed to Luther's lengthy rendering of the same thing. I remarked how beautiful it was, and with a pleased smile he at once read it again, and then translated it into Greek, lingering lovingly over each of the beautiful words. I sat listening in the cool of the dusty little gallery, gazing out at the summer fields and the glistening water of the Bodden through the open door. His gentle voice made a soft droning in the emptiness. A swallow came in and skimmed about anxiously, trying to get out again.

'The painted pulpit was also given by Wrangel,' said the parson, as we went downstairs.

'He seems to have given a great deal.'

'He needed to, to make good all his sins,' he replied with a smile. 'Many were the sins he committed.'

I smiled too. Posterity in the shape of the parishioners of Bobbin have been direct gainers by Wrangel's sins.

'Good, you see, comes out of evil,' I observed.

He shook his head.

'Well, painted pulpits do then,' I amended; for who that is in his senses would contradict a parson?

I gave a last glance at the quaint pulpit across which a shaft of coloured sunlight lay, inquired if I might make an offering for the poor of Bobbin, made it, thanked my amiable guide, and was accompanied by him out into the heat that danced among the tombstones down to the carriage. To the last he was mild and kind, tucking the Holland cover round me with the same solicitude that he might have shown in a January snowstorm.

Glowe, my destination, is not far from Bobbin. On the way we passed the Schloss with the four towers where the wicked Wrangel committed all those sins that presently crystallised into a painted pulpit. The Schloss, called the Spyker Schloss, is let to a farmer. We met him riding home, to his coffee, I suppose, it being now nearly five, and I caught a glimpse of a beautiful old garden with ancient pyramids of box, many flowers, broad alleys, and an aggressively new baby in a perambulator beneath the trees, rending the holy quiet of the afternoon with its shrieks. They pursued us quite a long way along the bald high road that brought us after another mile to Glowe.

Glowe is a handful of houses built between the high road and the sea. There is nothing on the other side of the road but a great green plain stretching to the Bodden. We stopped at the first inn we came to—it was almost the first house —a meek, ugly little place, with the following severe advice to tourists hanging up in the entrance:—

Sag was Du willst kurz und bestimmt.
Lass alle schöne Phrasen fehlen;
Wer nutzlos unsere Zeit uns nimmt
Bestiehlt uns—und Du sollst nicht stehlen.

Accordingly I was very short with the landlord when he appeared, left out most of my articles, all of my adjectives, clipped my remarks of weaknesses such as please and thank you, and became at last ferociously monosyllabic in my effort to give satisfaction. My room was quite nice, with two windows looking across the plain. Cows were tethered on it almost to where the Bodden glittered in the sun, and it was scattered over with great pale patches of clover. On the left was the Spyker Schloss, with the spire of Bobbin church behind it. Far away in front, blue with distance but still there, rose as usual the round tower of the ubiquitous Jagdschloss. I leaned out into the sunshine, and the air was full of the freshness of the pines I had seen from the heights, and the freshness of the invisible sea. Some one downstairs was playing sadly on a cello, tunes that reeked of *Weltschmerz*, and overhead the larks shrilled an exquisite derision.

I thought I would combine luncheon, tea, and dinner in one meal, and so have done with food for the day, so I said to the landlord, still careful to be *kurz und bestimmt*: 'Bring food.' I left it to him to decide what food, and he brought me fried eels and asparagus first, sausages with cranberries second, and coffee with gooseberry jam last. It was odd and indigestible, but quite clean. Afterwards I went down to the shore through an ear-wiggy, stuffy little garden at the back, where mosquitoes hummed round the heads of silent bath- guests sitting statuesquely in tiny arbours, and flies buzzed about me in a cloud. On the shore the fishermen's children were wading about and playing in the parental smacks. The sea looked so clear that I thought it would be lovely to have yet another bathe; so I sent a boy to call Gertrud, and set out along the beach to the very distant and solitary bathing-house. It was clean and convenient, but there were more local children playing in it, darting in and out of the dusky cells like bats. No one was in charge, and rows of towels and clothes hung up on hooks only asking to be used. Gertrud brought my things and I got in. The water seemed desperately cold and stinging, colder far than the water at Stubbenkammer that morning, almost intolerably cold; but perhaps it only seemed so because of the eels and cranberries that had come too. The children were deeply interested, and presently undressed and followed me in, one girl bathing only in her pinafore. They were very kind to me, showed me the least stony places, encouraged me when I shivered, and made a tremendous noise,—I concluded for my benefit, because after every outburst they paused and looked at me with modest pride. When I got out they got out too and insisted on helping Gertrud wring out my things. I distributed *pfennings* among them when I was dressed, and they clung to me closer than ever after that, escorting me in a body back to the inn, and hardly were they to be persuaded to leave me at the door.

That evening was one of profound peace. I sat at my bedroom window, my body and soul in a perfect harmony of content. My body had been so much bathed and walked about all day that it was incapable of intruding its shadow on the light of the soul, and remained entirely quiescent, pleased to be left quiet and forgotten in an easy-chair. The light of my soul, feeble as it had been since Thiessow, burned that night clear and steady, for once more I was alone and could breathe and think and rejoice over the serenity of the next few days that lay before me like a fair landscape in the sun. And when I had come to the end of the island and my drive I would go home and devote ardent weeks to bringing Charlotte and the Professor together again. If necessary I would even ask her to come and stay with me, so much stirred was I by the desire to do good. Match-making is not a work I have cared about since one that I made with infinite enthusiasm resulted a few months later in reproaches of a bitter nature being heaped on my head by the persons matched; but surely to help reunite two noble souls, one of which is eager to be reunited and the other only does not know what it really wants, is a blessed work? Anyhow the contemplation of it made me glow.

After the sun had dropped behind the black line of pines on the right the plain seemed to wrap itself in peace. The road beneath my window was quite quiet except for the occasional clatter past of a child in wooden shoes. Of all the places I had stayed at in Rügen this place was the most countrified and innocent. Idly I sat there, enjoying the soft dampness of the clover-laden air, counting how many stars I could see in the pale sky, watching the women who had been milking the cows far away across the plain come out of the dusk towards me carrying their frothing pails. It must have been quite late, for the plain had risen up in front of my window like a great black wall, when I heard a rattle of wheels on the high road in the direction of Bobbin. At first very faint it grew rapidly louder. 'What a time to come along this lonely road,' I thought; and wondered how it would be farther along where the blackness of the pines began. But the cart pulled up immediately beneath my window, and leaning out I saw the light from the inn door stream on to a green hat that I knew, and familiar shoulders draped in waterproof clothing.

'Why, what in the world——' I exclaimed.

The Professor looked up quickly. 'Lot left Sassnitz by steamer this morning,' he cried in English and in great jubilation. 'She took a ticket for Arkona. I received full information in Sassnitz, and started at once. This horned cattle of a coachman, however, will drive me no farther. I therefore appeal to thee to take me on in thy carriage.'

'What, never to-night?'

'To-night? Certainly to-night. Who knows where she will go to-morrow?'

'But Arkona is miles away—we should never get there—it would kill the horses'——

'Tut, tut, tut,' was all the answer I got, ejected with a terrific impatience; and much accompanying clinking of money made it evident that the person described as horned cattle was being paid.

I turned and stared at Gertrud, who had been arrested by this conversation in the act of arranging my bed, with a stare of horror. Then in a flash I saw which was the one safe place, and I flung myself all dressed into the bed. 'Go down, Gertrud,' I said, pulling the bedclothes up to my chin, 'and say what you like to the Professor. Tell him I am in bed and nothing will get me out of it. Tell him I'll drive him to-morrow to any place on earth. Yes—tell him that. Tell him I promise, I promise faithfully, to see him through. Go on, and lock me in.' For I heard a great clamour on the stairs, and who knows what an agitated wise man may not do, and afterwards pretend he was in an abstraction?

But I had definitely pledged myself to a course of active meddling.

THE NINTH DAY

FROM GLOWE TO WIEK

The landlord was concerned, Gertrud told me, when he heard we were going to drive to Arkona at an hour in the morning known practically only to birds. Professor Nieberlein, after fuming long and audibly in the passage downstairs, had sent her up with a request, made in his hearing, that the carriage might be at the door for that purpose at four o'clock.

'At that hour there is no door,' said the landlord.

'Tut, tut,' said the Professor.

The landlord raised his hands and described the length and sandiness of the way.

'Three o'clock, then,' was all the Professor said to that, calling after Gertrud.

'Oh, oh!' was my eloquent exclamation when she came in and told me; and I pulled the bedclothes up still higher, as though seeking protection in them from the blows of Fate.

'It is possible August may oversleep himself,' suggested Gertrud, seeing my speechless objection to starting for anywhere at three o'clock.

'So it is; I think it very likely,' I said, emerging from the bedclothes to speak earnestly. 'Till six o'clock, I should think he would sleep—at *least* till six; should not you, Gertrud?'

'It is very probable,' said Gertrud; and went away to give the order.

August did. He slept so heavily that eight o'clock found the Professor and myself still at Glowe, breakfasting at a little table in the road before the house on flounders and hot gooseberry jam. The Professor was much calmer, quite composed in fact, and liked the flounders, which he said were as fresh as young love. He had been very tired after his long day and the previous sleepless night, and when he found I was immovable he too had gone to bed and overslept himself Immediately on seeing him in the morning I told him what I felt sure was true—that Charlotte, knowing I would come to Arkona in the course of my drive round the coast, had gone on there to wait for me. 'So there is really no hurry,' I added.

'Hurry? certainly not,' he said, gay and reasonable after his good night. 'We will enjoy the present, little cousin, and the admirable flounders.' And he told me the story of the boastful man who had vaunted the loftiness of his rooms to a man poorer than himself except in wit; and the poorer man, weary of this talk of ceilings, was goaded at last to relate how in his own house the rooms were so low that the only things he could ever have for meals were flounders; and though I had heard the story before I took care to exhibit a decent mirth in the proper place, ending by laughing with all my heart only to see how the Professor laughed and wiped his eyes.

It was a close day of sunless heat. The sky was an intolerable grey glare. There was no wind, and the flies buzzed in swarms about the horses' heads as we drove along the straight white road between the pines towards Arkona. Gertrud was once more relegated to a cart, but she did not look nearly so grim as before; she obviously preferred the Professor to his wife, which was a lapse from the normal discretion of her manners, Gertruds not being supposed to have preferences, and certainly none that are obvious.

From Glowe the high road goes through the pines almost without a bend to the next place, Juliusruh, about an hour and a half north of Glowe. We did not pass a single house. The way was absolutely lonely, and its stuffiness dreadful. We could see neither the Baltic nor the Bodden, though both were only a few yards off on the other side of the pines. At Juliusruh, a flat, airless place of new lodging-houses, we did get a glimpse of a mud-coloured sea; and after Juliusruh, the high road and the pines abruptly ending, we got into the open country of whose sandiness the Glowe landlord had spoken with uplifted hands. As we laboured along at a walking pace the greyness of the sky grew denser, and it began to rain. This was the first rain I had had during my journey, and it was delicious. The ripe corn on our left looked a deeper gold against the dull sky; the ditches were like streaks of light, they were so crammed with yellow flowers; the air grew fragrant with wetness; and, best of all, the dust left off. The Professor put up his umbrella, which turned out to be so enormous when open that we could both sit comfortably under it and keep dry; and he was in such good spirits at being fairly on Charlotte's tracks that I am inclined to think it was the most agreeable drive I had had in Rügen. The traveller, however, who does not sit under one umbrella with a pleased Professor on the way to Arkona must not suppose that he too will like this bit best, for he will not.

The road turns off sharply inland at Vitt, a tiny fisher-hamlet we came upon unexpectedly, hidden in a deep clough. It is a charming little place—a few fishermen's huts, a minute inn, and a great many walnut trees. Passing along the upper end of the clough we looked straight down its one shingly street to the sea washing among rocks. Big black fisher-boats were hauled up almost into the street itself. A forlorn artist's umbrella stood all alone half-way down, sheltering an unfinished painting from the gentle rain, while the artist—I supposed him to be the artist because of his unique neck arrangements—watched it wistfully from the inn door. As Vitt even in rain was perfectly charming I can confidently recommend it to the traveller; for on a sunny day it must be quite one of the prettiest spots in Rügen. If I had been alone I would certainly have stayed there at least one night, though the inn looked as if its beds were feather and its butter bad; but I now had a mission, and he who has a mission spends most of his time passing the best things by.

'Is not that a little paradise?' I exclaimed.

The Professor quoted Dr. Johnson and Charles Lamb, remarking that he understood their taste better than that of those persons who indulge in ill-defined and windy raptures about scenery and the weather.

'But we cannot all have the tastes of great scholars,' I said rather coldly, for I did not like the expression windy raptures.

'If thou meanest me by great scholars, thou female babe, know that my years and poor rudiments of learning have served only to make it clear to me that the best things in life are of the class to which sitting under one umbrella with a dear little cousin belong. I endeavoured yesterday to impress this result of experience on the long Englishman, but he is still knee-deep in theories, and cannot yet see the simple and the close at hand.'

'I don't care one little bit for the umbrella form of joy,' I said obstinately. 'It is the blankest dulness compared to the joy to be extracted from looking at a place like Vitt in fine weather.'

'Tut, tut,' said the Professor, 'talk not to me of weather. Thou dost not mean it from thy heart.' And he arranged the rug afresh round me so that I should not get wet, and inquired solicitously why I did not wear a waterproof cloak like his, which was so very *praktisch*.

From Vitt the road to Arkona describes a triangle of which the village of Putgarten is the apex, and round which it took us half an hour to drive. We got to Arkona, which consists solely of a lighthouse with an inn in it, about one.

'Now for the little Lot,' cried the Professor leaping out into the rain and hastening towards the emerging landlord, while I hurriedly rehearsed the main points of my arguments.

But Charlotte was not there. She had been there, the landlord said, the previous afternoon, having arrived by steamer; had asked for a bedroom, been shown one, but had wanted better accommodation than he could give. Anyhow after drinking coffee she had hired a conveyance and had gone on to Wiek.

The Professor was terribly crestfallen. 'We will go on, then,' he said. 'We will at once proceed to Wiek. Where Wiek is, I conclude we shall ultimately discover.'

'I know where it is—it's on the map.'

'I never doubted it.'

'I mean I know the way from here. I was going there anyhow, and Charlotte knew that. But we can't go on yet, dear Professor. The horses would never get us there. It must be at least ten miles off, and awful sand the whole way.'

It took me some time and many words to convince him that nothing would make me move till the horses had had a feed and a rest. 'We'll only stay here a few hours,' I comforted, 'and get to Wiek anyhow to-day.'

'But who can tell whether she will be there two nights running?' cried the Professor, excitedly striding about in the mud.

'Why, we can, when we get there, and it's no use bothering till we are there. But I'm sure she'll wait till I come. Let us go in out of the rain.'

'I will hire a cart,' he announced with great determination.

'What, and go on without me?'

'I tell thee I will hire a cart. No time shall be lost.'

And he ran back again to the landlord who was watching us from the door with much disapproval; for I suppose Charlotte's refusal to consider his accommodation worthy of her had not disposed him well towards her friends, and possibly he considered the Professor's rapid movements among the puddles too unaccountable to be nice. There was no cart, he said, absolutely none; and the Professor, in a state of fuming dejection, was forced to what resignation he could muster.

During this parleying I had been sitting alone under the umbrella, the rain falling monotonously on its vast surface, running off the glazed lid of my yellow bandbox in streams, and dripping from the brim of August's hat down his patient neck. A yard or two behind sat Gertrud on the hold-all, dimly visible through the cloud of steam rising from the back of her soaked cart- horse. I could hear the sea at the foot of the cliff sluggishly heaving on and off the shingle, and I could see it over the edge of the cliff to the east, and here for the first time round the bend of the island to the north. It was flat, oily, and brown. Never was such a dreary sea or such a melancholy spot. I got out and went into the house feeling depressed.

The landlord led us into a room at the back, the room in front being for the use of fishermen wishing to drink. Clouds of smoke and a great clamour smote our senses when he opened the door. The room was full of what looked like an excursion; about thirty people, male and female, sitting at narrow tables eating, chattering, singing, and smoking all at once. Three specially variegated young women, dressed in the flimsiest of fine-weather clothes, all damp muslin and feathers, pretty girls with pronounced hair arrangements, were smoking cigarettes; and in the corner near the door, demure and solitary, sat another pretty young woman in black, with a very small bonnet trimmed with a very big Alsatian bow on the back of a very elaborately curled head. Her eyes were discreetly fixed on a Wiener Schnitzel that she was eating with a singular mincingness; and all those young men who could not get near the girls in muslin, were doing their utmost to attract this one's notice.

'We can't stay here,' I whispered to the Professor; 'it is too dreadful.'

'Dreadful? It is humanity, little cousin. Humanity at its happiest—in other words, at its dinner.'

And he pulled off his cloak and hung up his hat with a brisk cheerfulness at which I, who had just seen him striding about among puddles, rent with vexation, could only marvel.

'But there is no room,' I objected.

'There is an ample sufficiency of room. We shall sit there in the corner by the young lady in black.'

'Well, you go and sit there, and I'll go out into that porch place over there, and get some air.'

'Never did I meet any one needing so much air. Air! Has thou not, then, been aired the entire morning?'

But I made my way through the smoke to a door standing open at the other end that led into a little covered place, through which was the garden. I put my head gratefully round the corner to breathe the sweet air. The garden is on the west side of the lighthouse on ground falling steeply away to the flat of the cornfields that stretch between Arkona and Putgarten. It is a pretty place full of lilies—in flower that day—and of poplars, those most musical of trees. Rough steps cut in the side of the hill lead down out of the garden to a footpath through the rye to Putgarten; and on the top step, as straight and motionless as the poplars, stood two persons under umbrellas, gazing in silence at the view. Oh, unmistakable English backs! And most unmistakable of all backs, the backs of the Harvey-Brownes.

I pulled my head into the porch again with a wrench, and instinctively turned to flee; but there in the corner of the room sat the Professor, and I could hear him being pleasant to the young person in the Alsatian bow. I did not choose to interrupt him, for she was obviously Mrs. Harvey-Browne's maid; but I did wonder whether the bishop had grieved at all over the manifest unregeneracy of the way she did her hair. Hesitating where to go, and sure of being ultimately caught wherever I went, I peeped again in a sort of fascination at the two mackintoshed figures outlined against the lowering heavens; and as so often happens, the persons being looked at turned round.

'My *dear* Frau X., you here too? When did you arrive in this terrible place?' cried Mrs. Harvey-Browne, hurrying towards me through the rain with outstretched hand and face made up of welcome and commiseration. 'This is too charming—to meet you again, but here! Imagine it, we were under the impression it was a place one could stay at, and we brought all our luggage and left our comfortable Binz for good. It is impossible to be in that room. We were just considering what we could do, and feeling really desperate. Brosy, is not this a charming surprise?'

Brosy smiled, and said it was very charming, and he wished it would leave off raining. He supposed I was only driving through on my way round?

'Yes,' I said, a thousand thoughts flying about in my head.

'Have you seen anything more of the Nieberleins?' asked Mrs. Harvey-Browne, shutting her umbrella, and preparing to come inside the porch too.

'My cousin left that evening, as you know,' I said.

'Yes; I could not help wondering——' began Mrs. Harvey-Browne; but was interrupted by her son, who asked where I was going to sleep that night.

'I think at Wiek,' I answered.

'Isn't Wiek a little place on the——' began Brosy; but was interrupted by his mother, who asked if the Professor had followed his wife.

'Yes,' I said.

'I confess I was surprised——' began Mrs. Harvey-Browne; but was interrupted by her son, who asked whether I thought Lohme possessed an hotel where one could stay.

'I should think so from the look of it as I passed through,' I said.

'Because——' began Brosy; but was interrupted by his mother, who asked whether I had heard anything of the dear Professor since he left. 'Delightful genius,' she added enthusiastically.

'Yes,' I said.

'I suppose he and his wife will go back to Bonn now?'

'Soon, I hope.'

'Did you say he had gone to Berlin? Is he there now?'

'No, he isn't.'

'Have you seen him again?'

'Yes; he came back to Stubbenkammer.'

'Indeed? With his wife?'

'No; Charlotte was not with him.'

'Indeed?'

Never was a more expressive Indeed.

'My cousin changed her plans about Berlin,' I said hastily, disturbed by this expressiveness, 'and came back too. But she didn't care for Stubbenkammer. She is waiting for me—for us—at Wiek. She is waiting there till I—till we come.'

'Oh really? And the Professor?'

'The Professor goes to Wiek, too, of course.'

Mrs. Harvey-Browne gazed at me a moment as though endeavouring to arrange her thoughts. 'Do forgive me,' she said, 'for seeming stupid, but I don't quite understand where the Professor is. He was at Stubbenkammer, and he will be at Wiek; but where is he now?'

'In there,' I said, with a nod in the direction of the dining-room; and I wished with all my heart that he wasn't.

'In there?' cried the bishop's wife. 'Brosy, do you hear? How very delightful. Let us go to him at once.' And she rustled into the room, followed by Brosy and myself. 'You go first, dear Frau X.,' she turned round to say, daunted by the clouds of smoke, and all the chairs and people who had to be got out of the way; for by this time the tourists had finished dining, and had pushed their chairs out into the room to talk together more conveniently, and the room was dim with smoke. 'You know where he is. I can't tell you how charmed I am; really most fortunate. He seems to be with an English friend,' she added, for the revellers, having paused in their din to stare at us, the Professor's cheery voice was distinctly heard inquiring in English of some person or persons unseen whether they knew the difference between a canary and a grand piano.

'Always in such genial spirits,' murmured Mrs. Harvey-Browne rapturously.

Here there was a great obstruction, a group of people blocking the passage down the room and having to be got out of the way before we could pass; and when the scraping of their chairs and their grumbles had ceased we caught the Professor's conversation a little farther on. He was saying, 'I cannot in that case, my dear young lady, caution you with a sufficient earnestness to be of an extreme care when purchasing a grand piano——'

'I don't ever think of doing such a thing,' interrupted a shrill female voice, at whose sound Mrs. Harvey-Browne made an exclamation.

'Tut, tut. I am putting a case. Suppose you wished to purchase a grand piano, and did not know, as you say you do not, the difference between it——'

'I shan't wish, though. I'd be a nice silly to.'

'Nay, but suppose you did wish——'

'What's the good of supposing silly things like that? You *are* a funny old man.'

'Andrews?' said Mrs. Harvey-Browne, at this point emerging on the absorbed couple, and speaking with a languid gentleness that curled slightly upwards into an interrogation at the end.

Andrews, whose face had been overspread by the expression that accompanies titters, started to her feet and froze before our eyes into the dumb passivity of the decent maid. The Professor hardly gave himself time to bow and kiss Mrs. Harvey-Browne's hand before he poured forth his pleasure that this charming young lady should be of her party. 'Your daughter, madam, I doubt not?'

'My maid,' said Mrs. Harvey-Browne, in a curdled kind of voice. 'Andrews, please see about the luggage. She *is* rather a nice-looking girl, I suppose,' she conceded, anxious to approve of all the Professor said and did.

'Nice-looking? She is so exceedingly pretty, madam, that I could only conclude she must be your daughter.'

This elementary application of balm at once soothed Mrs. Harvey-Browne into a radiance of smiles perplexing in conjunction with her age and supposed superiority to vanities. Forgetful of her objections to German crowds and smoke she sat down in the chair vacated by Andrews, made the Professor sit down again in his, and plunged into an exuberant conversation, which began by an invitation so warm that it almost seemed on fire to visit herself and the bishop before the summer was over in the episcopal glories of Babbacombe. This much I heard as I slipped away into the peace of the front room. Brosy came after me. To him the picture of the Professor being wrapped about in Mrs. Harvey-Browne's amenities was manifestly displeasing.

The front room seemed very calm and spacious after what we had just been in. A few fishermen were drinking beer at the bar; in a corner sat Andrews and Gertrud, beginning a necessarily inarticulate acquaintance over the hold- alls; both window and door were open, and the rain came down straight and steady, filling the place with a soft murmuring and dampness. Across the clearness of my first decision that the Professor must be an absolutely delightful person to be always with, had crept a slight film of doubt. There were some things about him that might possibly, I began in a dim way to see, annoy a wife. He seemed to love Charlotte, and he had seemed to be very fond of me—anyhow, never before had I been so much patted in so short a space of time. Yet the moment he caught sight of the Alsatian bow he forgot my presence and existence, forgot the fluster he had been in to get on after his wife, and attached himself to it with a vehemence that no one could be expected to like. A shadowy conviction began to pervade my mind that the sooner I handed him over to Charlotte and drove on again alone the better. Surely Charlotte *ought* to go back to him and look after him; why should I be obliged to drive round Rügen first with one Nieberlein and then with the other?

'The ways of Fate are truly eccentric,' I remarked, half to myself, going to the door and gazing out into the wet.

'Because they have led you to Arkona on a rainy day?' asked Brosy.

'Because of that and because of heaps of other things,' I said; and sitting down at a table on which lay a bulky tome with much-thumbed covers, I began rather impatiently to turn over its pages.

But I had not yet reached the limits of what Fate can and will do to a harmless woman who only asks to be left unnoticed; for while Brosy and I were studying this book, which is an ancient visitor's book of 1843 kept by the landlord's father or grandfather, I forget which, and quite the best thing Arkona possesses, so that I advise the traveller, whose welfare I do my best at intervals to promote, not to leave Arkona without having seen it,—while, I say, we were studying this book, admiring many of its sketches, laughing over the inevitable ineptitudes that seem to drop with so surprising a facility from the pens of persons who inscribe their names, examining with awe the signatures of celebrated men who came here before they were celebrated,— Bismarck's as assessor in 1843, Caprivi's as lieutenant, Waldersee's also as lieutenant, and others of the kind,—while, I repeat, we were innocently studying this book, Fate was busy tucking up her sleeves preparing to hit me harder than ever.

'It was not Fate,' interrupted the wise relative before alluded to, as I sat after my return recounting my adventures and trying to extract sympathy, 'it was the first consequence of your having meddled. If you had not——'

Well, well. The great comfort about relatives is that though they may make what assertions they like you need not and do not believe them; and it was Fate and nothing but Fate that had dogged me malevolently all round Rügen and joined me here at Arkona once more to Mrs. Harvey-Browne. In she came while we were bending over the book, followed by the Professor, who walked as a man may walk in a dream, his eyes fixed on nothing, and asked me without more ado whether I would let her share my carriage as far as Wiek.

'Then, you see, dear Frau X., I shall get there,' she observed.

'But why do you want to get there?' I asked, absolutely knocked over this time by the fists of Fate.

'Oh why not? We must go somewhere, and quite the most natural thing to do is to join forces. You agree, don't you, Brosy dear? The Professor thinks it an excellent plan, and is charming enough to want to relinquish his seat to me if you will have me, are you not, Professor? However I only ask to be allowed to sit on the small seat, for the last thing I wish to do is to disturb anybody. But I fear the Professor will not allow——' and she stopped and looked with arch pleasantness at the Professor who murmured abstractedly 'Certainly, certainly '—which, of course, might mean anything.

'My dear mother——' began Brosy in a tone of strong remonstrance.

'Oh I'm sure it is the best thing we can do, Brosy. I did ask the landlord about hiring a fly, and there is no such thing. It will only be as far as Wiek, and I hear that is not so very far. You don't mind do you, dear Frau X.?'

'Mind?' I cried, wriggling out a smile, 'mind? But how will your son I don't quite see—and your maid?'

'Oh Brosy has his bicycle, and if you'll let the luggage be put in your luggage cart Andrews can quite well sit beside your maid. Of course we will share expenses, so that it will really be mutually advantageous.'

Mrs. Harvey-Browne being one of those few persons who know exactly what they want, did as she chose with wavering creatures like myself. She also did as she chose with Brosy, because the impossibility of publicly rebuking one's mother shut his mouth. She even did as she chose with the Professor, who, declaring that sooner than incommode the ladies he would go in the luggage cart, was in the very act as we were preparing to start off of nimbly climbing on to the trunk next to the one on which Andrews sat, when he found himself hesitating, coming down again, getting into the victoria, subsiding on to the little seat, and all in obedience to a clear something in the voice of Mrs. Harvey-Browne.

Never did unhappy celebrity sit more wretchedly than the poor Professor. It was raining so hard that we were obliged to have the hood up, and its edge came to within an inch of his nose—would have touched it quite if he had not sat as straight and as far back as possible. He could not, therefore, put up his umbrella, and was reduced, while water trickled ceaselessly off the hood down his neck, to pretending with great heroism that he was perfectly comfortable. It was impossible to sit under the snug hood and contemplate the drenched Professor outside it. It was impossible to let an old man of seventy, and an old man, besides, of such immense European value, catch his death before my very eyes. Either he must come between us and be what is known as bodkin, or some one must get out and walk; and the bodkin solution not commending itself to me it was plain that if some one walked it must be myself.

In an instant the carriage was stopped, protestations filled the air, I got out, the Professor was transferred to my place, the bishop's wife turned deaf ears to his entreaties that he might go in the luggage cart and hold his big umbrella over the two poor drowning maids, the hood became vocal with arguments, suggestions, expostulations, apologies—and 'Go on, August,' I interrupted; and dropped behind into sand and silence.

We were already beyond Putgarten, in a flat, uninteresting country of deep sand and treeless, hedgeless cornfields. I had no umbrella, but a cloak with a hood to it which I drew over my head, throwing Gertrud my hat when she too presently heaved past in a cloud of expostulations. 'Go on, go on,' I called to the driver with a wave of my hand seeing him hesitate; and then stood waiting for Brosy who was some little way behind pushing his bicycle dismally through the sand, meditating no doubt on the immense difficulties of dealing with mothers who do things one does not like. When he realised that the solitary figure with the peaked hood outlined against the sullen grey background was mine he pushed along at a trot, with a face of great distress. But I had no difficulty in looking happy and assuring him that I liked walking, because I really was thankful to get away from the bishop's wife, and I rather liked, besides, to be able to stretch myself thoroughly; while as for getting wet, to let oneself slowly be soaked to the skin while walking in a warm rain has a charm all its own.

Accordingly, after the preliminary explanations, we plodded along comfortably enough towards Wiek, keeping the carriage in sight as much as possible, and talking about all the things that interested Brosy, which were mostly things of great obscurity to myself. I suppose he thought it safest to keep to high truths and generalities, fearing lest the conversation in dropping to an everyday level should also drop on to the Nieberleins, and he seemed quite anxious not to know why Charlotte was at Wiek by herself while her husband and I were driving together without her. Therefore he soared carefully in realms of pure reason, and I, silent and respectful, watched him from below; only I could not help comparing the exalted vagueness of his talk with the sharp clearness of all that the old and wise Professor said.

Wiek after all turned out to be hardly more than five miles from Arkona, but it was heavy going. What with the bicycle and my wet skirts and the high talk we got along slowly, and my soul grew more chilled with every step by the thought of the complications the presence of the Harvey-Brownes was going to make in the delicate task of persuading Charlotte to return to her husband.

Brosy knew very well that there was something unusual in the Nieberlein relations, and was plainly uneasy at being thrust into a family meeting. When the red roofs and poplars of Wiek came in sight he sank into thoughtfulness, and we walked the last mile in our heavy, sand-caked shoes in almost total silence. The carriage and cart had disappeared long ago, urged on, no doubt, by the Professor's eagerness to get to Charlotte and away from Mrs. Harvey-Browne, and we were quite near the first cottages when August appeared coming back to fetch us, driving very fast, with Gertrud's face peering anxiously round the hood. It was only a few yards from there to the open space in the middle of the village in which the two inns are, and Brosy got on his bicycle while I drove with Gertrud, wrapped in all the rugs she could muster.

There are two inns at Wiek, and one is the best. The Professor had gone to each to inquire for his wife, and I found him striding about in front of the one that is the best, and I saw at once by the very hang of his cloak and position of his hat that Charlotte was not there.

'Gone! gone!' he cried, before the carriage stopped even. 'Gone this very day —this very morning, gone at eight, at the self-same hour we wasted over those accursed flounders. Is it not sufficient to make a poor husband become mad? After months of patience? To miss her everywhere by a few miserable hours? I told thee, I begged thee, to bring me on last night——'

Brosy, now of a quite deadly anxiety to keep out of Nieberlein complications, removed himself and his bicycle with all possible speed. Mrs. Harvey-Browne, watching my arrival from an upper window, waved a genial hand with ill-timed cordiality whenever I looked her way. The landlord and his wife carried in all the rugs that dropped off me unheeded into the mud when I got out, and did not visibly turn a hair at my peaked hood and draggled garments.

'Where has she gone?' I asked, as soon as I could get the Professor to keep still and listen. 'We'll drive after her the first thing to-morrow morning—to-night if you like——'

'Drive after her? Last night, when it would have availed, thou wouldest not drive after her. Now, if we follow her, we must swim. She has gone to an island—an island, I tell thee, of which I never till this day heard—an island to reach which requires much wind from a favourable quarter—which without wind is not to be reached at all—and in me thou now beholdest a broken-hearted man.'

THE TENTH DAY

FROM WIEK TO HIDDENSEE

The island to which Charlotte had retired was the island of Hiddensee, a narrow strip of sand to the west of Rügen. Generally so wordy, the guide- book merely mentions it as a place to which it is possible for Rügen tourists to make excursions, and proffers with a certain timidity the information that pleasure may be had there in observing the life and habits of sea-birds.

To this place of sea-birds Charlotte had gone, as she wrote in a letter left with the landlady for me, because during the night she spent at Wiek a panic had seized her lest the Harvey-Brownes should by some chance appear there in their wanderings before I did. 'I daresay they will not dream of coming round this way at all,' she continued, 'but you never know.'

You certainly never know, I agreed, Mrs. Harvey-Browne being at that very moment in the room Charlotte had had the panic in; and I lay awake elaborating a most beautiful plan by which I intended at one stroke to reunite Charlotte and her husband and free myself of both of them.

This plan came into my head during the evening while sitting sadly listening to something extremely like a scolding from the Professor. It seemed to me that I had done all in my power short of inhumanity to the horses to help him, and it was surely not my fault that Charlotte had not happened to stay anywhere long enough for us to catch her up. My intentions were so good. Far preferring to drive alone and stop where and when I pleased—at Vitt for instance, among the walnut trees—I had yet given up all my preferences so that I might help bring man and wife together. If anything, did not this conduct incline towards the noble?

'Your extreme simplicity amazes me,' remarked the wise relative when, arrived at this part of my story on my return home, I plaintively asked the above question. 'Under no circumstances is the meddler ever thanked.'

'Meddler? Helper, you mean. Apparently you would call every person who helps a meddler.'

'*Armes Kind*, proceed with the story.'

Well, the Professor, who had suffered much in the hood between Arkona and Wiek, and was more irritated by his disappointment on getting to Wiek than seemed consistent with the supposed serenity of the truly wise, was telling me for the tenth time that if I had brought him on at once from Glowe as he begged me to do we would not only have escaped the Harvey-Brownes but would have caught his Charlotte by now, seeing that she had not left Wiek for Hiddensee till eight o'clock of this Saturday we had now got to, and I was drooping more and more under these reproaches when, with the suddenness of inspiration, the beautiful plan flooded my dejected brain with such a cheerful light that I lifted my head and laughed in the Professor's face.

'Now pray tell me,' he exclaimed, stopping short in his strides about the room, 'what thou seest to laugh at in my present condition?'

'Nothing in your present condition. It's the glories of your future one that made me laugh.'

'Surely that is not a subject on which one laughs. Nor will I discuss it with a woman. Nor is this the place or the moment. I refer thee'—and he swept round his arm as though to sweep me altogether out of sight,—'I refer thee to thy pastor.'

'Dearest Professor, don't be so dreadfully cross. The future state I was thinking of isn't further off than to-morrow. Sometimes there's a cunning about a woman's wit that you great artists in profundity don't possess. You can't, of course, because you are so busy being wise on a large scale. But it's quite useful to have some cunning when you have to work out petty schemes. And I tell you solemnly that at this moment I am full of it.'

He stopped again in his striding. The good landlady and her one handmaiden were laying the table for supper. Mrs. Harvey-Browne had gone upstairs to put on those evening robes in which, it appeared, she had nightly astonished the ignorant tourists of Rügen. Brosy had not been seen at all since our arrival.

'What thou art full of is nothing but poking of fun at me, I fear,' said the Professor; but his kind old face began to smooth out a little.

'I'm not. I'm only full of artfulness, and anxious to put it all at your disposal. But you mustn't be quite so cross. Pray, am I no longer then your little and dear cousin?'

'When thou art good, yes.'

'Whom to pat is pleasant?'

'Yes, yes, it is pleasant, but if unreasonableness develops——'

'And with whom to sit under one umbrella is a joy?'

'Surely, surely—but thou hast been of a great obstinacy——'

'Well, come and sit here and let us be happy. We're very comfortable here, aren't we? Don't let us think any more about the wet, horrid, obstinate, disappointing day we've had. And as for to-morrow, I've got a plan.'

The Professor, who had begun to calm, sat down beside me on the sofa. The landlord, deft and noiseless, was giving a finishing touch of roses and fruit and candles to the supper table. He had been a butler in a good family, and was of the most beautiful dignity and solemnity. We were sitting in a very queer old room, used in past years for balls to which the quality drove in from their distant estates and danced through winter nights. There was a gallery for the fiddlers, and the chairs and benches ranged round the walls were still covered with a festive-looking faded red stuff. In the middle of this room the landlord had put a table for us to sup at, and had arranged it in a way I had not seen since leaving home. No one else was in the house but ourselves. No one, hardly, of the tourist class comes to Wiek; and yet, or because of it, this inn of all the inns I had stayed at was in every way quite excellent.

'Tell me then thy plan, little one,' said the Professor, settling himself comfortably into the sofa corner.

'Oh, it's quite simple. You and I to-morrow morning will go to Hiddensee.'

'Go! Yes, but how? It is Sunday, and even if it were not, no steamers seem to go to what appears to be a spot of great desolation.'

'We'll hire a fishing-smack.'

'And if there is no wind?'

'We'll pray for wind.'

'And I shall spend an entire day within the cramped limits of a vessel in the company of the English female bishop? I tell thee it is not to be accomplished.'

'No, no—of course they mustn't come too.'

'Come? She will come if she wishes to. Never did I meet a more commanding woman.'

'No, no, we must circumvent the Harvey-Brownes.'

'Do thou stay here then, and circumvent. Then shall I proceed in safety on my way.'

'Oh no,' I exclaimed in some consternation; the success of my plan, which was by no means to be explained in its entirety to the Professor, wholly depended on my going too. 'I—I want to see Charlotte again. You know I'm —fond of Charlotte. And besides, long before you got to Hiddensee you would have sunk into another abstraction and begun to fish or something, and you'd come back here in the evening with no Charlotte and only fishes.'

'Tut, tut—well do I now know what is the object I have in view.'

'Don't be so proud. Remember Pilatus.'

'Tut, tut. Thou art beginning to be like a conscience to me, rebuking and urging onwards the poor old man in bewildering alternations. But I tell thee there is no hope of setting sail without the English madam unless thou remainest here while I secretly slip away.'

'I won't remain here. I'm coming too. Leave the arrangements to me, dearest Professor, and you'll see we'll secretly slip away together.'

Mrs. Harvey-Browne sweeping in at that moment in impressive garments that trailed, our conversation had to end abruptly. The landlord lit the candles; the landlady brought in the soup; Brosy appeared dressed as one dresses in civilised regions. 'Cheer up,' I whispered to the Professor as I got up from the sofa; and he cheered up so immediately and so excessively that before I could stop him, before I could realise what he was going to do, he had actually chucked me under the chin.

We spent a constrained evening. The one remark Mrs. Harvey-Browne addressed to me during the hours that followed this chin-chucking was: 'I am altogether at a loss to understand Frau Nieberlein's having retired, without her husband, to yet another island. Why this regrettable multiplicity of islands?'

To which I could only answer that I did not know.

The next day being Sunday, a small boy went up into the wooden belfry of the church, which was just opposite my window, and began to toll two bells. The belfry is built separate from the church, and commands a view into the room of the inn that was my bedroom. I could see the small boy walking leisurely from bell to bell, giving each a pull, and then refreshing himself by leaning out and staring hard at me. I got my opera-glasses and examined him with equal care, trying to stare him out of countenance; but though a small he was also a bold boy and not to be abashed, and as I would not give in either we stared at each other steadily between the tolls till nine o'clock, when the bell- ringing ceased, service began, and he reluctantly went down into the church, where I suppose he had to join in the singing of the tune to which in England the hymn beginning 'All glory, laud, and honour,' is sung, for it presently floated out into the quiet little market-place, filling it with the feeling of Sunday. While I lingered at the window listening to this, I saw Mrs. Harvey- Browne emerge from the inn door in her Sunday toque, and, crossing the market-place followed by Brosy, go into the church. In an instant I had whisked into my hat, and hurrying downstairs to the Professor who was strolling up and down a rose-bordered path in the garden at the back of the house, informed him breathlessly that the Harvey-Brownes might now be looked upon as circumvented.

'What, already? Thou art truly a wonderful ally!' he exclaimed in great glee.

'Oh *that's* nothing,' I replied modestly; as indeed it was.

'Let us start at once then,' he cried briskly; and we accordingly started, slipping out of the house and round the corner down to the quay.

The sun was shining, the ground was drying, there was a slight breeze from the east which ought, the landlord said, to blow us gently to Hiddensee if it kept up in about four hours. All my arrangements had been made the night before with the aid of August and Gertrud, and the brig *Bertha*, quite an imposing-looking craft that plied on week-days, weather permitting, between Wiek and Stralsund, had been hired for the day at a cost of fifteen marks, including a skipper with one eye and four able seamen. The brig *Bertha* seemed to me very cheap. She was to be at my disposal from dawn till as far into the night as I wanted her. All the time the bell-boy and I were exchanging increasingly sarcastic stares she was lying at the quay ready to start at any moment. She had been chartered in my name, and for that one day she, her skipper, and her four able seamen, belonged entirely to me.

Gertrud was waiting on board, and had arranged a sort of nest of rugs and cushions for me. The landlady and her servant were also there, with a basket of home-made cakes, and cherries out of the inn garden. This landlady, by the way, was quite ideal. Her one aim seemed to be to do things like baking cakes for her visitors and not putting them in the bill. I met nothing else at all like her or her husband on my journey round Rügen or anywhere else. Their simple kindness shall not go unsung; and therefore do I pause here, with one foot on the quay and the other on the brig *Bertha*, to sing it. But indeed the traveller who does not yearn for waiters and has no prejudices against crawling up a staircase so steep that it is practically a ladder when he wants to go to bed, who loves quiet, is not insensible to the charms of good cooking, and thinks bathing and sailing agreeable pastimes, could be extremely happy at a very small cost at Wiek. And when all other pleasures are exhausted he can hire the *Bertha* and go to Hiddensee and study sea-birds.

'Thou takest the excellent but unprepossessing Gertrud with thee?' inquired the Professor in a slightly displeased voice, seeing her immovable and the sails being hoisted.

'Yes. I don't like being sick without her.'

'Sick! There will hardly be a sufficiency of wind for the needs of the vessel—

how wilt thou be sick in a calm?'

'How can I tell till I have tried?'

Oh gay voyage down the Wieker Bodden, over the little dancing waves, under the serene summer sky! Oh blessed change from the creaking of a carriage through dust to rippling silence and freshness! The Professor was in such spirits that he could hardly be kept from doing what he called manning the yards, and had to be fetched down when he began to clamber by the alarmed skipper. Gertrud sat watching for the first glimpse of our destination with the intentness of a second Brangäne. The wind could hardly be said to blow us along, it was so very gentle, but it did waft us along smoothly and steadily, and Wiek slipped into distance and its bells into silence, and the occasional solitary farms on the flat shores slid away one after the other, and the farthest point ahead came to meet us, dropped astern, became the farthest point behind, and we were far on our way while we were thinking we could hardly be moving. The reader who looks at the map will see the course we took, and how with that gentle wind it came to be nearly twelve before we rounded the corner of the Wieker Bodden, passed a sandbank crowded with hundreds of sea-gulls, and headed for the northern end of Hiddensee.

Hiddensee lay stretched out from north to south, long and narrow, like a lizard lying in the sun. It is absolutely flat, a mere sandbank, except at the northern end where it swells up into hills and a lighthouse. There are only two villages on it with inns, the one called Vitte, built on a strip of sand so low, so level with the sea that it looks as if an extra big wave, or indeed any wave, must wash right over it and clean it off the face of the earth; and the other called Kloster, where Charlotte was.

I observe that on the map Kloster is printed in large letters, as though it were a place of some importance. It is a very pretty, very small, handful of fishermen's cottages, one little line of them in a green nest of rushes and willows along the water's edge, with a hill at the back, and some way up the hill a small, dilapidated church, forlorn and spireless, in a churchyard bare of trees.

We dropped anchor in the glassy bay about two o'clock, the last bit of the Vitter Bodden having been slow, almost windless work, and were rowed ashore in a dinghy, there not being enough water within a hundred yards to float so majestic a craft as the *Bertha*. The skipper leaned over the side of his brig watching us go and wishing us *viel Vergnügen*. The dinghy and the two rowers were to wait at the little landing-stage till such time as we should want them again. Gertrud came with us, carrying the landlady's basket of food.

'Once more thou takest the excellent but unprepossessing Gertrud with thee?'

inquired the Professor with increased displeasure.

'Yes. To carry the cakes.'

'Tut, tut.' And he muttered something that sounded irritable about the *lieber Gott* having strewn the world with so many plain women.

'*This* isn't the time to bother about plain women,' I said. 'Don't you feel in every fibre that you are within a stone's throw of your Charlotte? I am sure we have caught her this time.'

For a moment he had forgotten Charlotte, and all his face grew radiant at the reminder. With the alacrity of eighteen he leapt ashore, and we hurried along a narrow rushy path at the water's edge to the one inn, a small cottage of the simplest sort, overlooking green fields and placid water. A trim servant in Sunday raiment was clearing away coffee cups from a table in the tiny front garden, and of her we asked, with some trembling after our many disappointments, whether Frau Nieberlein were there.

Yes, she was staying there, but had gone up on to the downs after dinner. In which direction? Past the church, up the lighthouse way.

The Professor darted off before she had done. I hastened after him. Gertrud waited at the inn. With my own eyes I wished to see that he actually did meet Charlotte, for the least thing would make him forget what he had come for; and so nimble was he, so winged with love, that I had to make desperate and panting efforts to get up to the top of the hill as soon as he did. Up we sped in silence past the bleak churchyard on to what turned out to be the most glorious downs. On the top the Professor stopped a moment to wipe his forehead, and looking back for the first time I was absolutely startled by the loveliness of the view. The shining Bodden with its bays and little islands lay beneath us, to the north was the sea, to the west the sea, to the east, right away on the other side of distant Rügen, the sea; far in the south rose the towers of Stralsund; close behind us a forest of young pines filled the air with warm waves of fragrance; at our feet the turf was thick with flowers,—oh, wide and splendid world! How good it is to look sometimes across great spaces, to lift one's eyes from narrowness, to feel the large silence that rests on lonely hills! Motionless we stood before this sudden unrolling of the beauty of God's earth. The place seemed full of a serene and mighty Presence. Far up near the clouds a solitary lark was singing its joys. There was no other sound.

I believe if I had not been with him the Professor would again have forgotten Charlotte, and lying down on the flowery turf with his eyes on that most beautiful of views have given himself over to abstractions. But I stopped him at the very moment when he was preparing to sink to the ground. 'No, no,' I besought, 'don't sit down.'

'Not sit? And why, then, shall not a warm old man sit?'

'First let us find Charlotte.' At the bare mention of the name he began to run.

The inn servant had said Charlotte had gone up to the lighthouse. From where we were we could not see it, but hurrying through a corner of the pine-wood we came out on the north end of Hiddensee, and there it was on the edge of the cliff. Then my heart began to beat with mingled feelings—exultation that I should be on the verge of doing so much good, fear lest my plan by some fatal mishap should be spoilt, or, if it succeeded, my actions be misjudged. 'Wait a moment,' I murmured faintly, laying a trembling hand on the Professor's arm. 'Dear Professor, wait a moment—Charlotte must be quite close now—I don't want to intrude on you both at first, so please, will you give her this letter'— and I pulled it with great difficulty, it being fat and my fingers shaky, out of my pocket, the eloquent letter I had written in the dawn at Stubbenkammer, and pressed it into his hand,—'give it to her with my love—with my very dear love.'

'Yes, yes,' said the Professor, impatient of these speeches, and only desirous of getting on. He crushed the letter unquestioningly into his pocket and we resumed our hurried walking. The footpath led us across a flowery slope ending in a cliff that dropped down on the sunset side of the island to the sea. We had not gone many yards before we saw a single figure sitting on this slope, its back to us, its slightly dejected head and shoulders appearing above the crowd of wild-flowers—scabious, harebells, and cow-parsley, through whose frail loveliness flashed the shimmering sea. It was Charlotte.

I seized the Professor's hand. 'Look—there she is,' I whispered in great excitement, holding him back for one instant. 'Give me time to get out of sight—don't forget the letter—let me get into the wood first, and then go to her. Now, all blessings be with thee, dearest Professor—good luck to you both! You'll see how happy you both are going to be!' And wringing his hand with a fervour that evidently surprised him, I turned and fled.

Oh, how I fled! Never have I run so fast, with such a nightmare feeling of covering no ground. Back through the wood, out on the other side, straight as an arrow down the hill towards the Bodden, taking the shortest cut over the turf to Kloster—oh, how I ran! It makes me breathless now to think of it. As if pursued by demons I ran, not daring to look back, not daring to stop and gasp, away I flew, past the church, past the parson, who I remember stared at me aghast over his garden wall, past the willows, past the rushes, down to the landing-stage and Gertrud. Everything was ready. I had given the strictest private instructions; and dropping speechless into the dinghy, a palpitating mixture of heat, anxiety, and rapture, was rowed as fast as two strong men could row me to the brig and the waiting skipper.

The wind was terribly light, the water terribly glassy. At first I lay in a quivering heap on the cushions, hardly daring to think we were not moving, hardly daring to remember how I had seen a small boat tied to a stake in front of the inn, and that if the *Bertha* did not get away soon——

Then Fortune smiled on the doer of good, a gentle puff filled the sails, there was a distinct rippling across the bows, it increased to a gurgle, and Kloster with its willows, its downs, its one inn, and its impossibility of being got out of, silently withdrew into shadows.

Then did I stretch myself out on my rugs with a deep sigh of relief and allow Gertrud to fuss over me. Never have I felt so nice, so kind, so exactly like a ministering angel. How grateful the dear old Professor would be! And Charlotte too, when she had read my letter and listened to all he had to say; she would have to listen, she wouldn't be able to help herself, and there would be heaps of time. I laughed aloud for joy at the success of my plan. There they were on that tiny island, and there they would have to stay at least till to-morrow, probably longer. Perhaps they would get so fond of it that they would stay on there indefinitely. Anyhow I had certainly reunited them— reunited them and freed myself. Emphatically this was one of those good actions that blesses him who acts and him who is acted upon; and never did well-doer glow with a warmer consciousness of having done well than I glowed as I lay on the deck of the *Bertha* watching the sea-gulls in great comfort, and eating not only my own cherries but the Professor's as well.

All the way up the Wieker Bodden we had to tack. Hour after hour we tacked, and seemed to get no nearer home. The afternoon wore on, the evening came, and still we tacked. The sun set gloriously, the moon came up, the sea was a deep violet, the clouds in the eastern sky about the moon shone with a pearly whiteness, the clouds in the west were gorgeous past belief, flaming across in marvellous colours even to us, the light reflected from them transfiguring our sails, our men, our whole boat into a spirit ship of an unearthly radiance, bound for Elysium, manned by immortal gods.

> Look now how Colour, the Soul's bridegroom, makes
> The house of Heaven splendid for the bride....

I quoted awestruck, watching this vast plain of light with clasped hands and rapt spirit.

It was a solemn and magnificent close to my journey.

THE ELEVENTH DAY

FROM WIEK HOME

The traveller in whose interests I began this book and who has so frequently been forgotten during the writing of it, might very well protest here that I have not yet been all round Rügen, and should not, therefore, talk of closes to my journey. But nothing that the traveller can say will keep me from going home in this chapter. I did go home on the morning of the eleventh day, driving from Wiek to Bergen, and taking the train from there; and the red line on the map will show that, except for one dull corner in the south-east, I had practically carried out my original plan and really had driven all round the island.

Reaching the inn at Wiek at ten o'clock on the Sunday night I went straight and very softly to bed; and leaving the inn at Wiek at eight o'clock on the Monday morning I might have got away without ever seeing Mrs. Harvey-Browne again if the remembrance of Brosy's unvarying kindness had not stirred me to send Gertrud up with a farewell message.

Mrs. Harvey-Browne, having heard all about my day on the *Bertha* from the landlady, and how I had come back in the unimpeachability of singleness, the Professor safely handed over to his wife, forgave the chin-chucking, forgave the secret setting out, and hurried on to the landing in a wrapper, warmth in her heart and honey on her lips.

'What, you are leaving us, dear Frau X.?' she called over the baluster. 'So early? So suddenly? I can't come down to you—do come up here. *Why* didn't you tell me you were going to-day?' she continued when I had come up, holding my hand in both hers, speaking with emphatic cordiality, an altogether melted and mellifluous bishop's wife.

'I hadn't quite decided. I fear I must go home to-day. They want me badly.'

'That I can *quite* understand—of course they want their little ray of sunshine,' she cried, growing more and more mellifluous. 'Now tell me,' she went on, stroking the hand she held, 'when are you coming to see us all at Babbacombe?'

Babbacombe! Heavens. When indeed? Never, never, never, shrieked my soul. 'Oh thanks,' murmured my lips, 'how kind you are. But—do you think the bishop would like me?'

'The bishop? He would more than like you, dear Frau X.—he would positively glory in you.'

'Glory in me?' I faintly gasped; and a gaudy vision of the bishop glorying, that bishop of whom I had been taught to think as steeped in chronic sorrow, swam before my dazzled eyes. 'How kind you are. But I'm afraid you are too kind. I'm afraid he would soon see there wasn't anything to make him glory and much to make him grieve.'

'Well, well, we mustn't be so modest. Of course the bishop knows we are all human, and so must have our little faults. But I can assure you he would be *delighted* to make your acquaintance. He is a most large-minded man. Now *promise.*'

I murmured confused thanks and tried to draw my hand away, but it was held tight. 'I shall miss the midday train at Bergen if I don't go at once,' I appealed —'I really must go.'

'You long to be with all your dear ones again, I am sure.'

'If I don't catch this train I shall not get home to-night. I really must go.'

'Ah, home. How charming your home must be. One hears so much about the charming German home-life, but unfortunately just travelling through the country one gets no chance of a peep into it.'

'Yes, I have felt that myself in other countries. Good-bye—I absolutely must run. Good-bye!' And, tearing my hand away with the energy of panic I got down the ladder as quickly as I could without actually sliding, for I knew that in another moment the bishop's wife would have invited herself—oh, it did not bear thinking of.

'And the Nieberleins?' she called over the baluster, suddenly remembering them.

'They're on an island. Quite inaccessible in this wind. A mere desert—only sea-birds—and one is sick getting to it. Good-bye!'

'But do they not return here?' she called still louder, for I was through the door now, and out on the path.

'No, no—Stralsund, Berlin, Bonn—*good*-bye!'

The landlord and his wife were waiting outside, the landlady with a great bunch of roses and yet another basket of cakes. Brosy was there too, and helped me into the carriage. 'I'm frightfully sorry you are going,' he said.

'So am I. But one must ultimately go. Observe the eternal truth lurking in that sentence. If ever you are wandering about Germany alone, do come and see us.'

'I should love to.'

And thus with mutual amenities Brosy and I parted.

So ended my journey round Rügen, for there is nothing to be recorded of that last drive to the railway station at Bergen except that it was flat, and we saw the Jagdschloss in the distance. At the station I bade farewell to the carriage in which I had sometimes suffered and often been happy, for August stayed that night in Bergen, and brought the horses home next day; and presently the train appeared and swept up Gertrud and myself, and Rügen knew us no more.

But before I part from the traveller, who ought by this time to be very tired, I will present him with the following condensed experiences:—

> The nicest bathing was at Lauterbach,
> The best inn was at Wiek.
> I was happiest at Lauterbach and Wiek.
> I was most wretched at Göhren.
> The cheapest place was Thiessow.
> The dearest place was Stubbenkammer.
> The most beautiful place was Hiddensee.

And perhaps he may like to know, too, though it really is no business of his, what became of the Nieberleins. I am sorry to say that I had letters from them both of a nature that positively prohibits publication; and a mutual acquaintance told me that Charlotte had applied for a judicial separation.

When I heard it I was thunderstruck.

THE END

www.ingramcontent.com/pod-product-compliance
Lightning Source LLC
Chambersburg PA
CBHW021231020726
47498CB00008B/2800